# also by hannah stone

The Space Between Our Hearts

# ERASE THE EMPTY SKY

# erase the empty sky

## hannah stone

FEATHER

*David*
*I'd do it all again.*
*All of it.*

# **one**

. . .

## ANNABELLE

If I had known Trent would be dead in less than twenty-four hours, I would have thrown his keys in the river.

Or glued my skin to his and stayed with him.

At the very least, I would have let him kiss me good-bye. But I didn't know.

I didn't know.

# two

. . .

# VANCE

I misjudged a leap across a section of the river, so now my left Chuck Taylor squishes with every step. In the daylight, Cut Canyon is not the most impressive main street around; it's a half-mile stretch of buildings, most with yellowing *To Rent* signs taped to their front windows. It looks better now at night, when the majority of shopfronts are dark, looking like a prize fighter's smile with too many missing teeth.

West Aldrin, Washington is a town that can take one on the chin, and I appreciate that.

Murphy's Café is on the west end, one block ahead of me, and all I have to do is keep walking forward. Then I can lie down, resume the documentary on the Pan-American Highway I started last night, and finally be able to fall asleep.

But I have one stop to make.

Trent and I were supposed to meet after third period, but I didn't go to school today. This morning a postcard from my mom waited for me on the kitchen counter, and I haven't been able to breathe since I turned it over and discovered she didn't write a single word. I've lived with Murphy for three years and this is the second card Nat has sent. Don't ask how many times she's called because it's fewer than two.

I've only been to Trent's house once. The garage is detached, offset behind his house and I don't think a car has ever parked inside. Instead, a foosball table sits in the center and a punching bag collects dust in the back. The garage door must be open because a soft orange light spills onto the gravel driveway.

I imagine Trent will be mad. I imagine he wanted to send me texts all day asking where I was, but last year, when this started, he was the one who said we should never contact each other and leave a trail. I joked that everything would be fine—I would save his number as Top Secret. He didn't laugh. But Trent's not wrong. We'd both be screwed if anyone found out.

At the side of the garage, I expect an Avicii song to fill the night, but it's Derek's voice I hear. "Why are we still talking about this? You've been beating this to death all week. Just cut your losses if you need to," he says.

"We're still talking about this because everything in

my life feels impossible right now and because I actually love Annabelle."

Trent sounds worn through, and I stop walking.

I'm still untouched by the light spilling into the night, so they haven't seen me. Before they do, I need to consider my options. I could leave the paper under a rock near the back porch and hope nobody except Trent finds it. I could walk away, leave Trent hanging, and not get paid, or I could interrupt their argument.

Trent and I are not friends; we have an arrangement. I write his papers, he pays me, and if word got out, both of us would be expelled. It might seem like being expelled would be an option I'd consider, but it's not. I'm not an idiot. I know my chances of making it in life go from small to zero if I don't at least graduate high school.

But Derek is in the garage with Trent, and I don't trust Derek.

Being the new kid was a normal part of life with Nat. I would appear out of thin air at a new school, before disappearing just as quickly when she decided to pull the rip cord, and we were off. On my first day at West Aldrin High, Derek told me to be careful with my clothes after we changed for PE, or who knows what might happen to them. But by then, I had an excellent education on what might happen. I soaked my own clothes, leaving them in a pile on the shower floor for all to see, successfully extracting the venom from a bite Derek promised to take and now never could.

I can't leave this piece of paper out in the open in case the wrong person finds it. But I need the cash, which means I have to trust Derek with what he's about to see.

I pull the sheet of notebook paper from my backpack, and I roll it in my hand, turning it into a baton so I can pass it over as quickly as possible and get out.

Derek is still talking as I step inside the light. "I get that you love Annabelle—" His eyes snap to my face, and he stands from the ripped leather couch, pushing curls off his forehead that instantly spring back. "You lost, MiniVan?"

I tap the paper against my leg at the mention of the nickname that no longer fits. I was a scrawny fourteen-year-old when I first arrived, thanks to a mom who forgot simple tasks like buying groceries or coming home, but I can't get sidetracked by Derek being Derek. Not now.

"I need a minute with your friend," I say, and for the first time, I look at Trent. His face is as pinched as his voice sounded.

Derek swings his head to Trent, but Trent is already walking over. "Do you have it?" he asks.

I hold out the rolled-up paper, and Trent takes it. As he scans the words, his eyebrows scrunch together. I had all the time in the world to write Trent's valedictorian speech, but I put it off until the last minute, scribbling it this afternoon along the river when I should have been at school. It's good, but it might not be what Trent imagined. I couldn't muster the energy I needed to write a speech worthy of William Wallace rallying a crowd into a frenzied freedom chant. It's more of an "I heard a Fly buzz - when I died -" kind of speech.

Derek snatches the paper out of Trent's hand, reads enough to understand, and flicks it with his finger. "What's going on?"

Trent steps toward his best friend and, before I can stop him, he tells Derek the truth. "Vance has been writing my papers."

Derek's dark eyes widen, but his shock quickly disappears, replaced by anger aimed at me. "You are such an idiot."

I should bite my tongue, but I don't. "Funny, because Trent told me it's the papers I write that nudged him ahead of Avery for valedictorian. So I don't think *I'm* the idiot."

People cheer when Derek flattens the opponent with a tackle on the football field, but he won't get into a fight, not here. He has too much to lose if he gets kicked off the team. But I don't miss him clenching his hands at his sides. Derek and I are both juniors, and he's more brain than brawn, though he has both in spades. If he keeps doing what he's been doing this year, he'll be our valedictorian next year.

Derek turns away from me, stepping closer to Trent. "Look what he's got you messed up in. You know what could happen, don't you?"

Trent's hands fly into the air. "Of course I know!" He drops his arms, yanking a set of keys out of his pocket and whipping them in a circle.

We both watch the repetitive arc Trent's keys make, and I feel the question building inside Derek before he asks it.

"How come you never asked me?" Derek moves the mop of curls off his forehead again with the same result. "If you needed help, I would have done anything to help, and you wouldn't have had to involve him." He spits the last word to the ground.

The keys fly off Trent's finger, and he scoops them up, starting to swing them all over again only faster. "I didn't need the help. It just made everything easier. It took the pressure off, left me a little more room to breathe, to be with Annabelle."

Derek's voice raises. "And got you a scholarship. Listen to yourself, justifying cheating so life would be easy and you could have more time with Annabelle. And you've been going off all week about breaking up with her."

Trent becomes a live wire of energy, his blue eyes

flair, and this seems like an excellent opportunity to make my exit. I'll get my money later. Stepping out of the garage, I walk along its side, headed to the alley when I hear Trent shout, "I don't need you in my face about this!" Derek might respond, but I don't hear it because a vehicle roars to life, tires flying across the gravel, then silence.

Watching a documentary until I fall asleep is not going to cut it tonight. Behind the café, I take the stairs to the apartment I share with Murphy two at a time and climb on top of the railing, leaning out for the wrought-iron ladder bolted to the bricks. The tar and gravel rooftop above Murphy's apartment is a sanctuary of open space, with old lawn chairs, a metal trunk, and a bench press in the middle. I spend as much time as possible up here.

Collapsing on the bench, I pull my black hoodie over my hair that's the same color. Murphy and my mom were together long before she met my dad, had me, and tried to be a mom, and this Nirvana sweatshirt is all I have left of her. I wad it up and press it to my face, trying to find the shape of my mother's love in the wearing-thin cotton. But I can't remember what that felt like in the first place.

Receiving a blank postcard from Nat this morning, three years after she walked out on me was a rotten way to start the day. One more reminder that I am expendable in everyone's life.

Even Derek and Trent extend the circle of their lives out to encompass each other. But Derek is angry Trent came to me. I have no idea what that would feel like, to have a friend furious with me because I didn't ask him for help. What really burns is knowing that they'll be fine. They both need to blow off some steam, but tomorrow they'll still be friends.

I don't have friends or a family; all I have are agreements. One that gives me a place to live, and one that pays me in cash.

I do reps until my arms refuse. Until my body aches more than my heart. Until sweat mats my hair to my head and drips down my face.

Laying on the bench, arms shaking, I search the sky for familiar specks of light that anchor me no matter where I live and trace an imaginary line down the handle of the Little Dipper.

I pull my backpack to me and rustle my hand inside until I feel the cylinder of a permanent marker and clamp my fingers around it. Taking out my wallet, I remove the first postcard Nat ever sent me. I could recite it without unfolding it.

*Never been this far north.*

*Can't stand the cold, need to find my way back to the sun.*

I remove the cap of the marker between my teeth,

and I run a black line over what Nat wrote until it says what she really meant to tell me.

*Never* ~~been this far north.~~

~~Can't stand the cold, need to~~ *find my way* ~~back to the sun.~~

There's one year left until my agreement with Murphy expires. He said I could live with him until Nat came back for me or I graduate, whichever comes first. I don't have faith in Nat like Murphy does. And none of this will matter if Derek decides to tell the truth about what he witnessed tonight.

*I don't belong here.*

The words pulse under my skin like an open wound, and if I said them aloud, they would sound like a pack of wolves howling at the moon above my head.

# three

. . .

## ANNABELLE

I don't have the energy for a shower. Trent has been avoiding my question all week. Last night I texted him: *Call me when you get this,* then stayed up playing a game on my phone, waiting for a reply that never came.

I scrub my face and French braid my honey-blonde hair, not caring that it ends up crooked and lumpy. I'll fix it for Meredith's inspection later.

I was nine when my sister moved away for college and, like everyone else in town, once she left, she didn't come back. Until now. Because apparently, woodland weddings are all the rage. West Aldrin is a small slice of life wedged between a river and a ridge, built on the back of a logging company that dissolved into thin air, and about all we do have are trees.

Back in my room, the screen of my phone lights up, and I pick it up with a sigh when I see her name.

Meredith: *rehearsal is 5 pm SHARP*

Meredith: *ride with Mom and Dad so you won't be late*

Meredith: *I won't tell you what to wear but NO CUT-OFFS*

I squeeze my eyes shut. It's not even five in the morning and Bridezilla is on the prowl. If I didn't have the energy for a shower, I don't know how I'll manage to deal with Meredith. She loves organizing everyone's lives on a regular day, and nothing about her getting married is an everyday occurrence. Part of me wishes today only belonged to Trent and his graduation. But I'd be lying if I said I haven't been counting the days until I can wear my bridesmaid dress and tomorrow I finally can.

The hangers screech as I search for an outfit Meredith would approve of, but I don't want to wear any of them. Turning to my dresser, I pull out a blue sleeveless top with orange bicycles printed all over it and a pair of cut-offs. I'm still her little sister, and making Meredith roll her eyes is one of my best skills.

Without answering any of her messages, I check again to see if Trent replied, but I'm left staring at my message from last night. I consider sending him another text, but I don't want to seem needy. Instead, I open Instagram and select the picture I snapped of Trent yesterday. We stood in the courtyard of the school. The sides of his hair were lit golden from the sun, his sea-glass blue eyes shining as he smiled at me.

I post his picture with the simple caption *forever is ours for the taking* and head to work.

The café is dark when I enter, but I could weave through the collection of tables, setting chairs on the floor as I go, with my eyes closed. The front wall is all glass with two gnarled-wood slab counters framing the front entrance. Every morning I stop here, pushing my thumb into a whorled knot, worn smooth from years of people doing exactly this, and watch the sun wake up the sky. I'm not big on habits, but this is my favorite morning ritual. I'm about to turn around when my phone buzzes in my back pocket. *Finally*, I think, but it's just another message from Meredith that I don't bother reading. After unlocking the main door, I head behind the counter and flick the grinder on.

When it stops, the café splits open with sudden silence, then Murphy's voice fills the space. "Sorry I'm late. The bakery was running behind this morning." He drops the pastry boxes on the table and runs a hand over his bald, dark head. After Trent and I binged *Luther*, I told Murphy he is Idris Elba's doppelganger, and all he did was laugh so hard he snorted. But it's true.

Murphy nods to the open bag of beans, silently asking me to put it away, a task I can never do without my head lingering over the opening. Closing my eyes, I breathe in the earthy aroma, wondering what Trent is dreaming about. If it were me graduating today, I'd be up with the sun, too excited to sleep. But if that were true for Trent, why hasn't he called me? All I did was ask him what he thought our relationship would look like after he left for college. He had reached into his pocket and grabbed his keys, swinging them in a circle instead of answering. He's been avoiding the topic ever since. But I've known Trent my entire life, and there's something in his eyes he doesn't want me to see, something he doesn't want to tell me.

Murphy hands me a doughnut hole as we walk to the counter where Miss Matcha-Latte is already waiting for us. Behind her stands Mrs. Only-Gets-A-Water (but Murphy lets her stay as long as she likes). Referring to customers as their drink order isn't exactly what you would call a thrill but small town, small thrills.

Apparently, everyone needs to be caffeinated today because the line never slows and before I know it, Murphy is nudging me out the door so I'm not late for school.

In the alley, my phone buzzes with another message from Meredith: *Are you ignoring me?*

Her detective skills are top-notch. I almost turn my phone to silent, but there's still time between now and my first class. Trent could still reply, so I leave the ringer on.

It's silly, but I wait for him under the canopy of the only tree in the school's courtyard. There is no need; graduation is later today, and no seniors are on campus. A hand taps my shoulder, and I spin, expecting it to be Trent, but it's Derek. Yesterday after I took Trent's picture, Derek appeared out of nowhere, throwing his arms around Trent and practically leveling him to the ground. There is no pretend tackle this morning, just Derek standing in front of me wearing a very wrinkled shirt and bloodshot eyes.

"Have you heard from Trent?" he asks.

I push away my annoyance and shake my head. "I texted him last night but he's probably sleeping."

Derek attempts a smile. "Tell him to text me when you hear from him."

Squinting my eyes at Trent's best friend I try to understand why I suddenly need to be their go-between. "Why don't you just message him yourself?"

Derek is a step ahead of me, pulling the door open for both of us to walk through. "Already did. Twice. I've gotten nothing back."

I stop walking. A crow caws, and then a second one, before the pair lift off the branch they shared. I haven't heard from Trent and neither has Derek. A dull roaring fills my ears, and I turn so I'm facing the street, ignoring Derek's offer of an open door. All I want is for Trent to walk around the corner so he can give me his lopsided grin as he runs to kiss my cheek. He'll smack his hand to his forehead telling me his charger wasn't plugged in and his phone died. My dad's first rule in assessing an engine is to look for the simplest solution first. Trent's phone isn't charged. He's asleep with his hair fanned across the side of his face.

It's the only thing that makes sense, but I shiver in the warm breeze and then the bell rings.

Paying attention to Mr. Bryant is impossible. My mind drifts to yesterday and instead of copying the equation he's reviewing for our final next week, I look at the list of plans Trent and I wrote for the summer. *Camping. Floating the river. Fire pit and s'mores. Friday night movies in the park. A day trip to Seattle to add our gum to the wall.* I flip the page, starting a new list like I do every day. I guess I have more routines than I thought I did.

*FRIDAY: Wake up. Work. School. Trent. Graduation. Rehearsal. Party.*

Not much is better than crossing things off a list, and I'm about to draw a line through the first two, when my phone chimes.

Snatching it from my pocket I almost tumble out of my seat. I forgot to turn it off and today of all days I cannot pay the price for forgetting.

"I'm sorry. I'm sorry. I'm sorry." Holding my phone, I see Meredith's name and kick myself for not silencing it earlier.

Mr. Bryant doesn't have a chance to say anything because the phone on his desk beeps and the secretary's voice warbles through its speaker. "Sorry for the interruption, Mr. Bryant, but please send Annabelle Davis to the office."

"On her way," he says, removing his glasses, cleaning the lenses with his necktie. "Isn't that convenient—now you can give your phone to Mrs. Milholland at the front desk."

Jason, sitting behind me, coughs the word *busted* into his hands and I snap my notebook closed, shoving it into my backpack.

Why am I being called to the office? Does it have something to do with graduation? Do they need me to help? As I walk under a *Congratulations Seniors* banner, I pass a science room. In the corner, a student is dropping a freeze-dried mouse to the coiled snake below. The lid of the cage hinged open at an odd angle makes me stop, and a seed of apprehension grows between my ribs, pulling them tight. I used to have a hamster that I should have named Houdini instead of Hamsterdam. Every time he escaped, I knew where to look. Until one day when I came home and found the lid askew, and something inside me knew there would be no more finding Hamsterdam.

That same feeling of knowing winds its long fingers around my neck, choking me. I rush to the drinking fountain and force my mouth under the arc of water, gulping so much I gag. Water drips from my chin while I type a message to Trent with shaky fingers: *Where are you? Why won't you answer?*

Then I type what I don't want to admit: *I'm scared.*

Ramming the button on the drinking fountain, I drink again, but I can't swallow. Water pools under my tongue, spilling out the corner of my mouth. I force the ball of it past the gate in my throat, swiping droplets over my flaming cheeks, and take a breath. There is no need for the memory of a hamster to spook me. Everything is fine. I'm fine. Trent is fine. I press my still-wet hands to my cheeks once more. There is nothing to worry about.

Alternating gray and white tiles pass under my worn-to-perfection Birks and there are no more thoughts in my mind of escaped hamsters or unanswered texts from the boy I love. There is only my heart beating, thudding, pounding secret messages I do not want to decipher.

Mrs. Milholland points to a chair but before my legs bend to its plastic, Mr. Logan opens his door. Why have I been called to the principal? Walking into his office, my face twists into a topographical map of confusion. My parents stand in front of his desk, and as soon as they see me, they wrap their arms around me. A metallic tang fills my mouth, another swallow I have to force down.

This doesn't make sense. Dad should be at his shop. My mom should be in the gymnasium with the other parent volunteers hanging streamers and balloons.

A man clears his throat. "Good morning, Annabelle."

I did not see Officer Daily-Drip-To-Go standing to the side of Mr. Logan's desk when I entered. The room spins and I crush my mom's arm in my grasp. I can't get a hold of Trent. No one can. Now Officer Dobb is at school. There has to be a simple explanation for all of this, but a trap door swings open inside my heart and I slip through.

My voice is pinched, almost unrecognizable. "Missed you earlier. Can't remember not seeing you first thing at Murphy's. I ground the Ethiopian beans this morning. I know you like those best." My eyes skip off every surface in the room, unable to find one thing to look at. Windows. Diploma. Globe. Stapler.

Officer Dobb's hat in his hands.

The principal, my parents, and a police officer. It's the beginning of a horrible joke and an egg of fear cracks open, spilling its slime down my back with a shiver. "Why am I here?"

"Have a seat." Officer Dobb motions to the tufted leather chair facing Mr. Logan's desk.

I don't want to sit, but my legs obey. Mom rests her hand on my shoulder, Dad rests a hand on my back, and Mr. Logan looks at me like I'm about to shatter.

Officer Dobb clears his throat again. "This is never easy and there is no way to make it easier, so I'm just going to say it. There was a single-car accident early this morning." He pauses to take a breath and time swirls around itself instead of marching forward, a clogged sink refusing to drain. "I'm sorry to have to tell you this, but Trent was killed."

The words land on me, disjointed syllables that mean nothing until they snap together and become every terrible thing I can imagine. I fold in half, clawing my hand at my throat as if something is clamped against it, stopping the air from flowing. Finally, I gasp in a huge breath that I push out in a scream.

This is not happening.

Trent cannot be dead.

I slide off the chair, but my dad falls to his knees, catching me, and my mom collapses next to me, holding me, rocking. "Shhh, I've got you," she says against my ear over and over. Turning the words into a circle, a mantra, a prayer.

This I understand, being held in my mom's arms. It's as familiar as looking at my own reflection. But the life raft of her comfort is too far for me to swim to and I don't think I'll be able to reach it.

"No, no, no," I moan, each word growing louder. "NO! I don't understand." Sobs roll through my body. None of this is real.

Lunging out of my parent's embrace, I shout, "You're wrong. You are all wrong. I sent him a message, maybe he sent one back." Panic, along with bile, raises at the back of my throat and I tear at my pocket. If only I could get it out, I would know for sure, but I give up on worthless fingers that will not do my bidding.

Everyone is wrong. Trent is at home, asleep. Where else could he be?

I leap over my parent's legs, running from the room.

I run for home, the safest place I know, and by the time my parents catch up with me I've swiped the majority of the photos off my wall. I'm out of breath. I have no stamina for heartbreak. Whenever I have experienced pain in the past, it was small enough that I could sweep it under my skin and ignore it. The pain had never been heavy enough to crush me.

But the weight of Trent's death is molten in my veins, flashing fire and cooling in an instant, turning me into a statue holding a single photograph, the tape on its back sticking to my fingers. I took this picture last summer. It's always been my favorite. Trent is blurry as he turned to the sound of his name being called. His focus extends past me, fixed on Derek flipping in the sky above a trampoline, his lopsided smile on full display.

Rubbing my thumb over all that is left of Trent, I start to feel the same spinning sensation I did in Mr. Logan's office. Shooting forward, I push open my window, leaning out, and gulping in mouthfuls of fresh air. More than once, Trent climbed the oak tree next to my house, clambering on top of the roof directly below my window. And more than once we sat out there, wrapped in a blanket kissing until our lips were raw. I can see the shadow of our bodies as I try to breathe. My phone chimes and I lurch back in surprise, smacking the back of my head on the window frame. Trent is finally replying, and everyone will see how wrong they've been.

But it is not Trent.

Bewildered classmates are texting me in droves. A new message appears on the screen, only for another to arrive and push it out of the way, followed by another. Then another. They become a tsunami pulling me out in a riptide far away from anything that makes sense.

I don't want these messages. I want Trent.

I want to rewind time, to go back to yesterday and stop this before it happened, but another message comes in, then another one. Regret surges through my body and I throw my phone. It thuds against the pale yellow wall opposite me with a crack, sliding to the floor. It's silent, then it chimes again. And again.

My heart threatens to rupture, and I cover my ears, making a sound close to a growl. I feel like I'm riding the Round Up at the state fair, pinned against the wall of a spinning wheel, eyes closed, waiting for it to be over.

I need all of this to stop.

The messages gathering like a storm.

The racing of my heart.

The truth about Trent.

What am I supposed to do now?

I fall to my knees, tipping to the ground, and curl into a ball. My parents lay next to me, one on either side, their arms overlapping me in a blanket of love.

Today was supposed to be a ceremony and a celebration. It was supposed to be a war with my sister over cut-offs instead of sun dresses, not a tragedy.

I'll never be able to survive this.

# four

. . .

## VANCE

By the time we are released from the emergency assembly, some parents are already standing in the hallway. Word travels fast in a town like this. Murphy leans against the wall at the far end, before the hall turns a corner, and my first thought is that he's here looking for Annabelle. She works for him, and he must want to check on her. He's wringing his hands together like he's rubbing hand sanitizer on them but stops when he finds me in the mass of bodies and strides over.

He never hugs me because I do not give off *please hug me* vibes, but now he wraps his arms around me, and I push away. Not because I don't want to be crushed in his hug but because that is exactly what I want. I don't know how to accept this kindness.

Murphy keeps a hand on my shoulder. "You okay?"

I have to turn away. The emotion I'm wrestling down

isn't because Trent is dead—it's because Murphy came looking for me, just like he did three years ago when I called him. I don't want Murphy to see my scrunched-up face. "I'm fine."

A shoulder knocks against mine and I look in time to see Derek. He doesn't glance at me, just keeps holding Sasha's hand, walking away. Derek, Trent, Sasha, and Annabelle. Even on my first day, I knew they were a pack. The four of them were best friends before they split into couples. Maybe this knock on my shoulder is purely an accident in a crowded hallway filled with off-kilter people, but something tells me it's more than that.

Murphy's voice brings me back. "They told us we can take our students home if you want."

I'm not sure what I want, but spending the rest of the day with Murphy's concern hanging over me like the jellyfish tentacles of blue and silver streamers dangling from the raised basketball backstops in the half-deco-rated gym is too much to consider. "It's fine. I'll stay." I think Murphy's shoulders fall, but it could be because he adjusted his position, so I add, "Plus if I need to, I can talk to one of the people they brought in."

Counselors came from Rye, a town between us and Seattle, a town big enough to have Target, Starbucks, and a surplus of school counselors.

Murphy's face lights up, glad that I would consider taking advantage of the help offered even though I only said it so he'd go back to work. "Okay." He slaps my back. "Okay then, I'll see you when you get home."

I watch him until I don't see him anymore, then turn to my locker. But when I reach it, Derek is waiting for me, arms crossed at his chest.

The hairs at the base of my neck shiver to attention. "We should stop meeting like this," I say.

But Derek doesn't take the bait as the hallway drains, leaving us alone. He's trying to be imposing, but I can tell it's taking every ounce of energy he possesses. "Let's get one thing straight: I could care less what happens to you."

I sway back, unsure where this is going, because I've never once thought Derek cared what happens to me. "Why is that something you needed to clarify?"

He taps a finger against my chest so light I hardly feel it. I think I'd like him better if he decided to hit me; at least I'd understand that. "Trent was my . . ." His voice breaks, his shoulders sag, and he doesn't attempt to finish his sentence. "I'm doing this for her. Because he loved Annabelle, and she doesn't need to know."

I can count on one hand the times I've spoken with Annabelle, and the majority of those conversations were, *"Do you have a pen I can borrow?"* Why does Derek think I'm suddenly going to strike up a conversation with her now, admitting I wrote her boyfriend's papers?

I don't have time to ask because Derek keeps going.

"He didn't mean it. Whatever you heard Trent say about breaking up with Annabelle, or think you knew about him because of your . . ." Derek flicks his hand back and forth, unsure what to say.

"Agreement," I offer.

He snorts. "Whatever. Just keep your mouth shut."

I thought Derek was smarter than this. It doesn't matter to me what Trent was or was not going to do. "Not going to happen, so relax."

Derek nods his head several times, satisfied, then pulls a folded sheet of paper out of his back pocket. I don't need him to twist it toward me to know he's holding the speech I wrote for Trent. Tipping his head in the direction of the main office he says, "I'll hold onto this in case you change your mind. Say one word to Annabelle and I take this to Logan."

# five

. . .

## ANNABELLE

My right arm is numb. It hangs off the couch and when I raise it, a shock of electric pain shoots to my shoulder. The living room is dark and quiet, except for a soft glow coming from the kitchen carrying hushed voices. It's my parents, my sister, and a voice I can't place before I realize it's Mateo, my almost brother-in-law. I can only make out some of what they are saying, but it's enough to know they are discussing canceling the wedding.

Trent hated being the center of attention. It was one thing for him to be the sun that I orbited around, but he wouldn't want to be the reason Meredith postponed her wedding. But how can my sister get married in the morning when Trent is dead? *Dead.* The word slams into my chest as a scream tears at the back of my throat, and I throw my hand over my mouth and bite into my palm. I cannot give my pain a voice so I bite until I almost break the skin.

When I try to roll off the couch, I discover all my bones have turned to concrete. It should not be this hard to stand up, but I guess this is what happens to your body when your world collapses. It takes more than one try for me to get up, and when I finally appear at the entrance to the kitchen, the look on everyone's faces make me turn and check over my shoulder. What could possibly make them look so shocked? Then I realize it's me. I'm a ghost standing in the doorway.

My words are drips of tar, slow and heavy. "Trent wouldn't want you to cancel your wedding. He'd hate to be the reason."

It's true, but the ground starts to slide away under my feet at the thought.

Everyone's opinion is written on their face. *Yes. No. Are you sure?* They never say it, but I nod, agreeing that plans should not be altered, and that seals the deal.

My mom walks me upstairs, tucks me into bed, and sits at the end, a hand resting on my foot, staying until she thinks I've fallen asleep. But I haven't. I'm stuck hovering between being asleep and awake, between memory and haunting.

The year I turned ten, my dad got me a butterfly kite for my birthday. I paced in front of the living room window for a week waiting for the wind to stir the branches. And when it finally did, I shot out of the door, running to Trent's house, monarch wings trailing behind me, never once noticing that the clouds rising over the ridge were angry. By the time we got the kite up, it was too late. The wind chomped through branches and made quick work of a single strand of string. The kite was gone, devoured by a storm I never saw coming.

Now Trent is the kite. Gone and never coming back. A jumbled slideshow plays on the track of my mind: Trent swinging his keys, Murphy carrying pastry boxes, my fingers locked between Trent's, a long stretch of road, Trent laughing in the courtyard, my bridesmaid dress hanging in my closet, sweeping under tables at the café, Trent biting his lip as he waited for me to finish making his cinnamon latte.

Every picture circles back to him and I throw the covers off. I need something I can hold on to, something that makes sense, something to make my mind stop churning, and I find what I'm looking for on the floor where I threw it.

A huff of air leaves my mouth as I pick my phone up, regretting my instinct to retrieve it, blinking fireworks at the sudden brightness of the screen. The number of accumulated messages is staggering. This is not a good idea, but I unlock it and stop breathing. My fingers tighten around the screen as the wallpaper image of my face next to Trent's appears. I tip sideways, reaching my arm to the frame of my bed to steady myself, but I can't put my phone down. I can't stop looking even when tears flood my eyes, and our faces rip apart into kaleidoscope pieces.

My heart thumps at the base of my throat and I open Instagram simply out of habit and picture after picture is of Trent. My pulse quickens at the repetition of his face. The endless sight of his smile, his eyes, and flop of sandy hair, is like walking over flames. Why is every post exactly the same? Trent stands outside, a shaft of light behind him, the tips of his hair brushed gold with sunlight. Something familiar nibbles at the side of my mind but the thought is too far away for me to grab.

The more I scroll, the more my fog burns away, and I remember that I took this photo. My stomach clenches. Why is everyone posting a cropped and filtered image that belongs to me?

Pushing my feed further up the screen, I find the original post. Everyone has reposted what Sasha shared. I cannot read the lengthy tribute she typed. I can't keep looking at Trent or an entire school's worth of gestures of solidarity that feel fake. I power down my phone, open a drawer, and slide it under a stack of folded shirts, closing everything away.

My concrete bones have melted, and I no longer have the strength to stand. I am slack, hollowed out. Life used to make sense. If you show up and pay attention, you'll pass the class. I thought that translated to all of life. If you hold on tight enough, you can't lose what you love.

I wrap the duvet tighter around my shoulders and when sleep finally grabs my ankles, pulling me under, it sails me across a choppy sea with iceberg stars to an island where nightmares are real and dead boys are always alive.

—————

All I need to do is walk, but the grassy aisle littered with petals seems impossibly long. The music of Yo-Yo Ma's cello fills the air. The notes flutter through the billows of lace strung between ancient fir trees standing like gnarled fingers poking out of the earth, forming a circular sanctuary. The score plays on and on and on. All I need to do is walk, but I am frozen in the sun.

The bouquet of ranunculus is heavy in my hands. and my feet refuse to move. I'm stuck replaying my last moments with Trent. We had been at the dock, and then he walked me home. He had kicked a rock across the driveway, his shoulders slumped, and he took out his keys from his pocket, swinging them over and over and over, something he only did when he was having a hard time making a decision. I was annoyed that he didn't want to talk about what a long-distance relationship would look like. When he leaned in to kiss me, I turned my head, his lips never finding my face.

That was my last moment with Trent.

This morning, no one knew how to include me as we waited for the ceremony to begin, and it's all my fault. I'm the one who said we should be here. But it's their fault for believing me. All of the bridesmaids were supposed to have matching, pinned-to-perfection hair, but I couldn't sit still, so mine hangs around my face, not even brushed. As they drained their mimosas, the other bridesmaids started bumping hips, gushing about this venue and Meredith's forever with Mateo. They kept saying that word: *forever*. It's true. No one comes to a wedding thinking, *Five years tops*. It's always forever and ever. Amen.

I buckle under the weight of that word because it's also true that no one waits for a text from their boyfriend thinking, *I bet he didn't live to see the sunrise.*

The truth crashes over me—forever is an illusion.

As we lined up, my mom had cradled my face in her hands, asking if I was sure I could do this. All I thought about was the silky feel of the coral chiffon on my skin. I had been waiting months to see Trent's reaction to me wearing this open-back dress. That's all I could think about, so I said yes. I wasn't thinking about the fact that I would have to endure the ceremony.

I still can't make my legs move.

If only roots would spread from my feet, tunneling into the dirt and attaching me to the ground, then I could be one of these trees instead of having to stand in front of the guests. My mom turns in her seat, tears on her cheeks, a sad, silent plea for me to take a step. The music ends, leaving in its place an overflowing silence, and that is what finally propels me forward. Halfway down the aisle, I kick off my shoes before resuming painfully slow steps to reach the place marked for me to stand.

I try to pay attention. I force my eyes wide open, staring at the tulle draped over the back of Meredith's head. I squeeze the stems of the flowers until my fingers hurt. I ride along in the low rumble of the minister's voice, but an invisible current continues to sweep me further away from where I stand.

Trent was supposed to be here with me. He would have been sitting next to my parents, watching. My head whips toward the guests. Is that him in the third row? I lunge toward the line of chairs. The sun glinting off his hair makes whoever he is look exactly like Trent. But he's not. It's a cruel craving to look for Trent in each face. The fact that I will never see him again is a lead ball through my chest. My eyes jump from face to face, searching, and in the last row, a pair of steel-gray eyes hold mine. My desperation to be found is mirrored in

Vance's eyes and, for a moment, the current dragging me under stops.

I'm no longer standing in my perfectly marked place, but I'm too unsteady to step back. So, I stay where I am as the vows are said, the rings are given. But an earthquake rumbles through my body. After Mateo dips my sister in a kiss, the mood shifts, and candles are distributed. Everyone is asked to stand—there will be a prayer for the boy who was taken from us far too soon. The forest is silent as each candle ignites, a collective benediction burning in grasped hands. I refuse to hold a candle, refuse to wrap my hand around the wax, not trusting myself to hold it, too afraid I'd let the flame fall and burn everything.

Dad sees me wilting under the prayer that curls in wisps toward Heaven, and he comes to my side, slipping his arm through mine, anchoring me in place. I want to tell him thank you, but the tears glistening in his eyes steal my words. We don't wait for the prayer to end. He just walks to the reception area and plants me in a chair with a kiss on my forehead. I slump down, the back of my head resting against the slat of white wood, arms skimming the grass like a rag doll tossed aside.

As the candles are snuffed out, the celebration returns in cautious increments. It creeps over the guests in the lyrics the DJ plays, smiles returning to faces, guests becoming alive to the moment, the dancing, the eating. The simple fact that they are alive stacks stones in my heart.

I don't know how much time has passed while I sit unmoving, enough to darken the sky by a shade. My mom has been sitting next to me since Dad led me here. But all of a sudden, Meredith's voice cuts over the opening notes of a song and she screams my name. It takes me a moment to place the synthesizer and the bells. Watching *Glee* used to be our thing. We'd sit on the couch and sometimes sing along. Even after she moved out, we still watched the show together over FaceTime. Meredith always said if she got married, she'd play *Marry You* and we could dance together.

I don't even lift my head from the back of the chair. My voice is husky from lack of use. "She's drunk."

I don't know if that is true. I'd rather blame her behavior on too many cocktails than willfully calling me to the dance floor. Mom squeezes my hand, and gets up, weaving her way between tables to quiet Meredith's request.

I shouldn't have said Trent wanted us out here cele-brating. Last night I was certain that was what he would want, but I have no idea about anything. Not anymore. Is this what Trent would want? He wouldn't want to be dead, but nobody says that.

Fairy lights twinkle through the branches as the sun continues to dip lower. The lights sparkling above my head bring back a memory, making me spin under a disco ball. Was it only a month ago that I wore a plum dress and white Vans to prom? Trent matched his shoes to mine and his tie to my dress. We danced and spun. Laughed and lived.

It's punishing to remember, but I'm afraid to forget, so where does that leave me?

It leaves me ripped open and spinning under wedding lights with memories that are too hard to hold.

I can't do this. I can't remember him, and I can't forget. I can't navigate my life anymore. Who will I be without Trent next to me? I spent my whole life with him. He was the knobby-kneed boy who dug pits with me when I was convinced I could trap a unicorn. He was my first love. The one person who knew me best and if he were here, he'd know exactly what to say to help me make sense of what I'm feeling. If only I could ask him.

The sky is cloudless when black stars explode. No, not stars—birds. Hundreds gather in a unit, swirling in their own gravity, morphing in rhythm with each other before breaking apart and scattering, turning into shrapnel against the fiery fabric of the sky.

*What would Trent want?* Tears roll down my cheek. What do *I* want? My heart pounds against the wall of my chest. I want to stop hurting. I want to see Trent again, to hold him, and keep him. But my heart is empty and so are my hands. I have nothing left.

There has to be a way out of my pain.

The birds are carried higher in the sky, riding an unseen current until, as quickly as they arrived, they are gone. What a simple pleasure to be a bird. To float and fly, to disappear from view. When I was a kid, Dad used to stand waist-deep in the river and launch me from his arms into the abyss of nothing until I splash-landed in the safety of the water. I would swim back to him, and he would do it again. Again. Again.

The shimmering black wings are gone. Vanished, a memory of a memory, and the sky is empty once again.

Empty. Forever. Dead. Gone. Trent. Float. Fly. Disappear. The words leapfrog in my mind, bending over each other, tying around themselves until they take up so much room inside my mind that I stand up and run.

# six

. . .

## VANCE

This morning, Murphy handed me a new shirt and tie, telling me I was his plus one to Annabelle's sister's wedding. As if I had a choice.

The ceremony is over, so I've removed my tie and myself from the party, sitting alone in the thick of the forest, my back against a tree, snapping a twig into smaller and smaller sections.

The sun is putting on a show with its flaming descent, and a hundred birds gather to dance. I watch them until a thud of feet against the ground, a heave and pull of air in and out of a mouth, and a rustle of fabric catch my attention. Annabelle is running. She careens between tree trunks, ducking under low branches, and if she were ten feet closer, she would crash into me.

But we are worlds apart and she rushes past.

I watched Annabelle erode during the ceremony. I watched her frantically scan the guests and I knew who she was searching for—we all did. Annabelle was always with Trent, not in an obsessive way but in a salt-and-vinegar-chip sort of way. They made a good pair.

I almost grab another stick and start the snapping process all over again, but Annabelle shouldn't be alone. I glance toward the reception, expecting to see someone running after her, but the woods are empty. I don't think anyone knows what's happening, except me, and I don't want to be the one to know. I just want to sit here snapping sticks until the sky is black then go find Murphy. There isn't a twig close enough to grab. I'd have to stand up anyway, and the pit in my stomach turns into a boulder I cannot ignore. Something's not right. People don't run through the forest unless someone is chasing them. Or they are chasing something themselves.

Forgetting my desire to be alone, I follow the map of her coral dress flashing between the ancient pines and emerge onto Ridgeline Road. There is nothing out here other than the forest, the road, and the bridge.

The bridge.

A sickening realization hits me. Annabelle is well ahead of me, bare feet carrying her fast along the pavement. I'm quick, but I didn't understand why she was running until it was too late, and she is still running.

Five steps and Annabelle is even with the bridge.

Four more steps and she's climbed atop the ledge. I yell her name in short barks between breaths, screaming for her to stop, but if she hears, she never slows.

Three steps take her to the center but there won't be enough time. I'll never be able to catch her.

# seven

. . .

## ANNABELLE

My toes curl over the rough stone edge as water swirls far below.

My mind is a tangle of questions and memories, and I can't find meaning in any of them. I don't know what to do. Or who I am. Not anymore. Trent was my foundation and yesterday, if you had asked me who I was, I would have said Trent's girlfriend. Of course, there were others—daughter, sister, friend, student, barista—but being Trent's girlfriend was my favorite.

Now I'm lost, confused, off balance, standing on the ledge of a bridge. How did I end up here? My heart is a drum, pounding Trent's name, pounding a list of words that could mean something. Or nothing.

I could step off the ledge toward the river or the road. What would Trent want me to do? What do I want to do? I close my eyes trying to quiet my mind and find an answer, but all I see is a black imprint of trees burning against my eyelids.

"Did you know the water in Lake Superior is so cold you can dump a dead body in it and the body will never surface?"

The voice next to me is unfamiliar, breathless from something—exertion? Fear? A breeze lifts the hair off my shoulders, and I open my eyes. It takes me a minute to remember my classmate's name. He hardly ever talks to anyone. Vance. I'm dizzy with confusion, and I scrape my feet across the rocks, inching sideways, away from this boy I barely know, frustrated that he interrupted my attempt to find an answer.

"You came up here to tell me about the Great Lakes?" I ask.

He makes a slow gesture between me and the river. "It's the first thing I thought of. If I had thought it through, I would have started with something less deadly."

This is not a conversation I want to have. I was looking for clarity and answers. I wanted to hear Trent's voice.

I close my eyes again, and it's quiet for so long that I forget Vance is there. Until he speaks again. "I'm sorry about Trent."

*I'm sorry.*

The words crack my heart open, and everything

rushes out. I cry, and not softly behind my hand, but in loud wrenching sobs that sound a lot like screaming. Vance doesn't move, he just lets me stand on the ledge of a bridge and come undone. When I finally stop, my entire body aches.

Vance holds out a hand reaching into the space I created between us, his palm up, an invitation. But all I see is Trent's hand and how I couldn't stand the sight of the swinging motion of his keys as we stood at the end of my driveway. I should have grabbed his keys.

I blink, and the hand waiting for me doesn't belong to Trent. It belongs to Vance, and below my feet, the river swirls and gurgles. Vance is saying something about chocolate-covered strawberries waiting to be eaten back at the reception. I don't want food. Or this outstretched hand that doesn't belong to the boy I love.

Loved.

I *loved* Trent, and he is never coming back.

Vance's hand reaches closer, and I don't want it. I don't want to be here. I don't want to be anywhere, except transported back to when my skin felt like my own, instead of a sweater stretched too small across my back.

Vance's hand touches my elbow, as slight as a feather, and I look into his raincloud eyes. "I'll take you back," he says.

I don't know how Vance understands my desire to go

back in time, back to my old life, where everything made sense, and my heart didn't feel like dynamite with the fuse already lit. I don't know how he'll manage to do what he's offered, but I want it more than anything, more than this bridge, or the river waiting below. I reach my hand toward his, stepping toward his offer, but my foot slips and I fall.

# eight

. . .

## VANCE

Annabelle is suspended in mid-air for the eternity of a single breath. Tendrils of golden hair float around her face while her arms bend up and out as if she is a marionette held aloft by invisible strings. As if I could reach out and grab her hand, pulling her safely to the edge.

But she is gone, disappearing in a rush.

I don't think twice before crossing my arms over my chest and jumping in after her. The water is shockingly cold as I slice the surface. My muscles stall before I force them to work, and in the muted stillness underwater, my heart beats as loudly as the repeated warning inside my head.

What if I should have gone for help? What if I can't find her? Why did I talk about dead bodies and snacks? I've never been able to save anyone. Not that Nat ever asked to be saved.

My body shouts for me to return to the surface when I see a pulse of color. Flares rupture at the edge of my vision as I swim toward it. My lungs demand I open my mouth and breathe. But I ignore the pain and the panic and push my arms farther, grasping first fabric, then a leg, and I pull Annabelle's body to mine, kicking for the surface.

We erupt from the river, the birth of a two-headed creature. I cough, gulping air into greedy lungs, rotating Annabelle so her face is free from the water. Thick ropes of hair cling to the sides of her waxy face.

*What if what if what if.*

And then she gasps, writhing in my arms, her eyes wild with fear. I try to say something, but she pushes against me, and I swallow a mouthful of water. Swimming behind her, I'm glad this section of the river is calm and I don't have to fight her and the current to steer us to shore. Throwing myself against the mud and rock, I roll onto the bank, never letting go of Annabelle. Looping my arms under hers, I gently drag her free from the river that almost consumed her. Safely on shore, I press my hands against my thighs, coughing, heaving air in and out.

She's stretched out on the mud, her dress cling-wrapped to her body, shaking but breathing. A thin line of spit drips from the corner of her mouth stretching to the ground. "I'm going for help. I'll be right back."

All she does is blink, and I take off running. I climb the bank, rush along the road, and crash through the trees, branches whacking against me that I don't even attempt to dodge. One whips across my cheek, slicing a line that trickles blood.

I burst into the circular clearing. "Come quick!" I shout over the music. "Annabelle slipped off the bridge!"

Annabelle's dad drops his plate, sprinting to me, but I've already turned back to the woods, running to where I left Annabelle. Her dad catches up with me between the branches asking questions. *Where? When? How?*

But he never asks why.

Cutting a path between the trees, we then race down the center line of the road. I point to the left of the bridge before scooping my phone and wallet from the side of the road, thankful I dumped them before climbing up. Annabelle's dad rushes to her side, his hands hovering over her skin. "I'm right here, sweet pea. I'm right here."

Annabelle's face is ashen, her lips a swirl of blue, purple, and white. The thin line of spit becomes a trickle and then a sudden torrent as she vomits, convulses, and vomits again.

I don't want to stick around and be part of a scene that doesn't belong to me. I don't have a dad who would race to my side or a mom who would pick her way down a steep embankment in heels to cry and pray and hold her hurting child.

This isn't a family portrait you would hang above your mantle. It is raw and it is love. It is family and it wrecks me.

I look up in time to see Murphy appear at the bridge, leaning over, searching. His hand presses to his heart and I back away, pushing deeper into the trees until they clump around me and I'm alone. All my strength is gone, and I fall to the ground. I cry for Annabelle. I cry for all the things I want but will never have. But mostly I cry for the vicious beast life transforms into when you least expect it, and everything it devours.

The sky is dark and growing darker when my phone rings. I'm still on the ground, hidden in the thick of the forest. How much time has passed? Five minutes? Ten? An hour? Figuring the call is from Murphy, I swipe the back of my hand over my face and answer without looking.

My breath rattles at the back of my throat. "What?"

"Baby, it's me."

Her voice turns me into a child. Nat is the only person who has ever called me *baby*. Three years, two postcards, and this is the first time she's ever called. I'm safe under the encroaching night, solid on the ground, but it feels like I have been shoved back into the river, and no one is coming to pull me out.

# nine

. . .

## ANNABELLE

All I want is the couch and as many episodes of *The Great British Baking Show* as it takes before I can have my next dose of pain medication and then fall asleep. But Sasha is sitting on our front porch painting her nails when we get home from the hospital.

My mom rests her hand atop Sasha's fiery hair before climbing the steps to the house. "Sasha, would you like to stay for breakfast?"

Something slides across Sasha's face, an expression I'm not used to seeing on my best friend's face, but she blinks and it's gone. "Can't. Sorry."

Mom smiles, pulling open the screen door when she turns to me, asking silently with her eyes if it's okay for her to walk inside, and I nod.

Sasha's hand is splayed on her knee as she paints

each nail with practiced strokes. "I tried calling you a million times," she says.

I suck in a breath like soda through a straw. "My phone is dead," I lie through clenched teeth as I lower myself to the step below her, taking my time, trying not to jostle my ribs which is impossible, but I try. Two broken ribs and a fractured left wrist. Last night the doctor told me I was lucky. But I think that's a warped version of the word. Luck is finding an empty parking space when you need one. Luck is four-leaf clovers, your favorite song on the radio, or a free scoop of ice cream.

Not dead boyfriends and a broken girl.

Sasha shrugs, accepting my answer, blowing on her nails. "Twilight Licorice, what do you think?" She rotates her hand for me to see. "I figured it needed to be something . . ." She stumbles over her words. "You know, something . . ."

"Dark?" I offer.

Dark, like the birds that fluttered across the sky. Dark, like Vance's eyes, the last thing I saw before being swallowed by the river. Dark, like the inside of my heart that I refuse to crack open ever again.

Sasha finally looks at me and that same strange something lurks under the surface of her eyes, and I turn away, afraid what I see is sympathy or worse—pain. She dips the brush back into the vial then drags it across my cast, painting a black river on the bumpy white surface, and a shiver rolls down my back. I'll never be free from the river.

"Sorry about . . ." She dips the tiny brush again, collecting more nail polish, and I'm amazed that even with these materials she can create something so beautiful. But her sentence is unfinished. I hold my breath, waiting for her to say Trent's name, wondering what it will do to my heart when she does. But she doesn't. This must be what it will be like from now on. Dreading the thought of Trent's name being spoken as if it's a prayer only I can say. Wishing everyone would say his name because if they did, they would bring him back to life, even if just for a breath.

At the hospital, there were scans and questions. *What was I thinking?* Concerned looks and strained conversations. *We should have seen this coming.* And. *Why didn't we see this coming?* What *was* I thinking? It hurts too much to try to remember anything from my life before, but the question leaps out. "Do you think Trent was acting weird? Like maybe hiding something?"

"He seemed fine to me." The brush hovers over my cast before Sasha says, "But if he was keeping secrets, you're better off not knowing." My body sways as if I'm slipping off the edge of the bridge all over again. Better off not knowing? What is that supposed to mean? She adds with a sigh, "It's not likely. Do you even remember how bad he was at two truths and a lie?"

This is true. Trent was painfully horrible at that game.

Sasha keeps talking as she finishes painting the river, but I'm not listening. A few wisps of words make their way into my head, the same sensation as listening to the breeze through branches. I hear her say Derek's name, but I'm thinking about when Trent used to hug me, and I felt like a letter tucked inside the envelope of his arms. Sasha says something about her dad, but I'm thinking about how Trent would grab my hand, and we'd run the length of the dock, laughing our way into cannonballs. But when I surface from that memory, Trent stays under the water.

Sasha wiggles her fingers in my face. "Are you even listening?" she asks.

My pain is an eclipse blocking out the sun, and I wasn't listening at all. I hold my breath, turning the lack of air into a knife between my broken ribs. "You said something about your dad."

A sound catches in the back of her throat as she stands from the porch pinching the nail polish between not-quite-dry fingers. "Right. Something about my dad. That about sums it up." She watches as I try to remember something, anything, that she said, but then she leaves. She is almost on the sidewalk when she calls out, "You're not the only one."

I'm not the only one? But that thought is pushed

away by something soft gliding against my hand, making me jump. I immediately brace my elbows against my sides as my ribs feel like they are cracking once again from my sudden movement. It's a gray fluff ball of a kitten that I had completely forgotten about. Mom brought her home the day before Trent died. She does this all the time—finds animals that need a home, then finds a home that needs an animal. The kitten nudges my hand with her head, and I scoop her onto my lap. She circles twice before settling, a rumbling purr vibrating against my leg.

Focusing on the kitten is a good distraction from my conversation with Sasha. "Maybe you can stay with us," I tell the kitten. If it were up to my dad, no animals would make it past the front door, but mom has a way of sneaking them in. "If I name you, you'll stand a better chance with Dad."

I used to spend afternoons talking to my dad's legs while he was working under a vehicle. He'd listen to me ramble about my day, and he'd tell me what he was working on, a hand poking out, asking for a tool. He was always happy when I'd let him explain mechanical things, thrilled that I seemed interested in what he did for a living. And that's how I know what to name the kitten.

Torque. The act of applying enough pressure until something rotates. It goes both ways—to loosen a bolt or fasten one firm, and I know which way my heart is rotating.

Mom comes out holding a quilt and a plate of waffles. She wraps the blanket around me, even though the June air is already tinged with heat and sits on the step so close our shoulders touch. "Sasha already left?"

I nod, once again reminded of her last words. *You're not the only one.* I don't know what she meant but I am the only one, can't she see that?

Mom takes my arm, looking at the river Sasha painted on my cast. There are tears in her eyes when she looks up. "Trent's mom just called. She's inviting you to the graveside service on Friday morning. But I don't want that to be too overwhelming for you."

Mom said Trent's name, and when I heard it, it was like she had opened a window on the first day of spring. I'm finally able to take a breath and I force myself to smile. My skin feels tight, sunburn tight, but I shift the corners of my mouth higher.

Mom's lie-detector skills are on high alert as she watches me, but, as good as she is, she can't see what I'm doing. It's not an easy task to shove Trent and the bridge far enough inside my heart that I can no longer feel the memories. I need my mom to let me go to his service, and she'll only do that if she thinks I'm okay. And I'll only be okay if I can't reach in and pull my memories to the surface. I have to lock them away.

"I need to be there. I'll be alright." My smile slips, but I push it higher and try to relax the rest of my face. "I'm feeling better." It's what everyone wants to hear me say, but it's not true at all, and I hold my breath until she squeezes my hand, agreeing that I can go.

Relief floods my body, and I lean my head on her shoulder. Everything is going to be okay. Time with Trent is exactly what I need.

# ten

. . .

# VANCE

I'm thirty thousand feet off the ground, sitting in 24C, wondering if Nat will recognize me. Or if I will recognize her. My mind pulses with the thought: *What if what if what if.* The same question that drummed through my heart last night as I searched for Annabelle in the water. The question no longer pulses for Annabelle's safety, but for a home, for my mom.

This is all Murphy's fault. This glimmer of *what if* is such a slippery idea. We fought as he drove me to Seattle this morning.

"This could be an opportunity," he said.

I couldn't tell if Murphy wanted that to be true so he can have his life back and stop being my makeshift parent. Or if he simply can't get over the hole Nat carved in his heart when she didn't agree to his plans of staying sober, left him, and never looked back.

"How can you do this? How can you hold out for something that will never happen? It's like you want her back. And for what?" I asked, my agitation bouncing my knee against the glove box.

His answer was quiet. "You don't know what she's like."

My fist slammed into the dashboard. "You think I don't know that when she's sober and she pays attention to you, it's like you're living under a heat lamp? Because she loves you like there's nothing else. She's the drug, and you'd do anything to feel like that again because she erases the emptiness in the sky and makes a constellation where you belong. She was all I had until she decided being my mom wasn't worth her time. So, no. You don't get to tell me that I don't know what she's like."

The speaker crackles between the captain's words, letting me know we are making our final descent and my stomach drops. What if Nat really is ready to stay clean this time? She called me from a rehab center last night, rambling on about being surrounded by so much goodness, so much beautiful light. Her words were bubbles that floated higher than I'd ever heard. She had a revelation about life, and she needed to tell me in person. Forget the past, forget that she walked out on me. Forget all that. Come now.

What will she have to say? I don't want to get sucked

into Murphy's all-consuming belief that people can change for the better. All the evidence I've accumulated points in the opposite direction.

My parents were never married or stable or sober. My dad left when I was eight, and Nat's rudder completely disappeared after that. Try as I might, I never knew how to be what she needed. She slipped deeper into her addictions until one day she left and never came home. I was young enough to convince myself that if I could have been different—if I could have figured out what she needed and bent myself into that—she would have stayed and been my mom.

Along with the ticket, I received an email from Gary, Nat's counselor at the center. He told me he'd be waiting at the main entrance of the airport, and then we'll drive north to the facility. The plane's wings dip, and my heart is stuck in my throat. What am I supposed to do when I see my mom after she abandoned me? Hug? Fist bump? Cross my arms and demand answers? Our reunion will happen later, but my palms are sweaty at the thought of seeing her, and I wipe them down my thighs.

At the airport exit, a lean gentleman stands in front of the automatic door wearing khakis and a plaid button-up, holding a wrinkled paper with Vance Powell scrawled across it. I have half a mind to keep walking, but I catch his eye and there's no point pretending I have somewhere else to be.

Gary rolls the paper in his hand. "Vance?"

"Yep."

Gary doesn't ask if I had a nice flight or if I need to collect a bag. The absence of all the words he could say but doesn't bristle between us as he adjusts his wire-rim glasses. "Not sure how to say this, but your mom left our facility earlier today. From what we can piece together, she convinced a groundskeeper—"

I want to shove the words away, or Gary for saying them, but I shove my hands into my pockets instead. "You don't need to explain." I plummet off the tightrope I had been walking that this time—this time—things would be different. That Nat would want me *this time*. I've felt this way before: destroyed and pretending like it's no big deal.

Like all the other times.

Months after Dad left, Nat couldn't make rent and she dragged the two of us from Portland to California. We drove all day, and I was tired and hungry when we arrived at the apartment she somehow got from a friend of a friend of a friend. A single light bulb flickered at the end of the long hall, and Nat didn't even unlock our door before she knocked on the one across the hall. A woman answered the door with a paintbrush in one hand and a cigarette in the other. Nat asked her to watch me while she ran to get groceries; she'd be right back. But one hour, then another, then another passed before the woman, Vivian, grabbed my hand and pulled me across the street to a boarded-up building where I discovered what Nat had really left to go do.

After that, Nat's leaving became the song playing on repeat in the background of my life.

And now it's playing again. Buzzing in my ear, low and slow, sounding for all the world like that Cranberries song piping through the overhead speakers. Why did I let Murphy convince me that Nat could be someone she will never be? People do not change, at least not in the way Murphy thinks they can. People change from bad to worse—from Mother to nothing.

I turn, searching for an arrow pointing toward the ticket counter, and start walking in that direction.

Footsteps follow behind me. "Where are you going?" Gary asks.

"To find a flight," I answer, unsure why he cares.

Gary reaches an arm to my backpack, stopping me. "Not tonight, I already checked."

So, I'm stuck. I shove a hand through my hair. "When?"

"The earliest flight is tomorrow morning." He pulls a folded paper from his pocket, handing it to me. "It's all booked. I called your guardian and he'll be expecting you. There's a hotel down the road." His chin tips toward the door. "I set you up with a room."

As we drive, Gary keeps apologizing for Nat's disappearance until I tell him to stop. It's not exactly shocking. Painful, yes. Surprising, no. He pulls into the parking lot and hands me cash from his wallet, saying it's to cover my trouble for coming all this way for nothing. One last apology and he drives away. In front of me waits a generic hotel lobby and to my side, a road stretches out farther in the distance than I can see an end to.

I look from one to the other and start walking.

The sky shifts from orange to denim to not quite black, and I've walked so far that a sweaty imprint of my backpack is stamped on my shirt. I think about the days when Nat was sober and she would scoop me up in her arms, whirling me in circles until I begged her to stop. We'd spend the day huddled in a fort made from cushions and blankets pretending we were adrift on a raft, or stalking lions in the savanna, or landing a lunar pod. I could never tell when a day like that would come along —they were mileposts strung too far apart to rely on.

The appeal of alcohol never made sense to me. All I saw were its ugly side effects. What euphoria could it possibly give my parents that they were willing to go to such lengths to chase it, even if it meant hurting everyone they said they loved?

Anger and sweat crust my skin as I pass a neon orange sign advertising an establishment called The Growler. Fangs extend into the open mouth of the G, and for the first time, I want to find out what it is that Nat can never leave.

Smoky air rushes against my face as I open the door. Several pool tables take up one end of the room, and scattered round tables fill the other half. A pot-bellied man is hunched over the bar, a thick braid hanging down his spine. He's wearing a leather vest covered in patches, no shirt underneath, unless you count the sleeves of tattoos on both arms. Several empty shot glasses line the wood in front of him.

The man in the leather vest raises one finger, circles it above his head, and thumps it on the bar.

That's my cue. As soon as the bartender places the shot in front of Leather Vest, I'm already at his side, swiping it and swallowing. I instantly double over, face contorted, throat on fire, my stomach a rolling sea. This has to be paint thinner or gasoline or regurgitated venom. It is not what I expected, and if this is what Nat always wanted more than me then I finally know how I rank.

My mom would rather ingest battery acid than look me in the face.

Leather Vest spins and jumps off his barstool. His words slop together into an unrecognizable tangle.

I feel sick. In part from whatever I swallowed and in part from the realization of how far gone Nat has always been. I shift my weight on the balls of my feet, my anger demanding an outlet, so I ram my body against Leather Vest, but the man is immovable.

It's a fast fight.

Leather Vest's fist lands with a nasty crunch against my face as blood spurts, but before I can take a swing, an equally stout man in a matching leather vest pulls me from the clutches of my opponent. Leather Vest The Second drags me to the door, shoving me out with a string of choice words about what will happen if I ever set foot in here again.

Dumped in the parking lot, I slap dust off my jeans as if that is my most pressing concern. *Why couldn't you love me more than the dragon inside of you? Why couldn't you stay, just this once?*

But there is no time for longing. Blood gushes into my eye, and I have to figure out what to do. I walk a few feet to the gas station next door, thankful that the bathroom around the back is unlocked, and assess the damage. My right eye is already swelling shut. A cut above my eyebrow is the blood-pumping machine. I almost break the lever on the dispenser to get enough of the small and never-absorbent brown paper towels to clean my face and stop the bleeding. The end result is not my best look, but I ruffle my hair so it flops to the side, almost covering the worst of it. Inside the gas station, I pull out some of the money Gary gave me and buy a package of bandages, some aspirin, and a bottle of water.

But before I swallow an aspirin, I lean over a bush at the edge of the parking lot, stick a finger down my throat, and hurl. I don't want a single drop of what Nat chases, and I make my stomach as empty as my heart.

Every step rattles my bones. My head throbs, and my face is mangled, and there is only one person I want to talk to.

Murphy answers on the second ring. "You okay?"

"Do you remember the first time I called you?" Three years ago, I had to borrow the phone from the minimart next to my building in Denver. The phone had duct tape wrapped around the receiver, and the plastic square over the number nine was missing, leaving an exposed mess of wires. I was fourteen, and Nat had been gone for three weeks. I stood next to a rack of potato chips I had no money to buy, my stomach too hungry to growl.

There was no need to take off the Nirvana hoodie that was too big for me and read the number. I had already memorized the *206-555-4663* that Nat had written in permanent marker on the back of the tag. After I dialed, I tugged the sweatshirt tighter, more afraid of someone answering than I was of the phone ringing endlessly. If someone answered, they could fail me. Probably would fail me.

"Of course I remember."

"Why did you listen to me? Why didn't you hang up?" I suddenly need to know. I've never asked Murphy why he listened to my story or why he bothered to drive an entire day to come find me.

"Are you sure you're okay? Gary said he set you up with a room for the night."

"Answer my question. Why didn't you hang up?"

Murphy's sigh is so loud I almost feel it through the phone. "When you told me who you were, who your mom is . . . I couldn't hang up."

Murphy did it for Nat. Everything in my life revolves around her, and I'm the fallout. My head is splitting open just like my heart. My words are a whisper. "She wasn't here, Murphy. She wasn't here." And I hang up before Murphy hears the gurgle in my throat that could be the start of a sob if I let it.

Thank goodness Gary felt guilty and left me this cash. The rest of it should be enough for an Uber. My exhaustion goes far beyond not feeling up for the long walk back to the airport. I'm tired of feeling like a guest living inside agreements, and before I check to see if a ride is available, I download an app, typing in my graduation date for next year, and watch the seconds start to fly by.

One year. That's all that remains, then I'll really be on my own. What would it feel like to have a home? To have people that belong to me instead of agreements and empty postcards. To know that I'm worth it, so they'll stick around and love me instead of convincing groundskeepers to unlock the gate.

My dad left. My mom left. I sit in the grass next to the gas station and schedule a ride before shoving my phone in my pocket. People walking out is hardwired in my DNA so I might as well embrace it because in one year it will finally be my turn to leave.

# eleven

. . .

## ANNABELLE

What do you wear to your boyfriend's funeral?

Would any outfit seem like the right thing when the person you love is being buried? I finally settle on a faded denim skirt, my white Chuck Taylors, and the Post Malone T-shirt Trent gave me. It seems a better way to honor him than monochrome sadness.

Dad drives me down Cut Canyon to the cemetery. "Mom told me it was your idea to name the kitten Torque."

I hope he's letting Torque stay since they've reached a sort of peace treaty. Dad gets his entire recliner while the cat is relegated to its pillow-top kingdom, and not just because he thinks getting rid of the kitten will be one more thing to make me sad. Either way, I'm glad. I like having the cat around.

He reaches for my shoulder. "Well played."

At the entrance to the cemetery, he brushes the hair away from the side of my face. "I'll wait here for you."

If he waits, I won't be able to get what I came for. "It's okay, Dad. I'll get a ride."

Reaching across the gear shift, he grabs my hand while his eyebrows mash together. I know that expression. It's how he stares at an engine when he's trying to figure out how to repair it, except now I'm what's broken and in need of fixing. He puts the car in park. "I'll rephrase. I'm waiting here for you, and then we'll go to the school together."

It sounds so normal, a dad offering to drive his daughter to school. But it's not normal when a community is about to gather in the gym to sit on the bleachers so they can remember and mourn.

I close the car door and force myself to take even breaths, grasping the hot chain-link gate to steady myself. A long, straight line of oaks guard the property, and it's too much for me to look at them, to think about all they have witnessed, knowing they will forever shelter Trent and I shuffle away from them as quickly as my broken body allows.

Trent was the oldest of four boys, all of them replicas of each other. They each have the same sandy hair, blue eyes, and mischievous smiles. A six-year gap separated Trent and his first younger brother. Reed, Brody, and Sawyer are clumped together, three years spanning them from tip to tail. I loved watching them love each other, a pack of bear cubs tumbling over one other, my own band of brothers when I was with them. They stand next to their parents, scrubbed clean with slicked-down hair, wearing ties and long faces. They make a picture of a table missing a leg, off-balance, and tipping toward the earth. It's hard to look at them and not fall to the ground.

Trent's mom starts to pull me into a hug but catches the sight of the cast and changes her mind mid-motion, rubbing my arms in motherly affection instead. "I'm so glad you're here."

*I'm so glad you're here* could mean at the service. Or. It could mean alive. I can't open my mouth without sobbing, and I don't want to do that. All I can give her in return is a smile that probably looks nothing like a smile.

"We're going up tomorrow to put a cross on the roadside. Would you and your parents want to join us?"

How do people have conversations like this without breaking in half? I'm having a hard time standing here listening to her words and what they mean so I hold my breath until my ribs burn. My voice is a thread, ready to snap. "I have to go sit down." I find a chair and dig my fingernails into the skin next to my cast. Everything is going to be okay. As long as I keep the pressure of my nails piercing my skin, I'm going to be okay.

The hearse winds its way to where we wait, and I raise my head to the sky, blinking, trying to keep the avalanche of tears from escaping. Fixing my attention on the perfect peacock blue above, I take a breath. It should be against the rules for the sky to look so beautiful on a day like today. It looks like summer, like a day at the river, like a blanket spread for a picnic. I'd prefer a gray bubble with dripping rain. Or at least a handful of clouds to disrupt its perfection.

Trent's dad stands as the casket is lowered into the grave. Watching it sink into the ground is excruciating. My chest clicks tighter with each inch gone until I no longer see the polished wood, and I am hardly breathing.

His dad's voice is sandpaper, grief punching a hole through every word of the poem he recites. I try to take a breath but choke on a sob I can't keep pressed back. By the end of the service, my lungs burn and I'm shaking. I don't know how to stand and carry on. Trent's mom offers me a ride, but I point past the winding path and line of trees to where my dad has been waiting.

Then I watch everyone walk away.

Now that I'm alone, I walk to the fresh gash in the ground and close my eyes, but all I see is water swirling under my feet. A rush. A river. Remorse. My eyes fly open and the only river here is the one Sasha painted on my cast.

On the day before my birthday, I used to spend the entire day keeping track of the last time I did something.

The last time I woke up as a nine-year-old. The last time I brushed my teeth as a nine-year-old. The list grew longer all day. Today is an endless list of lasts with Trent. The last time I saw him. The last time we kissed. The last time I heard his voice. The last time he made me laugh. The last time he took me by surprise. The last time he could have told me the truth.

A pin pulls loose, setting free a frantic need to leave part of myself with Trent forever. I rip at my cast until my fingers are raw and smudged black from the make-believe river, and I still try to pry it off so I can throw it down and give Trent a fraction of my brokenness.

I shout into the grave: "What am I supposed to do?"

It's shocking how forceful my panic feels, and I press my arms against my ribs to ease the throbbing. It is too dangerous to release my pain—look what happens when I try. I need to keep the pain to myself; it's the only way I'll be able to carry on. Whatever that means.

<hr>

My dad's hand is on the small of my back. He's not pushing me through the gymnasium, but he's making sure I keep walking forward. Everyone is inside this room for Trent. To honor him. To remember him. To let him go.

Officer Daily-Drip-To-Go catches my eye and tips his

head. Murphy stands behind a folding table because, of course, he is pouring cups of coffee. It's in his blood to serve. Miss Coffee-With-A-Carmel-Swirl is holding her daughter's hand, and when I pass her, the kindness in her eyes almost wrecks me.

I took longer than expected at Trent's grave, so the lights are already clicking off and a slideshow of Trent's life is beginning. My mom is sitting in the row behind Trent's family, but I don't want to walk any closer. When my dad's hand gently presses against my back, I stop moving and, thankfully, he lets us stay where we are.

I've already seen most of these pictures, thumbing through the albums on the shelves in Trent's living room. There is Trent's chubby baby face, his gap-toothed, first-grade grin, crooked even then. I look away. I hate being forced to remember that he is never coming back. I lean into my dad and tell him I need some water and escape to Murphy's table. But I walk past it and press my forehead to the wall, keeping my back to the room and the flickering pictures, when someone grabs my hand.

I don't recognize the feel of the paper-thin skin covering bony knuckles and look to find Mrs. Only-Gets-A-Water standing next to me. She does nothing to wipe the tears away that cling to her cheeks. She's watching Trent's life in pixels, but I turn once again to the blue and silver mats adhered to the wall meant to soften the blow of impact.

"It's okay to be sad, Capítuloito."

Capítuloito. I haven't been called "Little Chapter" in years. Mrs. Hernandez is a retired children's librarian, and when she read to us on Saturday mornings at the library, she offered each word as if it were a gift, or a key to unlock a hidden kingdom. Most people simply say words, but Mrs. Hernandez is not like most people. If words were snakes, she'd be able to charm them so they rise from the basket and dance. Her voice is her super-power and might be the reason that Murphy lets her sit sipping free cups of water all day in the chair by the window. If I could listen to her talk all day, I would let her stay too.

I don't want to be sad because being sad acknowledges all the truths I don't want to look at. Which is why I've turned my back on The Life and Times of Trent playing on the screen. I especially do not want to see that. I want to forget every last detail of the past few days so I'll stop suffocating.

I can't do what Mrs. Hernandez is asking of me: to accept my sadness. I want my life back—why doesn't anyone understand? Mrs. Hernandez releases my hand, finally wiping away the tears clinging to her cheek. She wasn't afraid to let them fall or let them stay. But I can't do anything she's suggesting and slip out through the open door.

75

# twelve

. . .

## VANCE

The side door of the gym is propped open, exposing a dark interior. Flickers of light streak across the polished floor, keeping rhythm with the piano music. Trent's life has become a photo montage.

I was going to step in and stand at the back, but Annabelle emerges through the door as if it is a portal into a world she is unfamiliar with, and I guess that is exactly what it is. She raises her cast-covered arm, shielding her eyes from the overabundance of sun, cocking her head to the side, her eyes running over my face as if she's trying to remember what I look like. She didn't return for the last week of school, and I haven't seen her since the bridge. My face is healing, but it's still an atlas of misery. My right eye is no longer swollen shut, but it is an ugly purple bruise, fringed with a northern-lights swirl of green and yellow. One scabbed-over cut dashes my cheek, another marks my forehead.

"Is your face because of . . . you know, because of me?" she asks.

I wasn't expecting that. Of all the things she could have asked, she wants to know if she is the source of my pain. "Are you a drunk biker twice my size?"

"No?" Her voice ticks up at the end, a question rather than a statement, then she steps closer, and I catch a hint of coconut from her hair. Her hand becomes a hummingbird over the hurt of my face. Quick. Tentative. Hovering. Never touching my skin, her fingertips are electric, and I force myself not to step back. Her hazel eyes never leave mine.

"Thank you," she whispers.

Thank you for seeing me, for helping me, for pulling me out of the river. Her two words are heavy with all of those. My nod is crisp before I rake a hand through my hair, but I wince as it pulls at the skin above my eye. I point at the open door behind her. "Didn't want to stay?"

She doesn't look over her shoulder, just shakes her head and I think that's it, that is all the conversation we'll have, and I start to leave.

"Wait. Your face." I turn, wondering what she wants. "You said it was a drunk biker. Any chance it happened at a bar?" I nod and there's a light in her eyes. "Can you take me there? I need to forget about today. This week. My life."

I can't help from laughing at the thought of strolling into The Growler, this time with Annabelle. "That's not possible."

Her face falls, and she is the one to walk away. "Fine, don't help. I'll go myself."

I cannot let her do that. Annabelle is not my responsibility or my friend, but I know what happens in places like The Growler or the abandoned train cars hidden deep in the woods further up Ridgeline Road. Even if it were legal, she is not in any state to go looking for trouble, thinking she can handle it.

Her steps are tiny and I feel like I'm not even walking when I match my pace to hers. "That's a really bad idea."

She grunts. "All of life is one bad idea after another. Don't feel like you need to change my mind, or stop me."

Call me a glass-half-empty kind of guy, but she sort of has a point about life being a string of bad ideas. And now that she's latched onto the idea of getting hammered so she can forget her life, it won't be an easy thought to dislodge. Those ideas have sticky edges that hang on tight, even when someone tries to shake sense into your head. Living with Nat taught me that. Which only leaves one option I can think of. "I'll drive you."

In the alley, I point at Murphy's truck and slide into the driver's seat. I flip the sunshade down, catching the key that falls while Annabelle climbs in. It's not the fluid step, bend, twist movement of someone getting into a vehicle. Her body moves as a solid unit, joints fused together, pressing her arms next to her side for support. Every movement she makes forms a letter spelling out pain, weary, broken.

"For the record," I say again, "this is a horrible idea."

It's quiet as we follow the river, silent as the two-lane road grows into four, and the buildings of Rye sprout from the earth instead of an endless display of trees. I don't say anything as we enter downtown, waiting for her to change her mind, to tell me to take her home, but she doesn't. We drive past an unremarkable building, its windows boarded over, and Annabelle tells me to stop when a random guy pushes himself out of the plywood-covered doorway.

She carefully unfolds herself from the truck and manages to pry the plywood far enough from the wall to slip through. I do not want to follow her inside, but I've been inside buildings like that and know what she'll find. She shouldn't go in there, especially alone.

Slits of light enter the room at odd angles, turning shadows into shapes. Broken bottles. Cardboard boxes. Wooden pallets. An old door. A tipped-over shopping cart. An old computer monitor next to a filthy mattress.

One of the shadows-turned-shapes is a man sprawled on the floor, making a passed-out snow angel in the dust, a needle dangling from his grasp. Annabelle sucks in a sharp breath and grabs my hand. I can almost feel the rings Vivian wore on every finger digging into my child-sized hand as she squeezed it when we found Nat passed out drunk, vomit down the front of her shirt.

I want to be impervious to the shock of searching for, and finding, and losing Nat. But I'm not. Those images never come to me as a healed or whole picture—how could they? They are fractured jigsaw pieces that never fit.

Kicking the foot of the man passed out on the floor is a release for my spiraling thoughts. "Wake up!" The man's eyelids flutter, and his arm jerks, but he does not wake up. My heart pounds with memories no childhood should hold. Grocery money spent on anything but groceries. Checking the inside of the toilet tank when Nat crossed her heart, telling me she didn't buy a fifth of vodka but finding one there every time. Skipping out of paying rent, driving away in the middle of the night, only being allowed to take what I could carry. Landing in a new town, a new dingy apartment, with a new set of disappointments and broken promises.

I kick the sole of the stranger's shoe again, whirling to Annabelle. "This is what you want? This?" My arms fly up to encompass the room. "If you're lucky, this will kill you straight away. More likely it'll bleed everyone you love to death. So if this is what you want, you're on your own. I won't be part of it." I shove myself out the narrow gap in the plywood leaving Annabelle alone in the dark.

Lowering my forehead to the hot metal of the truck's door, I wish the heat would singe away every memory that burns worse than the sun-scorched metal on my skin. But it doesn't and I drive away, ready to circle up the ramp to the freeway. I know what it feels like to want to forget your life. I grew up with a front-row seat to this kind of devastation, the kind Annabelle thinks is a legitimate way to forget. It's not her fault—isn't that how alcohol is advertised? I slam my fist against the steering wheel and turn the truck around.

She snail-steps along the sidewalk, honey hair hanging in curtains down the sides of her face, arms hugging across her stomach, crumpling Post Malone's face. I slow, rolling the window down.

"Get in," I tell her.

Annabelle keeps walking.

I throw the truck into park and hop out. I have no idea what to say, but something about Annabelle makes it hard for me to stay mad. Maybe it's the fact that when I look at her, I see the pain trapped inside her heart, something I know all too well.

"So, we're going to walk home?" I ask.

Her eyes shoot to mine. "You're such a jerk."

"Maybe. But driving's faster."

Annabelle snorts because I don't deny her accusation, and she turns to the truck. I wag my finger at her shirt while she crosses the seatbelt over her lap. "Don't think I'll feel sorry for you and play him on the drive home to cheer you up. Because that's not happening."

"You're really something, you know that?" She grabs the balled-up Nirvana hoodie I tossed between us. "You and your dead band."

Nat abandoned a lot in her life, but never the 90s. If you stumble across a picture of Courtney Love, you've seen my mom. Nat's music was the tell-tale heart living under our floorboards. Savage Garden, Gin Blossoms, Green Day. Those were good days. Radiohead. Pearl Jam. Red Hot Chili Peppers. Those were transition days. She only listened to one song by Soundgarden, but if "Black Hole Sun" played, it meant Nirvana was next and Nat saved Nirvana for the worst days. Except for her, they were the best. Kurt Cobain's gravelly voice meant locked doors and empty bottles.

"I never listen to them." The admission is out before I realize.

"You wear this every single day, and you don't even listen to them?"

I can't stand listening to Nirvana, and I can't stop wearing this sweatshirt. It's love and it's hate. I pull it from her grasp. She might be capable of understanding. "It's like comfort food, except I'm allergic."

Her nose wrinkles. "That's not even logical."

"Oh, right, I forgot you're winning at logic these days."

Her eyes narrow. I should have just gone with the easy answer to begin with. "They're legends. Even your boy Posty knows that."

"He's not my boy Posty," she says, mimicking my voice. Then she whispers, "He was Trent's favorite."

I meant what I said as a flippant comment, something to dampen the rush of memories that have crashed through my body, and now I've managed to mock the dead. I want to get out of the car and burn my forehead against the metal door one more time. I don't trust myself to say the right thing. This is the problem with spending time with people—you have to know what to say. I bring the truck to life and plug my phone into the cord hanging from the dash, scrolling until I find what I'm looking for. We pull away from the curb as the intro of Malone's song "Circles" fills the cab and Annabelle tips her head against the window.

She'll probably want to add this little excursion to the list of things she would like to forget about her life. But as we pass the storefront of one of my favorite used bookstores, I have an idea. I parallel park and exit the cab, but she's still sitting inside, her cheek squished against the glass.

I tap on the window. "Come with me."

I think she rolls her eyes, but the door clicks open and I watch her slowly unfold herself, and clap at her accomplishment. "Impressive."

"Because offering me a hand would be too hard?"

She freezes and is probably remembering the same thing I am. How we stood on the bridge together, me saying stupid things, holding my hand out, hoping she wouldn't jump. I ignore the jab because she has every right to call me out for clapping at her accomplishment of exiting the truck when her bones are broken.

Inside, we make our way to the back wall, and I run my hand along well-worn spines and pull one off the shelf. The cover is horrendous. How can there be so much flowing fabric and so much exposed skin at the same time? But in all my years of doing this, romance novels are the best.

I pull a permanent marker from my back pocket, watching Annabelle's eyebrow raise because who walks around with a marker conveniently tucked in his back pocket? Me. Exactly for this reason. I lick my thumb and scrape it across the pages, stopping when I feel like it. Then I drag it over the words I don't need, so I can tell Annabelle that I understand what she is going through in the only way I know how.

~~There was a moment when the room stopped spin-~~ ~~ning. When~~ **everyone** ~~faded to the background. Time~~ ~~stopped, and Adrianna's future~~ **has** ~~just begun.~~

**Something** ~~like an ache burst in her chest.~~ **They** ~~will~~ ~~call it love, but she will call it passion. Life gives lists of~~ ~~things to~~ **want**, ~~but none greater than this;~~ **to** ~~desire the~~ ~~affection of another. Adrianna will never~~ **forget** ~~the first~~ ~~time his eyes found hers.~~

"You can't do that." Her words are a hiss, as if I spray painted a glitter heart between God and Adam's finger on the ceiling of the Sistine Chapel.

I turn the book over for her inspection. "Calm down, I'll pay for the book. I'm not a monster."

When she looks at me after reading my message, her eyes look green instead of brown under a sheen of unreleased tears. Her voice is so soft that if there was more background noise in the store, I would have missed her question. "You have things you want to forget?"

"Pages." Forget about Lake Superior, this is the truest thing I've ever told her.

She blinks, and the tears slide down her face, but I hand her the marker and the book. It takes a very long time before she turns the page and blacks out anything.

The book is about to slip from her grasp, and I grab it before it falls to the ground, reading what she left behind.

~~Adrianna gasped. "I beg your pardon,"~~ **her glove fell to the floor,** ~~"you simply~~ **do not** ~~say such a thing."~~

~~Victor's eyes gleamed. "Rest assured, I~~ **know** ~~the proper course of action."~~

~~His eyebrow arches as Adrianna wondered~~ **who** ~~was this man?~~

Her voice is a whisper. "I don't know who I am anymore." She repeats it several times almost like she's forgotten I'm there. Then, as if awakening, her eyes find mine, her voice gaining strength. "You said *everyone* has something they want to forget. Do you really believe that?"

If there is one thing I know, it's that life sucks. "Absolutely."

I can practically see the wheels spinning in her mind. "And people don't want to admit the things they want to forget because they hurt, right?" She tucks her chin to her chest as if her next thought actually sucker-punched her. "Trent was acting strange the days before . . ." She doesn't finish, her eyes locking onto mine. "Do you think Trent had something he wanted to forget? Something he was hiding?"

My mouth goes dry with the truth I could tell and all the things I know about Trent. But Derek has a very specific piece of paper that I need him to keep to himself. My phone buzzes and I'm thankful for a reason to look away from Annabelle. I read a text from Murphy: *Going out on a limb—Annabelle left the memorial. Her folks are a little frantic. Any idea?*

I fire off a quick reply and tell her we have to go, that the town is looking for her. It might be an exaggeration —I don't expect the entire town to be looking for her. But then again, it is West Aldrin and maybe they are. This jolts her back to reality. Her question about Trent is forgotten.

But I know the answer.

# thirteen

· · ·

## ANNABELLE

The couch in Craig's office is blue velvet with armrests so tall they feel like barricades. Every Wednesday afternoon I sit on this couch, and every session starts the same way. He crosses his legs and leans forward ever so slightly as he asks, "So, how's your week going?"

And every week I tell the same lie. "Fine."

Craig settles back in his chair. "Tell me how you feel about summer ending. You'll be back to school, back to work."

I think about how this morning I sat at my desk, finally going through my backpack. I hadn't touched it since the day Trent died. I found crumpled sheets of paper, a textbook I never turned in, and my spiral notebook filled with lists from a life that is no longer mine.

"I used to make a list every day. You know, things like work, school." My voice catches on the first syllable of Trent's name because he used to be on every list. His name is the thread of a blanket, and if I pull it, I'll unravel so I leave it untouched. "I'm glad my parents said I could go back to work. School is school." I lift and lower my shoulders. "It should be fine."

"What about friends? Have you still been spending time with them?"

A few weeks ago, I told Craig that I got together regularly with Derek and Sasha. I thought the lie sounded believable, like something I should be doing. I can't even pull to mind the last time I saw Derek. Sometime in the *before* category of my life. The last time I saw Sasha, she painted me a river. I rub my arm, expecting to see the black paint smudged across my cast, but both are gone.

Spending the summer avoiding the entire town by hiding myself inside my house is one thing, but it's something else to avoid my best friend. My face flushes. "They've been busy," I say in a rush, but I have no idea if that is true and my stomach twists so I offer part of the truth. "I haven't left the house much." I don't tell Craig that I've spent the summer alone in my room, keeping my window open, an invitation for Trent to haunt me, but he already is. I can trace the outline of him everywhere I look. The doorway. The edge of my bed. The roof. My heart. But I've started sneaking out of the house at night, when the town is asleep, needing to be outside before my room full of ghosts smothers me.

Craig winces at my admission. Maybe he imagines me transforming into one of those people who keeps the blinds drawn, refusing to leave their own house. Which honestly doesn't sound like a bad idea. I don't like the way Craig is squinting his eyes at me. He probably wants to press into my admission. "It's not like I *never* leave the house. I went to the memorial."

That was months ago and I couldn't even stay. I needed to get as far away as possible from the gym that should have reeked of sweaty teens but instead smelled like lily-soaked grief. And then I ran into Vance. He seems to appear when I need someone. Never mind the fact that he left me in that abandoned building—at least he came back. And that makes me remember the bookstore. "Do you think everyone has something in their life that they want to forget?"

Now I'm the one pitched forward, waiting for Craig to answer.

His eyes get bigger for a second as if he's excited that we are actually talking about something instead of him trying to pry honest answers out of me. "What makes you ask that?"

I ignore the fact that he answers my question with a question and throw out another one. "And if everyone has something they want to forget, they would most likely keep it a secret, right?"

He rubs his chin. "It's true. I think most people carry weights that we know nothing about, and I would guess that most of those weights are events they would like to remove from their lives." His hands are laced together on top of his mousy hair, tipping his chair back on two legs, thinking. "But there are a lot of reasons why people keep secrets."

I try to think of all the reasons. Shame. Guilt. Fear. But then I think of another reason. Excitement.

What if I've been so focused on the accident and losing Trent that I can't see what was really happening? What if Trent wanted to tell me something amazing? He could have been planning a surprise. Trent loved surprises more than anyone I know, and he always roped Derek into being his partner in crime to pull them off.

Why didn't I think of this sooner? If anyone knew what Trent was up to, it would have to be Derek.

# fourteen

. . .

## VANCE

Will breaking into a church send me to hell?

Probably not, but it's what I wonder as I push myself through the window. They really should lock those.

Yesterday, as I walked the wooded path behind the church, the same window I just crawled through was shoved open and I could make out the shape of a woman hunched over an old upright piano. There wasn't anything fancy about the hymn she practiced. It sounded as soft as the underbelly of a cloud and made my fingers twitch.

I can't remember the last time I played and run my hand over the wood before pressing a key. My body stills as an amber sound fills the room. When Nat would disappear, I used to tell myself that everything was fine, that she'd be back soon. But hours would accumulate, and I could only wait inside the apartment for so long before I needed a change in scenery. That's when I started roaming.

In the basement of our building in Reno, next to piles of left-behind household items and a rat's nest or two, was an old piano. I spent a lot of time watching YouTube videos at the library and then running back before the information leaked out of my brain. Turns out there was no need to rush—music was a language I didn't know I was fluent in. The notes made sense in a way nothing had before. The best part was that, when I played, I wasn't alone in a rat-infested basement waiting for my mom to reappear. I was safe inside the music.

I slide a folding chair across the floor, push the sleeves of my sweatshirt up my arms, and dive headfirst into the notes. It's not a singular song but pieces I remember, and scales, and wrong notes, and chord progressions that feel right in the moment. It's an impromptu ballad that empties me, and for the first time in years, my heart stops compressing. I play it again and again and again.

By the time I exit out the same window, the moon has crested and my soul feels lighter. I might not even need a documentary to fall asleep tonight. Stepping onto Cut Canyon's sidewalk, my head is still wrapped in the sound of the notes when I hear her voice.

"Were you just—" Annabelle's thumb jerks sideways toward West Aldrin Presbyterian.

"Out walking?" I raise my hand in surrender. "Guilty." Music vibrates under my skin, and I wonder if the notes cling to me like too much cologne.

"Behind the church?"

Annabelle makes a face that says she doesn't believe me, and I'm about to list the merits of midnight hikes behind churches but a car slows, then comes to a stop. Derek and Sasha step out. Sasha leans against the side of the car, not walking toward where I stand next to Annabelle, but Derek jogs over.

There are questions written all over Derek's face, but he only asks Annabelle one. "What are you doing out here with him?"

She takes a small step back like she can't remember Derek's name. I watch her eyes squint as she shakes her head then says, "Nothing, I just ran into him, but I'm glad you stopped. There's something I need to ask you."

His eyes jump to mine and I raise my shoulders the smallest amount possible. Why should I know what Annabelle is about to say?

"Did Trent seem off to you the day before the accident?" She says *accident* as if it's a foreign word she doesn't know how to pronounce. She waits for Derek to answer, but he doesn't. "I couldn't figure out what was up with him. It was like there was something he wasn't telling me. I thought it was because I asked him a question he didn't know how to answer, but it was more than that." Her eyes dart to Sasha who now sits on the hood of Derek's car. Annabelle looks at Sasha for a long time before pulling her attention back to Derek. "Like he was hiding something from me. And what if he was?" She steps right up to Derek's chest. "What if he was planning a surprise? Something *you* were helping him with?"

I've never been hunting, but I imagine Derek's face is what a deer looks like when the hunter takes aim. The night I showed up at Trent's garage I was so fixated on Derek witnessing my encounter with Trent that my brain erased the fact they were already arguing about something. I don't think I would have ever remembered their conversation if Derek hadn't waited for me at my locker, revealing that he kept the trump card tucked inside his pocket.

Derek does not want Annabelle to know Trent was thinking about breaking up with her.

Annabelle is still waiting for Derek to admit that he was helping Trent to figure out how to fill her car with balloons or that he hired a mariachi band to follow her home from school. Or something equally thrilling. I suppose deciding to break up with your girlfriend could be considered planning a surprise for her. Just not one she'd be excited about. Sasha snorts from her perch on Derek's car and our attention flicks to her and then back to Derek. Annabelle isn't the only one holding their breath to see what he'll say.

Derek shifts his weight from his left foot and then back to his right—he's nervous. I open my mouth to say something. Not the truth, but something that could relieve the pressure building inside Annabelle and her desire to know. Derek gives an almost invisible shake of his head. It's the loudest warning he can give me right now.

Xylophone notes blast from Sasha's phone and she stops the alarm, lifting her phone in Derek's direction. "Curfew," she says, before climbing back into his car, and slamming the door.

Derek's gaze drifts from Annabelle to me. "We'll talk later."

He's practically running to his car and Annabelle shouts, "Just tell me what you know."

Annabelle's face is twisted in confusion, or maybe pain, and she spins to face me. "Was that weird? That was weird, wasn't it?" She pulls all her hair on top of her head and when she lets go it falls into her face. Swiping the strands away she asks, "You never knew Trent, but if you did, you'd tell me the truth, wouldn't you?"

The truth has never been an easy subject.

The truth is that Nat couldn't stand being my mom and shucked me off. The truth is that Trent was cheating, and I was helping. The truth is that Trent wanted an escape hatch from his relationship with Annabelle. I don't like agreeing with Derek, but maybe he's right and Annabelle is better off not knowing the truth.

I can't flat-out lie to her, so I offer a different truth. "Did you know the most frequent cause of power outages is squirrels?"

Her face is blank, probably from disappointment that no one is answering her questions. "Dead bodies. Squirrels. Is this why no one ever talks to you? You and your stockpile of worthless information?"

If only she knew the extent of my information. I should just offer every last detail to her and let her decide if it's worthless or not. But the corners of her eyes are still pinched in pain, so I tap my fist into her shoulder. "Yep, me and my worthless information. Come on, I'll walk you home."

# fifteen

. . .

## ANNABELLE

Stepping into Murphy's Café is a relief. If Heaven were a scratch-and-sniff sticker, it would smell like ground coffee mixed with old wood, which is exactly what this place smells like.

I push my voice toward the front of the shop as I tie my apron on. "Hey."

I expect Murphy's voice, but it's Vance who answers. I knew he picked up my shifts this summer, but I didn't think I'd see him here this morning. He looks out of place wearing a black apron instead of his black hoodie, stacking to-go cups. He kicks a cupboard door shut with his toe while reaching for the rag draped on the edge of the sink, and it hits me how familiar he is in this space.

He's not the one out of place right now—I am. My thoughts must be as a sign stamped on my face because he gives my elbow a nudge.

"Welcome back. I noticed we're out of punch cards. Want to restock them while I finish here?" he asks, giving me a task to do other than hugging my arms around myself wondering if I'll ever feel like I fit inside my own life.

I open the cash drawer, ready to reach in and grab more customer loyalty cards when a square of purple paper stops me. I jump back, my hand pressed to my lips, holding all the air inside my lungs.

Trent was alive when I slid that paper into the till. It was the morning before his accident. He came to walk with me to school. I made him a cinnamon latte, but he had forgotten his wallet and wrote an IOU that Murphy accepted without question. I'm afraid to pull the sticky note out, but I desperately want to hold documentation from a life that is no longer mine. Leaning my head closer, my hands shaking at my side, I examine the sloppy slant of the letter I. The incomplete circle of the O looks almost like the U next to it. Trent wrote it in a hurry.

My hand is still pressed against my mouth when a quick tap-tap-tap on my shoulder sends me leaping like a frightened cat again.

"Whoa, you okay? Why so edgy?" Vance asks.

Why am I so edgy? Because today is my first day back to reality after living inside the cocoon of my house. And sitting inside the register is the last thing

Trent handed to me. I point at it. "That note. The IOU. Trent wrote it the morning before he died."

Vance looks at the note and then at me. "Want me to grab it for you?"

I'm not superstitious—black cats, broken mirrors, cracks in the pavement that broke my mother's back— I'll take them all at once and still be fine. But I'm certain that if I hold the note, it will turn to dust in my hands. I don't want that to happen. "No. Leave it." I close the drawer. The note will be safe there, a treasure to uncover another day.

My parents agreed I could try coming back to work. But if it becomes too much, they said they'll pull the plug. I'm rattled by the IOU, and tears gather in my eyes. Crying on my first day back to work would be a really bad idea, a huge red flag of concern. So, I press my palms against my eyes. "You want the register or the bar?" My voice shakes as I ask.

"Register. I've been dying to see the designs Murphy says you pour."

My face warms with embarrassment, but I'm glad to be talking about something else. "He was being nice. My latte art is not impressive." I walk toward the espresso maker. "But they make me happy even if there's no point."

"I don't think art needs a reason to exist."

Vance turns his head at the sound of the bell above

the door and Officer Daily-Drip-To-Go's footsteps. I stare at Vance's black hair covering the side of his face, hiding his gray eyes that sometimes look as hard as granite and sometimes as full as the sky ready to burst. How does he always understand?

I would gladly spend the rest of my day making drinks instead of heading to school, but Murphy appears, tapping a screwdriver against his wrist, joking that he will not be held responsible if we are late.

"Senior year," Vance says as we exit the alley.

I cinch the straps of my backpack so tight I feel my pulse throb under the fabric. I thought the start of my senior year would feel like a victory, but it doesn't. Walking to school from Murphy's is as familiar as pulling on my favorite jeans, but right now it's like putting them on straight from the clothesline—stiff and uncomfortable. Not stretched and worn the way I like, when they feel as relaxed as a second skin. In a matter of moments, I'll be surrounded by classmates I've grown up with, lost teeth with, and sat on the dock with, but who I haven't seen in months, not since my life became small and unrecognizable.

I stop moving forward and my breathing becomes shallow and fast. The halls inside West Aldrin High, the ones lined with blue and silver lockers, have been my home for three years. I've always known who I was and where I belonged inside those halls, but I have no idea who I am right now, inside those halls or not.

"I can't do this."

"Can't keep walking?" Vance looks at the red blotches of panic I'm scratching on my neck. We're standing at the edge of the street. All we have to do is cross the road and step onto the campus. Vance puts a hand on my shoulder. It feels heavy, weighted with his own understanding. "People see what they want to see," he says.

That does not sound comforting, and I scratch my neck again. "What is that supposed to mean?"

"It means everyone is going to look at you and already have their minds made up. So who cares? Let them think whatever they want."

I study his face. Nobody knows anything about Vance. Rumors flew around the school when he arrived. It didn't help that Vance kept to himself, never talking to anyone. Eventually, people didn't care enough to invent new theories about where he came from.

His eyes look cold but kind as I say, "That's what you do? Let people think whatever they want about you?"

He nods and I let out the breath I had started to hold, bending my forehead to his arm before smiling at his attempt to steady my nerves.

I know what everyone will see when they look at me and they'll be right. *Let them think whatever they want and then tell them what they want to hear.* It sounds simple enough.

School is an unending repetition of the same encounter. No one asks how my summer was because everyone already knows. No one gives me a hug or tells me it's great to see me. No one does anything except keep their eyes down and avoid standing next to me in case the tragedy that now brands my life happens to be contagious.

Every time I enter a classroom, the conversation dies then restarts, and I know what it has shifted to—me. Teachers look at me with apologetic glances, unsure if they should say something or not. Finding words to say to the girl whose boyfriend died is not a simple task. Finding words to say to the girl who slipped off the edge of the world because her grief was too heavy to hold must seem unimaginable. So, I give everyone the same pasted-on smile, absolving them of their silence.

*I'm fine. I'm smiling. See what you want to see.*

By lunch, I'm drained. I spin the numbers on my locker, wanting to grab my things, and retreat to the cocoon of my room. When I whip the metal door closed, Sasha is leaning against the locker next to mine. This is the first time I've been this close to her in weeks. Months. Her hair used to be flames of red shooting down her back but now it's cut bluntly just above her shoulder. This is something we normally would have discussed. We would have spent hours scrolling through the images she found that inspired the new look; I would have sat with her at the salon.

Did her hair look like this last night when she and Derek pulled up along the sidewalk? It must have, but it was dark and she never came over. I could have walked to her but nothing inside my heart propelled me in the direction of my best friend. *You're not the only one.* Her words from months ago are marbles in my mind and I swallow past a rising sensation I don't want to name.

"I like your hair," I say, offering a branch we could both perch on.

She flicks my comment away. "You have time for midnight strolls and who knows what else with Vance," she says, "but you can't return a single message."

The air huffs out of me. I haven't missed my phone at all. I've liked the silence of not having it turned on, but I never considered what it means to everyone else that I've been unreachable. Plus, it's not like I was out with Vance, I just happened to bump into him.

"It's not like that," I say.

"Really? Because I'm pretty sure I know what I'm talking about." She waves her phone in the air between our faces. "And now, so does everyone else." Sasha opens an app and a blurry zoomed-in video plays. It's from this morning. I'm talking to Vance at the edge of the school. His hand rests on my shoulder, my head slumped on his forearm. Then Sasha's recorded voice. "You don't think that they—"

The recording stops abruptly.

I can't see the number of views the post has generated, but I can guess—everyone. I repeat myself. "It's not like that." I don't want people to think whatever they want to about me if this is what they are thinking.

For a moment, Sasha and I are stuck staring at each other like when we were little and had staring contests. I want to reach out and give a friendly tug to the freshly cut ends of her hair to bring us back to something that makes sense. It's something I would have normally done, but it seems as if *normal* is a ship that sailed a long time ago.

Sasha lets out a long sigh. "Could have fooled me," she says, pocketing her phone, a strange smile twisting her face.

"Why are you doing this? My life is hard enough right now without you making things up about it." My voice climbs the stairs of my frustration.

"Your life is hard enough right now." Her tone has teeth that bite. "Always thinking you are the only one, aren't you? Tell me one thing that is happening in my life right now. One thing." I stare at her, biting the inside of my cheek so hard I'm about to draw blood. She pushes herself off the bank of lockers that she was leaning against. "That's what I thought."

"Fine. You're right—is that what you want me to say?" My stomach twists. I've never been this mad at Sasha in my life. "You want me to admit that you know everything, and I know nothing. You could tell me and then I'd know one thing about your life." She's silent and then walks away. I yell at her back. "Fine! Think whatever you want to about me, but you're wrong."

She doesn't even turn around when she says, "We'll see about that."

I can't tell if her words are a promise or a threat. Neither option seems good, and goosebumps rise along my arm as I stand in the empty hall. I hold my breath again until the pain of it transforms into a red-hot poker between my ribs. My ribs are nicely healed; that's what the doctor told me. As if healing is something pleasant instead of a reminder that I was broken in the first place. All my bones are calcified back together but my life isn't, and I can't stop holding my breath. It brings the pain back so it's sharp and close to the surface.

*People see what they want to see.* I let my breath out. *Even when it's a lie.*

If this is what the school year is going to be like, I will not have the energy required to endure it.

By the end of the day, I'm a strange combination of exhausted and antsy. I feel like I could either hibernate or climb a mountain. At a recent appointment with Craig, I offered the same generic statements: *I'm fine.* Or:

*It helps when I focus on my breathing.* Leaving out the detail that I hold my breath until I almost split in two. Craig nodded and explained the benefits of adding constructive ways to manage my emotions.

He mentioned running.

My spiral notebook is open on my desk when I get home; the list I wrote this morning is pathetically short. Wake up. Work. School. I grab a pen and add *Run* and change my clothes. I'll cross them all off when I get back.

I don't stand on the sidewalk and stretch or wonder which way to go, I just run. Pushing my body down the street, replaying my day in my mind. I've never doubted videos posted online until today. What happened this morning between Vance and me and what Sasha is implying are worlds apart. Does she normally do that? It's no secret that Sasha rules all her social media accounts like a queen. She has a way of making even the most embarrassing moments entertaining. My heart is pounding in my chest and not just from exertion.

*What is happening to my life?* The question flutters against my ribs and I swing around the corner of Third Avenue and barrel down the sidewalk trying to ignore my thoughts until my lungs burn with a welcome sting. Reaching the end of the street, I whip around its corner, pushing myself along. Making my way up the residential streets, I become the lace of a corset constricting with every step, every street, every breath. Tighter. Tighter. Tighter.

A tide has shifted at school, and I've been pushed out past the safe harbor. I was never particularly close to anyone other than Derek, Sasha, and Trent. They were all I needed. Sweat slides from my forehead, stinging my eyes, confusion curdling in my stomach. If Trent were alive, I'd never be wondering any of this.

If Trent were alive.

Why can't those words be true? And what secret was he keeping from me? I still need to talk to Derek. He wasn't acting like himself last night. Or maybe he was, and I just don't know how to recognize my own friends.

I throw myself around the next corner and run faster on spent legs until every thought slides off the shelf of my brain. My heart is simply for pumping blood, not for holding fragments of a life I can't let go of. My lungs are a well-lit fire fueling me, but I've reached the last of the residential streets. There are no more laces of the corset to run. Only Ridgeline Road, which would take me through the trees and eventually to the bridge, something I can't face.

I come to a stop, gasping for air.

Then out of nowhere, I'm nauseous. I vomit on the sidewalk in front of a well-manicured bush. Spitting the last of it out, I stagger a few steps away and lower myself to the curb, lying flat on the sidewalk, my chest heaving up and down.

When will being alive stop hurting?

As soon as my pulse returns from its trip to the moon, I stand on rubber legs and walk across the pavers leading to the house I just puked in front of.

There are three houses in town I love above all others. First, mine—a white two-story with purple trim. Dad had to draw a line at the trim color or mom would have used the blank white surface as another one of her canvases. Second, Trent's, because it was his and it always smelled like cinnamon from his mom's constant baking. Third, this house. It's a hunter-green bungalow with black shutters and a porch wrapping around it. The yard has several raised garden beds with more flowers than I know how to identify. It seems like it should be in a children's book, which is fitting, considering who lives here.

Scuffing my feet across the porch, I wait for her to respond to the doorbell, my stomach cramping from violently being emptied. It takes a long time, but the door finally opens and I start talking straight away. "Do you have a bucket of water I can borrow?"

She covers a cough with her hand. "Hello, Capítuloito," she says, her voice scratchy.

I had forgotten my manners. "Oh, sorry. Hi, Mrs. Hernandez."

Height is not my strongest feature. I'm constantly trying to stretch the truth along with my spine in an attempt to reach five foot three, but never manage. It's not often I get to tip my chin down to look an adult in the eyes. Mrs. Hernandez would have a hard time reaching five feet with her shoes on. Her long black hair is streaked with silver and is pulled into a loose bun.

"That's better. Now. What is it you were asking? You look awfully pale. You feeling okay?"

I wipe the back of my arm across my face. "I went for a run, but maybe exercising doesn't agree with me because I threw up in front of one of your bushes. I'll clean it up, but I need a bucket of water. I'm so sorry."

"First things first. Sit." She nods to two rocking chairs on the porch and goes inside, returning with a glass of water for each of us. She hands one to me that I down in a single swallow. Wide-eyed, Mrs. Hernandez offers me her glass.

"Oh, no thank you. Guess I needed it though." I set the empty glass next to the rocker.

"Yes, I think you did." The wind chime hanging from the eave makes a gentle tune. "It was nice to see you back at Murphy's this morning. You've had a rough summer."

Today at school no one acknowledged me and now that someone is, I'm not sure I want them to. Maybe being ignored is actually better. I don't want to talk about my summer, so I think back to sitting criss-cross applesauce on carpet squares while she read to us.

"How come sometimes you read to us in Spanish?"

"Could you not understand?"

I shake my head. I only remember being wrapped up in whatever story she read, never feeling confused.

Mrs. Hernandez's eyebrows rise, her face opening in a smile that draws wrinkles around her eyes. "I think there are stories our hearts understand, no matter the language."

She holds my gaze and I can't look away. No words vibrate in the air between us, nothing but the soft clink of notes in the breeze. But I hear her voice as if she were actually speaking. *I see you. I see your pain. I understand.*

It makes me tremble. I'm an open book in front of her well-read eyes and I jump from the chair. If she can see inside me, she'll see that my heart is bulging with everything I refuse to acknowledge. Maybe she already knows.

Mrs. Hernandez senses my need to escape and directs me to the shed behind the house, and I rush to clean up my mess.

After returning her bucket to the shed, I thank her, and she takes my arm in her hand.

"Answers are worth discovering," she says out of nowhere.

Sasha told me I was better off not knowing when I

couldn't understand Trent's behavior, and her face from this afternoon flashes through my mind. Anger at Sasha glues my vertebrae together until my spine is a rod that will not bend. I've hardly spent any time with Mrs. Hernandez and yet she sees right through me, interpreting the beats of my heart. Something you would think your best friend would be able to do. But instead, my best friend is posting lies about me online.

I swallow the lump in my throat. "Would knowing the truth ruin what I remember about a person?"

Mrs. Hernandez pats my arm. "Does the sunrise make the birds forget the moon?" Is answering questions with questions how you know you've reached adulthood? My eyebrows bunch together, and she laughs at my expression but gives my arm another pat. "The truth is always worth knowing, even if it brings its own pain. Living inside a lie is no place to build a house."

Derek. Trent. Sasha. Me.

Those were the pillars that built the house I used to live inside of. Trent is dead. Sasha is spreading gossip. I need answers, which still only leaves one person.

# sixteen

. . .

## VANCE

The cookie Mrs. Hernandez gave me in exchange for the used coffee grounds from the café left a sweet taste in my mouth. It's not that Murphy doesn't keep treats in the house but, more often than not, they're something like zucchini muffins and not cookies. After I dumped the grounds in her compost pile, she invited me in for a snack, and I wasn't about to refuse that. Even better than the baked goods were the walls in her living room lined with books.

"Hey, MiniVan." Derek's voice interrupts my thoughts as I walk past his yard.

The sweet taste in my mouth is replaced by a sour tang at the sight of Derek. He motions me over and I raise an eyebrow. I'm not sure this is a good idea.

"It's the first day of school and you're already

causing a commotion with Annabelle. How is that staying away from her?"

I saw the video Sasha posted—everyone sees what Sasha posts. But that's not what bothers me. "You never said anything about not spending time with her."

I guess he doesn't like my smirk because he steps into my personal bubble. "I don't think you understand," Derek says. "You cannot tell—"

A blur of motion at the end of the driveway catches my eye. It's Annabelle jogging toward us, so I shove my hand into Derek's chest in an attempt to shut him up.

"What can't you tell?" Annabelle asks.

Derek rubs his chest where my hand made contact. He was about to tell me off for pushing him, but now he's choking on his own spit from Annabelle materializing at his side.

"He ... uh ..." Derek gestures toward me. His words are slow until he picks up steam, taking off like a runaway train. "Vance is helping me get a keg for Sasha's birthday. She wanted something big this year and I'm going to surprise her with a party up at the ridge."

Annabelle winces at the mention of Sasha as if she has stepped on a thorn. She bends, plucking a dandelion from the yard, twisting it between her fingers. "So, about my question. Were you helping Trent plan something?"

"I wasn't the one helping him!" The words are lava

bursting out of the volcano that is Derek's mouth and as soon as he says them, he looks like he's going to pass out.

Annabelle's eyes turn into planets with their own gravitational pull and Derek is stuck in her gaze with nowhere to hide.

She gasps. "What do you mean? Who was helping him?"

I don't make it a point to go to our school's football games. I can think of better things to do than sit in the bleachers pretending to throw an axe when a West Aldrin Lumberjack makes a touchdown. But I hear enough to know that Derek has good hands and rarely fumbles a pass. Those skills do not translate into him back-peddling out of this conversation.

"That's not what I meant. No." He presses a hand to his forehead. "What I was trying to say is . . . Trent was —he was doing something."

It's painful to watch Derek try to salvage the conversation but Annabelle doesn't pay attention to anything except Derek's last words. "I knew it!" She does a little leap. I've never seen her this happy. She's practically floating and Derek pulls his phone out, looking at a blank screen. "I gotta get this," he says, and as he retreats into his house, Annabelle crash lands back to reality and we are stuck standing together on Derek's lawn.

She looks like she is going to follow Derek up the steps, so I put a hand on her shoulder. "I'm glad I ran into you. Murphy wanted you to stop by. He's headed to a conference in Seattle but wanted to give you something before he left." The only direction Annabelle wants to go is into Derek's house, but I won't like the truth she discovers if she does. "You can talk to Derek any time, but we probably only have a few minutes before Murphy leaves."

I know it was low to play Murphy like that, and I wasn't even out looking for her. She's still twirling a dandelion between her fingers.

"Did you know they're edible?" I ask.

She snorts. "So many facts with you." But she looks at me then back to the flower, snapping the yellow head off the stem, popping it in her mouth, and chewing before extending her neck for a big swallow. "Kinda bitter."

"Maybe it was jilted by its lover in a previous life." Annabelle laughs and the sound creates stepping stones across a lake. She leans down, plucking another dandelion from the next lawn we pass, offering it to me and I shove it in my mouth without batting an eye.

Murphy is throwing his duffle bag into the bed of his truck as we enter the alley, and I shout his name.

"Perfect timing," Murphy says. "I was just heading out." He fishes in his pocket and pulls out coins that he sorts through on his palm, pinching one between his finger and his thumb. "I wanted to give this to you this morning, but it took me longer than I expected to fix the ice machine, and then I forgot. Anyway." He extends his arm to Annabelle, and she grabs the coin.

"You wanted to give me a penny?"

Murphy scratches his fingers through the goatee he's decided to grow. "Look closer."

She tips her head to the coin. I didn't know what Murphy planned to give Annabelle, but I know what this coin is. I know that right now Annabelle is looking at the number twenty-four inside a circle, and the circle is surrounded by a triangle with the words *unity, service, and recovery,* etched on each side.

"It's my twenty-four-hour sobriety coin," Murphy says, and Annabelle's head whips up. "Recovery is as different as the people going through it. Some quit cold turkey and never look back. Others—" He gives a low whistle. "Well for others, recovery is its own kind of torture for a time." He takes a step closer and puts both his hands on Annabelle's shoulders. "There's a reason programs give out twenty-four-hour coins. That first day can be harder than you imagine. But if you make it through one day, you can do it again."

"One day," Annabelle whispers.

Murphy and I repeat the words like a prayer, and it becomes a cord tying the three of us together.

Annabelle shakes her head. "But this is yours. You shouldn't give it to me. I bet it means a lot to you."

Murphy folds his hand over hers so she's clutching the coin. "I want you to have it, kiddo. We all need a reminder of hope from time to time. One day at a time. Don't let go of that, okay?"

She doesn't say anything but throws her arms around Murphy, and strangely, I want to add my arms to the pile but take a step back instead.

Murphy steps out of the hug and into his truck, rolling down the window. "Benji will be in tomorrow to cover for me. I won't be home until late." He nods and I nod back, and then he's gone.

Annabelle rotates the coin from heads to tails and back again. "Did you know Murphy had this?" she asks.

Two identical coins have sat on the windowsill above the kitchen sink the entire time I've lived with Murphy. I asked him about them once and he explained what they were. One for him. One for Nat. Murphy kept them both. Too bad Nat didn't hold onto hers. Maybe her sobriety would have stuck.

"Yep." It's all I can offer without unzipping memories of Nat. When Annabelle looks at me, it's like she is dredging my depths for more, not realizing she holds the answer in her hand.

"What? That's it? You're not going to tell me some

worthless tidbit of information, like that the national animal of Scotland is a unicorn?" she asks.

I kick a toe at the gravel. "I mean I *was* going to tell you that, but I'm glad I didn't waste a fact." I shake my head, attempting to give her a very disapproving expression while trying not to smile. "You are so ungrateful for the opportunity to learn new things."

She doesn't hide her smile. "That's me, so ungrateful."

I'm not going to touch that sentence in case there's a hidden meaning lurking under the surface so instead I ask, "Want to see if there are any leftover pastries from this morning?"

Her eyes brighten a little. "A sour cherry tart would be a lot better than a dandelion."

I hold the back door of the café open. "Hey, at least now you know so when you're stranded on a dandelion-infested island, you'll be fine." She laughs the same stepping-stone laugh. "Then when you write your survival story, you better thank me in the acknowledgments because without me, you'd be a goner."

"In more ways than one," she says, and opens the old bread box where Murphy keeps any pastries that didn't sell from the morning. Unfortunately, there isn't a cherry tart, but Annabelle grabs a lemon scone, then breaks it in half and hands me a section.

She's still chewing when she says, "You're the only

person who talks to me like I'm still a real person." She picks apart the scone. "It's nice because then I forget how messed up my life is when I hang out with you."

I always figured Annabelle was a One Direction song. Chart-topping. Overplayed. Predictable. And it's not a matter of me being right or wrong about that. Maybe she used to be or maybe I assumed that about her. But the thing about power ballads is that, like it or not, you know them by heart and can't help but sing along.

"Same." I slide myself onto the counter. "I know this is going to be a shocking revelation, but I don't really let anyone into my life." I raise my hands as her mouth drops open in mock surprise. "I know, I know. I understand this is a lot to process. Do you need to sit?" She joins me on the counter, the breadbox of pastries between us. "Most of the time, I don't even know what normal is supposed to feel like. But I guess this"—I knock my fist into her shoulder—"is as close as it gets."

Annabelle pulls out two doughnut holes and passes one to me. When I grab it, she taps hers into the one I'm holding. "Cheers to *as close as it gets*."

We pop them into our mouths at the same time. "Should we see how many we can eat before we hurl?" I ask.

Her face almost turns green, and she moans. "Please

no, I already did that this afternoon." I lift an eyebrow, and she shakes her head. "Don't ask."

# seventeen

. . .

## ANNABELLE

Five months ago, Trent was alive, and every day since has been like walking through a forest shrouded in fog. Every once in a while, I have a moment of clarity and find my bearings but usually, I feel lost, unrecognizable, clinging to the coin I had my dad drill a hole through that now rests on a chain above my heart.

One day at a time.

It's a motto that moves me forward as slowly as turtles walking in a circle, but I keep pressing my fingers to the metal—a reminder that I've made it another day.

The air has shifted from the heaviness of summer to the crisp bite of fall, and every morning before leaving the house I pull on a charcoal sweater that I pilfered from the back of Dad's closet. It's several sizes too big and drapes across me in a soft layer of protection that feels like home.

School isn't any better but it's not any worse, and I guess that is as good as I can ask for. Today the entire school is gathering in the gym for a special assembly. Mr. Logan stands at the door greeting us with hellos, high fives, and reminders that this is not a free pass to zone out and scroll. He catches my eye and cuts his way through the stream of students to stand next to me.

"Sasha gave me a heads up and I want you to know that I support you. We're with you." He pats my shoulder before stepping toward a group of loitering freshmen.

I'm pushed along by classmates behind me. Did I misunderstand him? He supports what? I haven't talked to Sasha since the first day of school and my stomach clenches. What did she tell Mr. Logan?

Sometimes when I hung out with Trent and his brothers, we watched clips from an old show where people competed on obstacles. One obstacle had two competitors trying to knock each other off a balance beam with what looked like gigantic cotton swabs. This is what my life feels like: keeping my head down and a smile plastered on my face while being knocked off balance.

I take a seat and brace for whatever is going to happen next.

Mr. Logan raises his arms, quieting the students, tapping the mic, sending out a screech of feedback. "Today one of our seniors and the president of The Key

Club, Sasha Brooks, will be leading our assembly so please give her your attention."

Sasha walks to the middle of the gym where a blue L is encircled in silver. Before she gets to the microphone, she whips her arm back and forth while shouting, "Chop, chop!" And the student body yells, "Timber!" Sasha missed her calling—she would have made an excellent cheerleader.

"Thank you, Mr. Logan." She grips the mic stand. "As you know, every year the senior class presents a gift to the school. Last year's class commissioned the mural in the entrance to be painted, and the next time you sit on the bench outside the locker rooms you can thank the class of 1998. Those are just two examples. This year, the Key Club unanimously voted to rename Senior Hall."

Senior Hall is the shortest hall on campus connecting our two main buildings, but it has what all good real estate has—location, location, location. Only seniors get assigned lockers in this centrally located stretch and occasionally there are not enough, causing enterprising classmates to sell their lockers off to the highest bidder.

Sasha reaches to the table behind her, pulling something out from under what looks like a towel, and turns it for everyone to see. My breath catches at the sight of Trent's senior picture enameled on a piece of wood. "This plaque will hang in honor of our friend for years to come." Sasha's voice warbles. "The Trent Walker Memorial Hall."

Trent's name vibrates in the space between my ribs as if my body constantly hums it under its breath. There is no time to react to what Sasha just unveiled because she keeps talking and says my name. "Annabelle asked to come forward and share a few words of what this means to her."

In fifth grade, we had to make our own vocabulary lists from the books we read as a class. The best words I remember discovering were *veranda* and *sabotage*. I glue my lips into a smile, and my heart thumps a warning as I walk to the center of the gym. Sasha's smile is as fake as a toothpaste commercial. "Annabelle Davis," she says into the mic, her phone out and poised to record this moment.

I feel every set of eyes drilling into me, waiting for me to speak, but I don't say anything. I can't. What does this mean to me? It means Trent is dead and this is one more reminder that I hate. My cheeks ache from keeping them stretched up and out. And they are not the only thing aching. My entire body hurts, not to mention my bulging heart. I'm so tired of holding myself together and for a moment I let it all go.

"I don't understand what you're doing." I'm not exactly screaming, but it's close and the mic ricochets my voice around the gym. "Why are you hurting me like this? What did I do to you that was so awful that you feel the need to ruin my life?"

Before I can step away from the mic Mr. Logan grabs it. "Thank you, ladies." He stammers something else than starts in on a list of upcoming announcements. But I don't bother standing there to listen. Or be watched. Let Sasha post my outburst online—everyone witnessed it anyway. What do I care if it becomes another viral sensation?

I push myself out the double doors, needing to get home, and drown the day with spoonfuls of Nutella. I haven't made it very far down the sidewalk before Vance runs up beside me. "Come with me," he says.

I want the couch and the remote and all the scoops of chocolate I can manage before I feel sick. I don't want whatever he is going to say. "Why?"

He makes a circling gesture that whirls around me. "That was some show in there and now you're walking like gravity is winning and you are going to end up on your face. So. Follow me."

I rub my fingers over a headache marching a line across my forehead. "Follow you where?"

He's already walking. "The river."

The river holds so many of my favorite memories. Summers with my family, learning to swim, standing on the bank when Trent slipped his arm around my waist for the first time. I've avoided the river like I avoid everything else in my life. Just at its mention, my heart threatens to open, revealing more snapshots of a life that used to be mine.

"I can't," I say.

Managing to avoid the river this long is a triumph in itself. Even if I refuse to stand at its edge, the water comes to me every night. Cold, rushing, expecting. Carving a line through my dreams. Sometimes I float on its surface. Sometimes I stand next to it. Sometimes I'm submerged. But it is always there when I close my eyes, waiting.

Vance doesn't turn around. "Sure you can. Plus, you can't pass up a day like today."

True. For the past several days the wind has ravaged the trees, pulling leaves loose, whipping them into small cyclones. The rain came down in fat splats, then sheets. Today is a fantastic November gift of blue sky, cotton ball clouds, and surprisingly warmer temperatures. A vivid reminder that so much can change in a matter of hours. It's hard to pass up a day like today when you know tomorrow it will be gone.

Everyone will want to hang out at the dock on a day like today. It's bad enough that I have to endure the heaviness of being talked about behind my back all day at school. I am not signing up for more of the same in my free time.

I don't move.

Vance is already walking and can apparently read my mind. "I didn't say we were going to the dock. I said we were going to the river. Start walking."

We enter the parking lot that leads to the boat ramp, and I have to swallow my heart before it jumps out of my chest. I've been here countless times, but never since Trent died. We walked here hand in hand hundreds of times, but now my limbs feel heavy and I wonder if Vance brought me here to feed me to the sharks sitting on the dock. *Sabotage* flickers through my mind again. He wouldn't do that, would he? I wouldn't have thought Sasha would want to sink her teeth into me either, so I'm clearly not the best judge of character. And just like that, we are past the parking lot stepping onto an unmarked path where a carpet of still-damp leaves squishes beneath my feet.

We walk further than I expected. Some time ago we left what little of a trail we followed and now our progress is slower as we navigate through the untouched forest. Dense trees spread themselves apart with wider reaches as the ground expands, then cracks, revealing the river. My breath catches at the sight. It's bloated from the rain, surrounded on both banks by a mixture of evergreen and deciduous trees. I've never been to this stretch and, with no trail marking the way, few have. A small waterfall, more of a stair step than a rushing majestic cascade, is in the distance. It's not the kind anyone would build a monument for or clear a path to so you could find it. But it makes me smile in a goofy, look-at-this-waterfall-I've-never-seen-before, sort of way.

For a moment, nature strips away my headache, mending my rupturing heart by giving me something beautiful in spite of my pain.

"How did you find this spot?" I ask.

Vance bends down, black hair hiding his face. He examines rocks, selects one, and sends it over the glass top of the water. "Sometimes I don't know how to sit still with myself or stay in one place, especially if that place happens to be quiet. So, I wander."

"Like when you *wandered* behind the church?" I air quote the word.

His reply is a small nod and another skipped rock. I count the bounces, ten. "Not bad," I say. Dumping my backpack next to his, I look for my own rock. I pick one, but let it fall with a clink before selecting another. Trent was the one who taught me to skip rocks, but I don't hold onto that thought and send my rock across the water. It skips eight times, but I can do better than that. "Wait." I hunt for a new rock and slide my thumb over it. Then I flick it across the water before I'm forced to remember the way Trent slid his thumb over the back of my hand the last time we were at the dock. "Eleven!" I shout, my fist flying up in victory.

Vance has a rock in his hand and a curious smile on his face. His next rock skips twelve times before disappearing.

I pull the sleeves of my too-big sweater over my hands, making them each a cave. "Who's counting?"

He laughs, giving me a little shove. "You are."

I lower myself onto a boulder jutting from the earth as Vance drifts further upstream, every so often stopping to send another rock skipping. Pulling my knees to my chest, I tuck them under the canopy of my sweater, scraping tufts of moss off the rock with my fingernails.

The only sounds are chirps from birds hidden in the branches above or the occasional gurgle from the river. I am alone in the quiet. But not alone in the same way I spend every day, aware that I am untethered and drifting away. This is a tranquil kind of alone, to be surrounded by hundred-year-old trees and a river that can't be erased even if you tried.

The river.

It constantly moves, constantly calls. What would it feel like to push my hand into its depths? To have the silky water wash over me again? I shudder and rise from the rock, making my way to the edge. The reflection of my hair wavers in long wet ribbons next to my face. My hand lingers before one finger touches the surface, sending out a circular shockwave and without another thought, I plunge my hand in. The water sucks and pulses around my skin. It is deep and frigid, and I wait until my fingers tingle, then throb and go numb before pulling my hand out.

Vance is watching. "Did you shake and make up?"

Wiping my dripping hand against my jeans, I look at him, really look. His T-shirt pulls tight across his chest, his head is sort of tipped to one side, and his hair is angled across half his face. There is so much unspoken between us about this river and maybe more. He understands me in a way no one else seems to and yet I hardly know anything about him. He saved my life when I fell. I'm not sure how to fill in a gap that large, but I start by telling him something I haven't told anyone.

"Every night before I fall asleep, I hear the river whispering my name. I used to love this river. But now . . ." I fold myself back onto the boulder. "I used to love so much." I stop talking because I don't want to recount everything I used to love and lost and say something easier: "I used to not hate going to school."

It's silent between us, but not strained. It's the kind of silence between friends when you hold open a door, waiting for them to walk through. Inviting them into your messy room with lit candles, discarded blankets, and ghosts who refuse to leave.

Vance sits on the boulder next to me. "For what it's worth, I think it's just a river."

If a river cannot whisper my name at night, why does a chill run across my shoulders?

I close my eyes, trying to imagine that it is only a river—the same as it has always been. But nothing is that simple. Nothing is the same as it has always been. Not school. Not the river. Not my dreams. Nothing. I take a breath to steady myself.

"It's only a river." I echo Vance's words even though I'm not sure I believe them. But I say them because I do believe that sometimes saying words aloud brings them to life. Like when you love someone, and the words are trapped dandelion seeds floating inside your chest until you are brave enough to give them breath. Turning the words into arms and skin that you can hold, lips you can kiss.

*It's only a river.*

Vance stands, picking up a rock at his feet, and hands it to me. It's bigger than my fist—this is not a skipping rock.

"Throw it," he instructs.

I fling it and watch it land with a satisfying sploosh. He has another one ready that I grab and throw. Again. Again. Again. Relishing the sensation of throwing something so solid and heavy. My arm aches but I somehow feel lighter.

As a kid, I would press my arms against the door-frame while my dad counted and, when I stepped forward, my arms floated up on their own. It made me laugh, imagining balloons tied to my wrists. How hard would I have to press to make myself fly away? No matter how many times I did it, no matter how many times Dad explained the science behind it, it was always a surprising kind of magic.

It feels like that now, standing in the forest, throwing rocks with the boy who saved my life. We both chuck them, letting them fly and sink and I find the same surprising kind of magic in throwing something, in letting it go. It is easy enough to grab a rock and throw it. Could I open my heart, scoop out everything trapped inside, and release that too?

"Keep doing what you're doing," Vance says.

There isn't a rock in his hand for me to grab. Keep doing what? My face curves into a question mark.

"At school. Keep ignoring everyone. They're not worth your time." He's serious. "Sooner or later, they'll get bored and move on. So forget about them."

This is his answer. My heartache is their entertainment and one day it won't even be that. It will be nothing. Forgotten. Ignoring what people think about me is the only thing I can do. Maybe that could become its own brand of magic. Not the kind that leaves my head spinning in awe, but the kind of magic that will let me survive.

I drop the rock I had been holding. It's one thing to

ignore what strangers or the people who live on the fringes of my life think about me. It's another thing entirely to ignore what my friends think, and based on today's encounter, Sasha doesn't think much of me.

"I don't think Sasha will let anyone move on from me anytime soon." I wind a strand of hair around my finger.

"Sasha's got her own stuff to figure out, you know?" I have no idea what he's talking about and don't ask because right now I don't want to understand Sasha. "Besides, two hundred and five days. You can make it."

"Until what?"

Vance looks at the fading light, swinging his head down to where our backpacks rest near his feet. "Graduation." He picks his up, and I understand—we've been here long enough.

This is another marker of time I have blinders to. Graduation is a finish line I'll limp across, not a launching pad of excitement. Of course it would be on Vance's mind, it's on every senior's mind. I have no idea what will happen after high school. I can't think that far ahead.

"How come you're already counting days? Graduation is ages away," I say. Vance's eyes glint in the late light, becoming stairs carved from bedrock leading someplace deep underground. I'm not sure it would be okay for me to follow.

He chews his bottom lip and doesn't answer.

These fall days are short and there won't be much light left. What light there is soaks through the leaves still clinging to branches, turning them into individually hung sunsets. Just this week I started tucking my phone into my pocket. I still haven't turned it on—I'm just getting used to the weight of having it with me again.

I pull it out, extending it toward Vance. "It's charged but I haven't turned it on since the day Trent died. I don't think I can face everything I left unread." I remember the tidal wave of messages and my heart speeds up. "Could you delete everything? Messages? Apps? Photos? All of it?"

He cocks his head to the side. "All of it. Are you sure?"

I take a step closer and grab his hand, putting my phone into his palm. "I'm sure."

Turning my back, I watch the sun filtering through the leaves and not Vance who is erasing the last remaining connections I had to my old life. When he's done, he taps me on my shoulder and slides my phone into my hand. Now it is simply a phone, a search engine, a calculator, a camera, and it could belong to anyone. Every trace that it is mine has been removed.

Vance starts walking but I stay a moment longer watching the leaves dangle in the light. I open my camera and take the first photo of my new life, holding my breath until the pain in my lungs burns as bright as the leaves, then I follow Vance out of the forest.

He holds back a branch for me to step around as we emerge from between the trees, and it makes my mind skip back in time. That last afternoon I shared with Trent, we stood at the boat ramp and he lifted a hand like he wanted to get someone's attention. I turned in time to see Vance appear between two trees in roughly this same spot.

I lean closer to Vance's face, squinting, looking for hidden answers written across his skin. Why would Trent have wanted to get Vance's attention?

Vance lifts a hand to his face. "Why are you looking at me like that?"

"Do you . . ." This is stupid. What am I about to ask? *Do you know what Trent was up to?* Why would I ask him? Vance wouldn't know. I never once saw Trent speak to Vance. I spent every waking moment with Trent, and I have no idea why he was acting strangely. I'm so desperate for answers that I'm looking for them wherever I can.

I close my eyes and exhale. "Do you really think it's just a river?"

Vance squeezes my shoulder. "I do."

I open my eyes and let that be enough.

# eighteen

. . .

## VANCE

I've snuck into the church as often as possible. But now, I'm standing outside of it on a windy Sunday night in need of help. Murphy and his truck would be a perfect solution except neither are available. That leaves one person I can text: *Can you meet me at the church?*

Annabelle: *???*

Me: *Needs to be now*

Annabelle: *Cryptic - on my way*

The security light hums above me as I lean against the peeling gray paint. Outside the reach of the light, I'm tucked in a fold of the night. What will Murphy say when he finds out what I'm up to? It's not like I asked his permission.

The wind pushes over my face, and I close my eyes, scrunching the hood of my sweatshirt against the back of my neck. Then there's a subtle shift in the air, a hit of coconut instead of a sky threatening to rain and that means Annabelle is here.

Her voice is playful. "Are you having a crisis of faith?"

I take a large step to my left so I'm ringed in the light. "That's me in the spotlight. Losing my religion."

I watch a story play across her face. She had been joking but that turns into confusion, followed by concern and now she's landed on what-do-I-do-if-he-is-having-a-crisis, and I can't hold in my laughter.

"Does the name R.E.M. mean anything to you?" I ask.

She shakes her head, still worried she walked into a dilemma way above her pay grade.

Somewhere along the way, I decided that if I couldn't have Nat, I could at least have her music, and it became my own. "Kids these days—no musical appreciation. We're going to have to fix that. But first, I need your help." I push off the side of the building and head to the back of the church, winding up the wheelchair ramp, and bang my fist on the door.

When it opens, I tip my head in Annabelle's direction and talk to the man who opened the door. "Found a helper. Mind if I take it now?"

The man scoots himself and his mop back, allowing enough room for Annabelle and me to enter. "She's all yours," he says.

I lead Annabelle past stacked tables, racks of folding chairs, and handmade banners hanging from the walls like retired jerseys. This room has become familiar to me over the past several months and I'm going to miss sneaking in.

"What are we doing here?" she whispers, as if that is as loud as one can be inside a church.

"Heard they were getting rid of this old piano and when I stopped to ask, Glenn said I could take it. But it would have to be tonight before he locked up or it'll go to a donation center in the morning. Ready to push?"

"Push what?"

"Keep up. This beauty." I flap my hands in front of the standing piano trying to be a convincing gameshow host.

"Push that? To Murphy's?" I nod, but Annabelle only blinks. "You're kidding."

"Nope. Come on." I walk to the far end of the piano and start rolling it across the floor. "Can you go prop the door open?"

The piano rolls closer and she puts her hands up in a stop sign. "Hang on a sec. Can you even play?"

I open the fallboard, a smile curving my lips. There's a moment of hesitation when I realize Annabelle will be the first person I've played in front of. What if my music only sounds good inside my head? I press a single key, letting the sound rub the tarnish off my doubt and then I play. My fingers pull notes from a long-forgotten song and right before the melody should take flight—I stop. The last note trembles over the hardwood before falling silent.

Glenn leans against his mop, clapping, I forgot he was there.

"Satisfied?" I ask.

Speechless, Annabelle spins, propping the door open. Getting the casters over the threshold is slow going. It requires both of us to push from one end. We're so close our shoulders rub and the hint of coconut swirls around me fusing with the leftover music pumping through my veins. It's a combination I could get used to.

Easing the piano down the ramp I tell Annabelle, "That was the easy part."

It's only four blocks from the church to Murphy's. Four blocks would be a non-distance if you were out for a walk to kill time. But four blocks while keeping a piano from veering off the edge of an uneven sidewalk stretches the word *only* into a tedious pull of taffy. Doing it in the dark doesn't make it any easier. We inch the piano down Cut Canyon, from one circle of light from a streetlamp to the next.

We wrangle it through the door into the café and push it past tables to its new resting place against the wall, and Annabelle gives a hoot of success.

"Thanks, muscle," I say, clapping her on the back.

"Couldn't have managed that on my own. Want something hot?"

She nods and I slip around the counter to turn on the electric kettle.

"What I don't understand is if Murphy wanted a piano so bad, how come he couldn't have moved it in his truck?"

"Didn't ask if he wanted it. But look at it. That empty wall needed a piano." I'll need a better reason to explain the piano to Murphy. I don't think selling it to him as wall decor will cut it.

"The wall needed a piano?" She cocks her head. "Or *you* needed a piano?"

I push the hair off my forehead before snapping the lids on two steeping cups of tea. "Look at you and your questions. Have time for one more thing?"

"Please don't tell me you need me to move something else."

I jut my head to the back door, and she moves around the counter, reaching for one of the cups in my hand as she passes. "I'll hold on to these for now. You'll need both your hands."

Out back I lead her up the steps, past the door to Murphy's apartment, motioning with my elbow to the wrought-iron ladder. "You'll have to stand on the railing to reach. Ladies first."

As soon as she's on the railing, my stomach sinks. I

blink and, for a second, I see Annabelle silhouetted against the blazing summer sky, disappearing off the ledge of the bridge. Now, she leans into the darkness, grabbing the side of the ladder. It's a stretch, but her body follows the momentum of the swing and she's on the ladder climbing up, and I'm glad I didn't watch her fall again. I stack the to-go cups one on top of the other, resting my chin on the top. My longer limbs span the distance with ease, even while balancing the leaning tower of tea.

Annabelle scoots one of the random seat cushions that are scattered around, eyeing the bench press and then me, her eyebrows going up with understanding. As she sits, I plug in a cord, turning on the outdoor lights that are strung across the air, making a ceiling of glittering bulbs.

I finally hand her a cup, and she wraps her hands around the warmth, taking a sip, her eyes opening in surprise. "Peppermint tea—I wasn't expecting that."

"I hate coffee, but this—" I take a sip. "Always makes me think of—" Annabelle loosens my tongue with memories I never share and I'm about to stop myself from saying anything else. But Annabelle is different. I think she and I might be notes in the same song. "It makes me think of the first night I lived here."

I had escaped to the roof to sit alone and count the stars, distracting myself from thinking about the fact that

Nat would never choose to find me. Murphy appeared over the rim of the roof holding two takeaway cups of peppermint tea. He didn't pretend everything was okay. He looked me in the face and said, "Pretty crap thing for your mom to do." That's what made me like him, even if I didn't know how to trust him. It was the first time I had peppermint tea, and that first sip tasted bitter, a penance. The next sip tasted sweet, a desire. I can never decide if I like peppermint tea or not. Every time I drink it, it tastes different.

She pulls her knees to her chin. "How come you live with Murphy?"

The rumors swirled off the ground, a man-made dust devil when I arrived in West Aldrin. Everyone in town wondered where I came from, and what I was doing living with Murphy. I started some of the rumors myself, never denying any, the more the better. Because the truth was worse than any of the rumors. Each thought leads to another, turning into a spiral staircase deep inside my chest.

Maybe Annabelle understands my silence as a reservation to answer her question, or maybe she's just tired of waiting and asks another. "When did you learn to play the piano?"

I take a too-big sip, and the tea scalds all the way down. "Nat, my mom, she wasn't around much." I don't explain that it was always her choice to leave me behind.

"There was an old piano in the basement of a building we lived in, and I spent a lot of time down there." Living in that building didn't last because nothing with Nat lasts. When we drove away, I drew a keyboard on the back of a notebook so I could keep practicing, hearing the music in my mind.

I take a non-scalding sip. "I had a lot of free time, so I taught myself."

I've never told anyone this before. It's one thing to let Annabelle past my walls when we are talking about her life, but talking about mine is harder than I thought. There are flecks of green in her eyes that spark under the lights, wheels turning in her mind. I bet she's wondering why I call my mom by her first name. I'll never be able to stretch my mouth around the words required to explain that so I ask, "Have you ever seen *Fight Club*?"

She shakes her head. "Nope."

"Really? Come on, it's such a classic. Brad Pitt. Edward Norton. Besides, how can you have known Murphy for as long as you have and never seen that movie?"

"I work for him. I don't live with him." As soon as she says it, her face breaks into a sweeping smile, and she dissolves into laughter. A tiny dimple blooms under her left eye. I've never seen her smile freely enough to create the crater. "That sounded so wrong." Her laugh is deep in her chest.

I never care what the documentary is about when I start one. Orcas. The collapse of the education system. Migratory patterns of geese. The subject doesn't matter, all I need is the narrator's voice so I can fall asleep. There is something similar about Annabelle's laugh. Her happiness could become my favorite narrator, and my back relaxes against the bricks.

"Why did you want to know if I've seen it?"

"I can't remember anymore. But it's like a religion for Murphy. Since living with him, I've watched it more times than I can count."

It feels like a stupid slip, another cord to be grasped and pulled, making answers spill out. I try to look past the glowing bulbs above us to the sky. "Do you ever wonder if the light we see from a star is already dead?"

She runs her hands up and down the thin cotton of her long-sleeve T-shirt. The tea isn't keeping her warm anymore. "No, not really."

I pull my hoodie off, handing it to her. It drapes on her, reminding me of the day I pulled it on for the first time, and how baggy it was back then. I reach over, unplugging the lights. My eyes adjust and I make out the puncture wounds of starlight littering the sky. "I come up here sometimes to look at the stars, wondering about the light traveling through time. Wondering if the light I see is an orphan because its star is already dead." It's not all I wonder about and I'm silent, waiting to see if the sky will offer a shooting star as an answer. "Maybe she's already dead."

"Maybe who's already dead?"

I meant to keep that last thought to myself, but I might as well land the punch. "Nat," I say.

Annabelle covers her mouth with her hand. "You wonder if your mom is dead?"

This is the most information I've ever offered anyone about Nat or my life. I need to get up and do reps on the bench to calm myself. I cannot sit here and have a conversation about Nat like it's perfectly normal for a son to be okay with the fact that his mom might be dead. As if that could be the least painful explanation.

Annabelle's phone chimes and she pulls it out, huffing so loudly she could be blowing out candles three rooms away. I bump my shoulder against her arm. "Everything okay?"

"It's my sister." She angles the screen so I can read the message: *Sunday sister check-in. There can only be rainbows after the rain! Don't lose hope!*

"Jeeze."

Annabelle's free hand lifts to the sobriety coin around her neck, rubbing it against her lips. "Tell me about it. At least she tries, right?" The words are heavy, like she's convincing herself they are true, and her hand falls away from her necklace. "What does that even mean—don't lose hope?"

I grab Annabelle's phone and tap random emojis. Mermaid. Coffee. Fire. Snowflake. Sushi. I hit send and hand it back with a wry smile. "I don't really know, but you should leave people guessing."

"Great, now she's going to call and want an explanation for that."

"Do you have to give her one?"

Right on cue, Annabelle's phone rings, and Meredith's picture lights across the screen. "Oh, I get it. You want me to take a page from your book and evade questions at all costs."

I clink the edge of my paper cup against hers. "You're a fast learner, little grasshopper."

Annabelle stands, brushing dust off the backs of her legs. "I should go. She'll keep calling until I answer."

I watch Annabelle swing herself over the lip of the roof and tap my head against the bricks. Today was surprising. I never would have heard about the piano if Murphy hadn't needed me to cover the counter so he could fix the grinder. And Murphy never would have asked me to do that before I started working for him. And I only started working for him because of Annabelle. Everything traces back to Annabelle. I reclaimed a lost piece of myself because of her. Maybe I should have told her that.

Annabelle shouts my name from the alley, and I peer over the roof. "Yeah?"

"I have your sweatshirt." She lifts her arms and elephant trunks of extra material spill down her arms.

"Then it's a good thing I know where you live." She smiles, and I wish I was close enough to see if the dimple emerged. I know what tonight's documentary will be about—the creation of a supernova. "Bring it back tomorrow."

"Okay, see you in the morning."

I lean over the edge. "Hey, Annabelle?" She turns. It's easier to say this when she's further away instead of next to me searching my face for answers I do not want to share. "It's not that I hope Nat is dead, but it's complicated."

"Be careful, little grasshopper. That was an answer."

I watch the night swallow her and finish the last of my tea, licking my lips. Today, peppermint tea tastes like the start of something unexpected.

I didn't tell Annabelle everything. There are secrets locked inside my chest, and stacked around my own are the secrets that belonged to Trent. Would Annabelle be better off knowing the truth? Would knowing the truth become a weight she couldn't let go of or would she finally be able to set her questions down and move on? Maybe I should tell her, but how could I do that without Derek finding out?

I lay down at the bench press, lowering the bar to my chest, lifting it skyward. There is a lot I want to tell

Annabelle but can't. And then there's the app on my phone, the one keeping a running tally, letting me know my days here are numbered.

My arms shake but I don't want to leave the roof, and I lift the bar for another set. Some days I think I should talk with Murphy and ask about the agreement we made. But he's never brought it up and I can only assume that means he doesn't want it to change. My breath is a puff of air as I stand.

Could I turn off the app and ask Murphy if I could stay? Should I really keep the secrets of a dead boy when Annabelle has every right to know what Trent was planning to do? Now that I've seen it appear, will I ever be able to stop thinking about tracing my finger around the small dimple under Annabelle's eye? I don't think so. I'm not so sure. Not a chance.

The sky is dark, filled with stars racing to bring their light to the earth. A light that could already be dead and it's only a matter of time before that will be true. One day the star will die and so will Nat. The wind picks up and I wish I had my sweatshirt to pull across my skin so I could suffocate the ache expanding inside my chest.

# nineteen

. . .

## ANNABELLE

The start of a run always annoys me. My body rebels against the effort until, somewhere in the middle of pumping arms and heavy breathing, I accept the struggle, settling into a stride. I'm getting stronger and the discipline of making my body work in a new way is strangely addicting. My favorite route is the zig-zagged incline of Ridgeline Road. I have yet to reach the summit, where the ground levels before weaving down to the opposite end of town. The goal of running that entire loop looms in my mind. But to complete the circuit I'll have to run across the bridge, and I'm not sure I can do that.

I reach the turnout of an old logging road and need to stop. So many of these overgrown roads snake through the forest. Trent and I spent many afternoons up here. He would choose an old access road and drive along it until the trees reclaimed the land, forcing us to turn around. I spin away from the sight of the road and the memories it brings. I gulp in the brisk fall air while bending into an angle, stretching my hamstring, and pick a rock from the ground. I toss it and catch it, enjoying the soft plunk of it landing in my palm.

Everything is so close to being its own opposite.

One minute the rock is in my hand. The next minute it is in the air.

One minute Trent was hugging me. The next minute he was dead.

Part of me wants to wander into the access road, to uncover hidden remains of time spent with Trent that have become fossilized relics. But what if I find more than I bargained for? What if poking around under the trees rouses more pain instead of sun-soaked memories with Trent?

It is impossible to separate the two—heartache and memories, so I stretch my other leg and head back the way I came.

Yesterday, we celebrated Thanksgiving and every chair in our house was occupied. We gathered to give thanks and eat more in one sitting than should ever be allowed. My cousins played rounds of charades that I watched from the couch. I am my own world-class champion of the game, except nobody knows I'm playing.

I sat, holding my breath, watching as they pantomimed. Trying to convince myself that the smile on my face was real.

My family took turns going around the table sharing what we were thankful for. My sister held Mateo's hand and said marriage. My uncle said the surgery that repaired his Achilles. One cousin gave thanks for being accepted into a juried exhibition. Another cousin gave thanks for learning to tie his own shoes. When it was my turn, all we heard was the clock above the fireplace.

Everyone blinked, waiting for my answer, and a light flickered to life inside the locked room of my heart. A light I didn't ignite myself, one I had not felt in months. And at that moment I realized something surprising—I am thankful. Thankful to be alive, to have a body and breath. Thankful, I still have time to spend with my family. But Trent was trapped, banging against that locked door. How could I admit I'm thankful for anything when Trent is dead?

Guilt rattled in my chest.

If only life was one of those choose-your-own-adventure books I used to devour. Unhappy with the current situation? Flip back and pick a different path. If only I could go back to the moment when I stood with Trent in our driveway and make him stay. Make him tell me why he kept whipping his keys. My chest tightens. *What if he was going to tell me something I didn't want to hear?* But I push that thought away.

Now, my phone chimes with a message from Meredith. It's a picture I don't remember. I must have been five, maybe six, and I'm riding on top of Dad's shoulders. It's from Mom's *film-only* phase. Meredith took the albums home with her so she could scan them onto her computer.

I tap out of the image, seeing last Sunday's sister check-in message. *Don't lose hope.* I still don't understand what that means.

The words ought to take shape in my mind, but they don't. There is no structure, no meat on their bones. Pain. Suffer. Heartache. Those make sense. I can draw a picture or make a list of what those words translate to.

*Ignore. Survive. Keep doing what I'm doing.*

That is a list I understand.

I run, and my legs throb and my lungs gasp but I force myself faster. Faster. Faster. Turning the music up louder. Louder. Louder. Pushing my emotions further. Further. Further. Until I simply become arms and legs and a heart that burns. This is how I can give thanks. Not with words or memories, but by dripping sweaty drops like tears.

Strands of hair slip from my ponytail, fluttering before sticking to the side of my face. I snap photos of my feet flying across the ground, trees blurring at my side, and clouds accumulating in the sky. Keepsakes from miles earned that prove I am alive. Images I can look at to remember the way my body hurts and the way it is being rebuilt.

A new song plays and the wind surges, but I force myself to keep going. The song is catchy and popular, and I immediately think about how much it would annoy Vance. I record a clip of myself singing, stuttering the words along with the band, and send it to him.

His reply is quick: *Have I taught you nothing?*

My smile is real, not pinched or fake. I like that Vance has become the person in my life who can make me smile. He doesn't expect me to, but still finds a way, and when I'm with him I don't hold my breath. He started sending me playlists to broaden my musical self. Each new musical offering settles inside my heart feeling like a memory I didn't know I forgot. I haven't told him how much I love the songs he sends but, somehow, I think he already knows.

The residential streets are in view, but I'm not ready to be home. I need more time, more road under my feet, more sweat to expel. As soon as I'm home I'll just be Annabelle inside the walls. Annabelle inside my head. Annabelle stuck on the couch.

But when I run, I'm someone else—someone free.

I turn onto Eighth Avenue, intending to wind down to my house on Second and throw myself against the wall of wind. But at the end of the street, a gust over-turns a recycling bin, sending papers shooting loose across the pavement. They are alive, being picked up and carried, dancing circles before landing, scooting away. I chase and gather as many as I can, but some are already lost. Pressing the stack of papers to my chest, I look for the bin that toppled over and find it at the end of Mrs. Hernandez's driveway.

As I wheel the bin to the curb, the wind shifts, carrying a voice that rises and falls like a tide from behind the house. I've been too afraid to return to her house since the day I threw up. That day, Mrs. Hernandez held the manuscript of my life, but instead of reading the words I painstakingly print for everyone to see, she read the spaces in between. The white gaps between every word, the place where my pain breathes.

The voice drifts past me again, and I follow.

Mrs. Hernandez sits in a deck chair pulled onto the grass next to Vance, who is turning dirt with a shovel. She is reading. "A honeybee, after finding an abundant source of pollen, will fly back to the hive, performing a dance for the other bees which supplies them with the directions they need in order to find their way to the nectar themselves."

Vance's back rounds as he plunges the shovel into the ground. "Huh."

"Those bees." Mrs. Hernandez taps her temple with a

bent finger. "There are more messengers than we can see trying to give us maps, but maybe we don't understand the dance."

Vance has his back to me, but Mrs. Hernandez notices me, standing, listening to her read, and she clasps her hands to her heart, the book falling to the ground. "You came back! You do have wings," she says.

What is she talking about? What wings?

I shake my head as Vance turns to look at me, leaning against the shovel. I don't have wings. I would be the first to know if that were true. I would have seen their nubs protruding from my skin. Trent would have traced his hand over them. Talking about the bridge is not something I do, but Vance was there that day, and a certain knowing radiates from Mrs. Hernandez. I can't stand in front of her pretending to cover myself with see-through words.

"I don't have wings because if I did, I would have . . ."

"Flown?" Vance is the one to fill in my sentence.

I tie my arms in a knot across my chest and nod.

"There's still time to fly, Capítuloito," Mrs. Hernandez says.

None of this makes sense. Wings and bees and Vance and Mrs. Hernandez. What he is doing here, which is exactly what I ask.

Vance kicks his foot against a bucket, one I recognize

from the café. "I bring the used coffee grounds for her garden." He jabs the shovel into the dirt of a raised bed, and turns it over, then repeats the process. "She pays me in books. Sometimes there are baked goods involved."

Mrs. Hernandez waves a wrinkled finger in his direction. "You know what he asked me the first time?" She doesn't wait for me to answer. "Romance. He wants to know if I have romance novels." A laugh bubbles out of her like spring rain. It blooms daffodils but catches on a storm, cracking into a cough that overtakes her body. She presses a palm to her chest, takes a deep breath, wheezes, and then stands, extending her hand for me to grab. "Come, we'll get something warm to drink."

Her house smells like one of those souvenir shops at the coast that sells Christmas ornaments year-round, bathed in spice and pine. She walks to the stove and lifts the lid of a pot, letting out a wave of steam, and my stomach gurgles. Whatever it is, I want it. She stirs, then taps the wooden spoon against the side, stirring again.

Her back is to me when she asks, "You don't believe me about having wings do you?"

I shake my head, then remember she can't see. "No." My voice sounds small, and hollow.

"Maybe I'll be able to convince you." She pulls three mugs down from the cupboard next to the stove and turns to me. "How many days now?" she asks.

I rest my hip against the counter, uncertain of what she is asking.

She walks to me, her wrinkled finger lifting the chain of the necklace that I didn't realize I was grasping between my fingers. She asks again, "How many days?"

My breath catches in my throat. I haven't been counting, afraid to watch the number grow and acknowledge the distance between this new life of mine and the one I wish I could have back. I shake my head. "I don't know. Only one. Only today." It's the only measuring stick I can hold onto.

She presses her hand to my cheek. "Good girl." Back at the stove, she ladles liquid into a teapot, setting it and the mugs onto a tray that I pick up so I can stop my hands from trembling. She's doing it again, peeling back my skin, revealing my battered and bruised heart that is trying to hold on but feels like it is disintegrating with every beat. She sees me, really sees me, and somehow, she understands.

Mrs. Hernandez holds the door open. "Sometimes questions hurt, and the answers take time, but there is hope to be found, even in the darkness of searching for it."

Her words are a blade that cut me open and a needle that stitches me back together. I collect all the air in my lungs as I walk outside, holding it until I'm forced to exhale.

When Meredith texted me about hope it felt like a child's game—climb the ladder, spin the wheel, earn the prize—something I should have mastered by now.

"I don't understand what hope is," I blurt, as we walk back to where Vance has been working.

Mrs. Hernandez's smile is sad. "I said that same thing when my husband died." She crosses herself, kissing the tips of her fingers.

I am so surprised at her admission that I almost dropped the tray. To know I'm not the only one who has wrestled with this is a pump of helium inflating my heart. But her smile doesn't reach all the way to her eyes like it normally does. Maybe there are no answers to questions like this. My heart isn't floating anymore; it constricts. She said she asked the same thing, not that she found any answers.

Vance jogs to the deck and drags over two more chairs, making the start of a circle. He pulls his sweatshirt over his head, collapsing in the chair, and accepts the mug Mrs. Hernandez hands him. She pours one for me, then herself, wheezing as she lowers herself into her chair. I rest the lip of the mug against my chin, wondering about hope while savoring the fruity, spicy smell.

Vance is the first to drink, closing his eyes at the taste. "This is amazing. What is it?"

Mrs. Hernandez answers after taking her own sip. "Mulled wine."

Vance spits a mouthful of liquid to the ground like it's poison, and Mrs. Hernandez's laugh is loud and contagious, taking away some of the tightness in my chest.

"Don't worry," she says, taking another sip. "I made this batch with juice. If I started serving you alcohol, Murphy would force me to buy those five-dollar coffees of his instead of supplying me with a chair and all the water I can manage."

"And coffee grounds," Vance adds.

Mrs. Hernandez raises her mug in agreement. "He's good like that, a man of his word."

They are comfortable in each other's company, a quiet conversation bouncing between them that I don't pay attention to, my eyes locked on the garden bed. The wind pushes against me, making me swipe errant strands of hair away from my face every time I take a sip. What did Mrs. Hernandez mean about wings? All I can see is the butterfly kite, the one I begged for and waited for, taking flight against a stormy sky. Why did everything have to go wrong then, and now? Why didn't I get more time with Trent?

Time was something that always seemed available in bulk supply, a two-pack—there had always been more than enough. I never imagined time was a limited edition.

"Capítuloito?"

My head jerks up. "Sorry. What did you say?"

"I asked, what answers have you discovered in that pile of dirt?"

Vance sets his mug on the tray, pulls his sweatshirt back over his head, and picks up the shovel, starting to mix coffee grounds into another bed of soil. He looks at me over his shoulder. "Maybe you should ask her what questions she is asking the dirt."

I have questions, lots of them, and my eyes stay on his. "What was Trent hiding?"

One of Vance's hands slips from the shovel, and he blinks several times. I think there's a lift in his shoulders —a shrug—or maybe it's the wind lifting the hood of his sweatshirt. Either way, he returns to digging. Why do I keep thinking Vance will have anything to tell me?

Mrs. Hernandez picks up a book from the grass at her feet. It looks familiar, like a textbook I used to shove into my third-grade desk. It's what she was reading from when I arrived. She flips several pages, and smooths her hand across the one she was looking for.

But she looks at me, not at the book. Whatever she has to say, whatever she learned from this page and wants to tell me, has been transcribed into her heart. "Seeds," she says, "when dropped into a crevice of a rock are strong enough to split the stone, allowing space for the plant to grow."

It's an elementary school science book, not a holy text, but as she speaks, goosebumps wash over me while Vance keeps digging and the clouds press together in a gray band covering the entire expanse of the sky. Mrs. Hernandez doesn't read anything else. She said what she needed to say and simply pulls the shawl draped on the back of her chair over her shoulders, while strands of silver and black hair dance a whirlwind around her face.

A seed can crack a rock? It is as unimaginable as wings sprouting from my back. But Mrs. Hernandez believes in things I cannot see or understand. What if her belief is a seed being dropped into my stone-cold heart? Is it about to split me open? And what wild plant will grow out of my cleaved-in-half heart?

# twenty

. . .

## VANCE

After polishing off a plate of leftover turkey and stuffing, I leave before Murphy can ask if I want to do something together.

The ridge is the destination of choice for parties involving red plastic cups and I generally avoid wandering up there on the weekends, but it's the way I start walking, zipping a down vest over my hoodie. If only I had a thermos of the mulled wine Mrs. Hernandez gave me this afternoon to keep the chill out of my bones.

I was shocked by the intensity of Annabelle's eyes when she looked at me, asking what Trent was hiding, and I can't believe she let me return to digging without pressing me for answers. I won't lie to her and I'm tired of carrying Trent's secrets, but Derek tied them to some secrets of my own. If I can just make it to graduation this will all be behind me. I don't know where I'll go, but I know I can't stay here.

That thought isn't as comforting as it used to be. These woods have become a friend if I can call them that. Is that what Annabelle is becoming—a friend? I'd like to think she is, but I also don't like to think about it.

A loud grunt up ahead pulls me from my thoughts, followed by what sounds like a branch snapping, and a thud, and a string of curses. I knew I should have stuck to the river and not wandered along the ridge. Bumping into a band of drunken classmates is not my idea of a good time.

There's another thud and grunt and burst of angry words and this time I recognize the voice. Derek doesn't know I'm out here or that I hear him. It would be so easy to slip behind the trees and put more distance between myself and him but whatever he's doing isn't going well and I can't just leave.

Stepping over a stump, I see Sasha slumped against the base of a tree, her body crumpled in an almost passed-out sort of way. Derek whirls at the sound of my feet finding a twig of my own and snapping it in half as I step.

It's hard to read his facial expression while he's covered in shadows. "I can handle this," Derek says, swiping the back of his arm across his forehead and pushing aside a tuft of curls.

"Really? Because it doesn't look that way." Derek pulls himself to his full height, but I raise my hands, palms up, a white flag. "I didn't mean it like that." When I look at Sasha slumped against the tree, all I see is Nat. "Let me give you a hand."

The seconds tick by as Derek considers my offer before finally letting his shoulders fall. "Fine. I parked in the gravel lot."

I am not a human compass, but I know enough to know he's headed in the wrong direction. Everything out here looks the same, and if you are deep enough into the woods, and if you've downed one or more of those red party cups, it's easy to get turned around.

Derek growls, kicking the ground, when I tell him he's been walking away from his car, not toward it.

We make an awkward basket out of our arms, scooping Sasha inside. She's small, but the limp weight of her is a brick between us. The ground is uneven, there is no light to guide us, and we're both walking sideways, facing each other, which makes our progress extremely slow.

"You and Annabelle have been spending a lot of time together these days," Derek says to break the silence. "Small town, lots of eyes, don't think I'm not watching."

I have nothing to hide, at least not from Derek. "Watch all you want."

He grunts a little, shifting his arm under Sasha. "Just

making sure that even with all that quality time you haven't said anything to her."

My foot catches on a tangle of roots, and I lurch forward. "I think Annabelle has a right to know the truth, but I'd really like to graduate so I can leave this town and never look back." This idea is not comforting at all tonight. What I really want is to stay, but no one has ever asked if that's what I'd like. "So, relax, I'll keep Trent's secrets for whatever it's worth."

"For whatever it's worth?" Derek's voice raises like this is personal or I'm too dumb to understand his frustration. "Look what knowing the truth does to people. Look!" Derek stops walking, and I'm forced to look at Sasha instead of where I'm walking.

Sasha is not unconscious, but she's not coherent either. Every so often she slurs something that doesn't sound like English and after a minute Derek says, "She's not normally like this." Sasha's head bumps off his shoulder, dangling back, her mouth gaped open. "When she found out the truth, she stopped caring about her life."

"I know about her dad," I say.

Derek isn't surprised because everyone heard about Sasha's dad. It came out around the same time as Trent's accident. The week after he died the school still smoldered in grief but wafts of a scandal started to drift in.

Sasha's dad. His hot intern. Affair. Divorce. It rose like a phoenix out of the ashes of tragedy and Sasha shot it down as quickly as it took flight by aiming the school's collective attention at Annabelle's grief.

At least now I understand where Derek is coming from and his desire to keep the truth from Annabelle. He thinks he is protecting her from the same self-destructive behavior Sasha turned to after the truth of her dad's affair was revealed. I don't agree with him, but it makes sense.

As we enter the edge of the parking lot, Derek says, "Seems like you've had plenty of practice getting drunk girls home."

He means it as a joke, to make the heavy situation somehow feel lighter and my reply sounds like its own punch line. "Only one."

It makes him laugh, like now we're the kind of buddies who share stupid banter about drunk girls. We're at his car and Derek shoulders the full weight of Sasha while I open the passenger door, pushing the seat all the way back, reclining it as far as it will go. He lowers Sasha in, stretching the seatbelt across her. She mumbles something and he rests his hand on her cheek.

Derek stops before getting in the car himself. "Thanks."

I fold my arms into a line. "Don't leave her alone and

keep her head tipped to the side, in case she finally does pass out and then pukes."

"Your girl teach you all that?" He winks.

He's still trying to cover up the things he doesn't want to think about—Sasha giving up, Annabelle's search for the truth, dead best friends—with jokes. The wind pushes the clouds apart and there's enough light from the moon for me to notice the weight in Derek's eyes.

"Yep. Life lessons from my mom," I say.

I want to take it back as soon as I've said it. My admission becomes a tightrope strung between us, and to my surprise Derek takes a step onto it, testing his weight. "I'm sorry, man. I didn't know."

That's just it. We never really know what anyone else is facing or has hidden inside their heart do we? If Derek looked at Annabelle, instead of Sasha, I think he'd realize that she needs to know the truth. It's the not knowing that is killing her and it's killing me to keep the truth from her.

Derek drives away, pumping the brakes once, sending a flare of red into the night and I turn to walk home.

It's not the jokes that became a thread between Derek and me tonight. It's our lousy luck for loving someone who happens to love a cruel master named alcohol. Maybe Sasha will find her way out before she hollows out her bones, pouring in their place the liquid liar that tells her this is who she is meant to be. Maybe it's just a phase, a teenager being a teenager. Maybe it's an expression of her grief—her rage. And maybe this is exactly what Murphy thought about Nat, all those years ago.

# twenty-one

. . .

## ANNABELLE

Vance told me he was put on the planet so I would finally listen to acceptable music. For the rest of the winter, he only lets me listen to Death Cab for Cutie, Tracy Chapman, The Shins, and Janis Joplin. But now that it's spring and the earth is waking up from hibernation, he says it's time to shift gears. So, the playlist we listen to together every morning as we work is filled with The Flaming Lips, Beck, Moby, and his favorite of the bunch, Pixies.

But this morning, it's not the playlist that fills the café, it's Vance playing the piano, and when I return from the back room, Sasha has her hip leaned against the counter, watching him. I grab my mug from beside the sink and take a swig of the lukewarm coffee to fortify myself before I'm forced to talk to her.

"What can I get you?" I try to keep my voice light.

She answers without turning. "Tape." Her finger taps the counter. "He's an odd mix, isn't he? There's something"—she swirls her hands in front of her heart—"inside him, something hidden." She turns to me. "Do you ever wonder why he's kept to himself all these years?"

She gives me a Cheshire Cat smile—all teeth, no heart—extending her hand. My face is blank, and she's annoyed she has to ask again. "I need tape so I can hang these." She pulls a folder out of her messenger bag and lays down a poster advertising the Founder's Day bonfire and dance. "The printer messed them up twice, so they're late, but these little beauties are worth the wait. It's going to be so good this year."

I set a roll of tape on the counter. "It's exactly the same every year."

Every year the old Ridgeline Logging camp is decorated with the same handmade banners and gold, black, and pink streamers. It's a strange combination of collected Valentine's hearts and handmade, glitter-covered signs that sparkle under the disco ball. My favorite is a poster of a cherub chopping down a tree, arrows strapped to its back.

Sasha rolls her eyes, enunciating her words as if giving directions to a child through a pane of glass. "It's going to be so good this year."

I fight the urge to roll my eyes back. "Whatever. Hang your poster and go."

"Do you mean *whatever*, as in, 'Whatever, I'm not going this year?' Or, 'Whatever, Sasha, the poster you designed is spectacular.' Or, 'Whatever, I'm going to stand here and listen to my hot coworker play the piano?'"

I push the tape closer to her. Vance never lifts his fingers even though I'm pretty certain he hears our conversation. He remains hunched over the keys replaying a string of notes he is trying to work out, and I'm jealous he has something to occupy himself with other than Sasha's antics.

She tapes the posters up, sets the roll on the counter next to the door, and swings her head back to me. "You can't play a song that moody without having a bunch of stuff buried inside that you don't want anyone to know. Just saying."

The notes stop and Vance's chair scrapes against the floor, and he looks at me behind the counter. He opens his mouth, but I raise my hand, cutting off whatever he is about to say.

"I know, I know. Ignore her."

There's a slight curl to his lip. "Always a solid plan. You going?"

My nose turns up as if the idea is rancid. "No."

"Not buying what you're selling. Try again." He

settles back into his chair, playing a string of scales, waiting.

I want to go because I've always gone. But it won't be the same because nothing is the same. Except if I go Sasha will see me, one more person in the crowd, blending in, celebrating. And if my life is as normal as can be, maybe then she'll release me from her grip. Something pulses through me, excitement or fear, I can't tell. I take another sip of my coffee, but it's cold and I dump it down the drain. "I'll be there."

Vance cracks his knuckles and plays a melody of dark notes that run together. I push Sasha's assessment aside because it seems as if Vance has taken my pounding heart and transformed it into a song. How does he know the right notes to play? It's strangely intimate like the song is my reflection. His back slopes over the keys, and I wonder what it would feel like to press my hand to the skin at the base of his neck. The mug clatters into the sink—why did I think that?

My mom has the unique ability to find exactly what people are looking for. Thrift shops, the mall, garage sales. She'll walk into any store and pluck out a gem. Every dress in my closet has a memory attached to it, and they all belong to Trent. So, when I told her I needed a dress for the dance but didn't want to go shopping, I knew she'd come back with something amazing.

The dress is the night itself, dark and shimmering with a scoop neck, cap sleeves, and it falls in ruffles to my knees. I twist a few loose braids to frame my face, rim my eyes in black, and finish with a dab of berry across my lips. Then I slip my feet into blue ballerina flats and look in the mirror. For almost a year I've waited for a moment when I look at my face and think, *Oh, there I am.* Tonight is as close as I have come. But it's still not the same, and maybe it never will be.

Yesterday afternoon, Vance, Mrs. Hernandez, and I sat in her living room. We each pulled a random book from her shelf, taking turns reading one sentence at a time, making our own story. It's become an unexpected routine, the three of us spending time together, and it steadies me, giving me shelter from facing my empty life.

But yesterday after Vance left, Mrs. Hernandez asked me if I was any closer to understanding what hope looked like. I'm not. I still don't understand what it is. She said I should keep my eyes open and tell her what I discover. How am I supposed to find something if I don't know what it looks like? It feels a lot like snipe hunting with my dad, some sort of practical joke.

My notebook is splayed open on my desk. I grab a pen and write: *What does hope look like?* My pen hovers over the page, and I wait for inspiration to leak words onto the page. But all that happens is a shiver pushing its hand down my spine, and I drop my pen.

I can't do this on my own.

The bedroom at the end of the hall has not been Meredith's bedroom for a very long time. It's my mom's studio because it soaks itself in the late afternoon light which vanished hours ago, so the overhead light is on instead. An apron is tied around Mom's waist, her back to the door, as she smudges a glob of blue acrylic across a canvas. She doesn't turn to the sound of me entering, but that's not surprising. Her focus narrows to the movement of her hand when she paints. It's been a long time since I've watched her.

I should curl up with Torque, who slinks over, weaving around my legs, and stay here all night, watching whatever is in Mom's head be born in front of me. And for a time, I lean against the doorframe doing just that. But I came in here for a reason and start rummaging.

The noise gets mom's attention, and she greets me with a wide smile. "It fits you perfectly," she says.

I give a small twirl. "I love it. Thank you. Do you have a marker?" I pull a small tub across a table and dig into its contents. "Can I ask you a question?" She nods. "What do you do when you are trying to figure out what something looks like in order to paint it?"

She tips her head to the standing collection of narrow drawers under the window. "I guess it depends. Maybe there's an emotion behind what I'm creating that gives me a color or a shape and I go from there. Why? What are you trying to figure out?"

I swallow back the worry of what might be revealed if I tell her the truth. "Hope."

Mom bites her brush between her teeth, pulling open a drawer of her own, and grabs two tubes. She walks to me and sets her brush on the table. She unscrews the tubes and squirts a small dab of both onto the back of her hand. "Chinchilla and Nimbus Cloud." She smears them into lines across her skin. "Hope," she says.

"You think hope looks like light gray paint?"

"Among other things. But these two always catch the colors around them and it's where I would start." She raises her eyebrows. "You want to borrow these?"

I tap a marker I grabbed in the air. "Just this."

Mom inspects her other hand before touching the back of a knuckle against the tip of my nose. "I'm glad you're going tonight. The bonfire has always been a part of you and even after everything that has happened, this is still your life. I want to hug you, but I won't because I'll get paint all over you."

I point at her face. "You have some on your cheek."

She swipes her thumb across her face, capturing the

renegade paint. "Cerulean. My favorite. But not for rouge."

I lean, kissing her other cheek, the one that is flesh and not the beginnings of a Smurf. "Love you. Will you and Dad come?"

She nods but also waves a hand toward her easel. It's a yes but maybe not. I'm at the door when she says, "Call if you need to."

A lump forms at the back of my throat. There is a lot hidden in those five words. Call if it's too hard to breathe. Call if I'm afraid. Call if the room is filled with ghosts. Call if you need me next to you. I hold my breath, so Mom won't see me caving under the pressure of remaining upright, and keep my breath trapped until my chest hurts. I walk back, kiss her cheek again, and head to my room.

With the marker I write the same sentence across my mirror: *What does hope look like?* The words overlap my face, so hope looks like my reflection. It looks like trying to live after being sideswiped by grief. Maybe I've been looking at this all wrong. Maybe hope is right in front of me.

On the blank notebook page, I write, *Maybe hope is staring me in the face,* and leave for the party.

The old logging dormitory is practically a sauna from all the bodies packed inside. Hanging up my coat, I accidentally bump into a woman gathering two matching jackets, one falling from her grasp. "Oh, gosh, I'm so sorry." I bend to pick up the small jacket, handing it to her.

"Don't worry about it." There's a slight pause. "It's good to see you. I'm glad you're doing better and moving on with your life." She walks away and then calls over her shoulder, "Happy Founder's Day."

Here is what I know about this woman. She comes to the café every morning, a green yoga mat rolled under her arm. She has recently moved here and apparently has two young kids. I cross my arms over my chest. Ms. Iced-Oat-Milk-Lavender-Latte is a stranger. Someone I serve but know very little about. Even strangers have opinions about my life and are glad to see me out tonight, dressed up and presentable. Don't they know that moving on is not the same as slipping on a party dress? What is so great about moving on? Every day that passes takes me farther from the place where Trent and I stood together. But that's what everyone wants me to do —move on.

I walk a circuit around the room and am back to where I hung my coat. The room sways with activity. Classmates drift around the room in tied-together knots as the disco ball catches light, spinning it in different directions. I've stood in this room celebrating the birth of my hometown every year of my life. Before Trent. With Trent. And now, after Trent.

It's only nine o'clock. I could go home, and say I tried. Convince my dad to start a James Bond marathon if he hasn't already, or maybe Mom is still painting, and I could watch colors appear and blend into something new. I walk another slow circle around the room. I don't want to give up, but I don't know how to stay.

The secretary from school spins by with her son. She stops dancing and wraps me in a hug that pins my arms at my side. "I'm so happy to see you enjoying yourself." After releasing me, she grabs her son's arm, spinning back into the crowd.

I'm standing alone against the wall, not exactly the picture of enjoying myself. *People see what they want to see.* I wish Vance was here, or Mrs. Hernandez, then I wouldn't feel so alone.

A few other people catch my eye as they dance by and I lift my chin, smiling, giving them what they want, playing the part. I'm fine. I'm normal. I'm having a fantastic time.

Isn't that why I came? To prove all of this to Sasha?

But standing here against the wall, I realize it's not the only reason. I'm not only here for myself; I can do this for Trent. I can stay and bear witness to something he will never experience again—something I almost missed myself.

So, for that reason, I'll stand alone and wait.

# twenty-two

. . .

## VANCE

I don't like parties. Not that I have a history of attending parties, so I can't prove my distaste for them since I never get invited. But in theory, I do not like parties.

I've paced from one side of my room to the other for the past hour, arguing with myself. Should I go? Should I stay? Neither seems right. I just downloaded *Absolute Garbage*, the Garbage greatest hits album. That album will not disappoint, but the party very well could. But what would happen if I tried something new? Made new plans? Set new goals?

Part of me wants to believe it could be that simple. That showing up to the bonfire could translate into fitting in and turning over a new leaf. Nothing in my life works like that, but I slide a necktie around my neck, twisting, folding, scooting the knot to my throat, then flip the collar down. Would it be too much to ask that just this once, my life could be that simple?

There is only one way to the abandoned logging camp where the party is held. Any other night of the year you can drive yourself up the winding switchbacks of Ridgeline Road but not tonight. Tonight, a school bus ferries people up and back. When the local fire department hosts an event where alcohol is served, safety comes first, and no one is allowed to drive themselves.

I round the corner of the alley to join the line waiting for the bus on Cut Canyon in front of the café, but I stop short. I'm not used to joining in. Sure, it's just a line, and even with the buffer of a family between me and the people I go to school with, I know looks will be shot my way and I could do without the looks right now. Retreating to the alley, I enter the café and watch instead. I watch Annabelle run across the road and then I watch her find a seat as the bus drives away.

I'm not ready to go.

This is still *my* life. The one where nothing is as simple as showing up. I run my fingers over the ivories and call notes to mind, spilling a song into the emptiness surrounding me. When the bus returns twenty minutes later, I have half a mind to stay where I am and play for the night. But as the last note drops from my fingertips, I run to catch the bus before it pulls away.

Everything is in full swing when I arrive. Families

with small children claim the first half of the night, giving way to others who keep the party going well into the early morning hours. I walk past a bulking old steam crane that, in the daylight, is simply faded yellow metal covered in patches of rust and spray paint. Tonight, it is covered in tinsel and fairy lights. An ogre dressed up in a suit and tie but still an ogre underneath. Absurd, but I can relate.

I cut my way around the large open space to the far side, scanning the room. I look past pink and black balloons bouncing on strings, past people dancing, and past clusters of classmates I could do without before I spot her. Annabelle stands alone in the opposite corner from me, one arm hugged around her middle, making a pale slash across the dark of her dress. The light fluctuates in constant circles. Her dress is black, it's purple, it's black. It doesn't matter.

As I approach, her face goes from surprised to relieved. "What are you doing here?" she asks.

"Why so shocked? You know I am a party aficionado. In fact, stamped on my birth certificate it says, *The party starts with me.*"

Her smile is sudden and sweeping. The tiny dimple under her eye emerges, and I'm glad I came.

"You look . . ." I don't know how to fill in the blank I just created.

She takes a guess. "Like I'm having the time of my life?"

"Nope, not what I was going to say."

What was I going to say? The disco ball throws make-believe stars against the ceiling, the floor, the wall. Against Annabelle. The black purple of her dress shimmers under the lights. Maybe it's blue? The colors morph like a river and my eyes widen. Annabelle is the river shifting and changing. One day the water can be hard and angry, another day it will be a murky mix of mud and rock. Come back later and it could be sweeping, idyllic blues. The earth's very own mood ring. Maybe I think this about Annabelle because the first time I touched her skin we were held under the river's clutches.

It's not her standard-issue T-shirt and jeans, so I offer the simplest truth. "You look different."

She picks at the skin next to her thumb. "My goal is to blend in."

I tip my head to the dance floor. "Blending in is out there. Not standing here trying to hide."

The light fluctuates again and her dress glints black, purple, blue. She closes her eyes and when she opens them, they spark.

"I will if you will," she says.

Her words are fast, and it takes me a second to digest what she's suggesting. She is calling my bluff, bending my words back to me. I ignore my internal warning bell because this is me trying something new, and I take her hand.

"Fine, but if the songs start calling me 'shorty' or telling me to drop it like it's hot, I'm leaving."

She gives me another smile. "You and your moral high ground."

My hand is rough and warm, hers is small and cold, and I steer us toward the center of the floor. "It's not morals. It's principles."

"Whatever you say. But if the songs tell you to get low, I promise we can leave."

We.

Annabelle's hand slips from mine, and she goes from hugging herself against the wall to giving herself over to the music in the span of a breath. I could stand and think and watch.

Or I could dance.

It is wild and free and would earn us zero points in a competition. Our legs spin and step, and our arms flail, sometimes grazing each other, sometimes bumping into the people around us. It's the sort of dancing I imagine you would do with your best friend. You don't care how frenzied you look because you are doing it together and that feeling hooks itself under my skin.

For once I am not alone.

I lose count of how many eye-rolling, trending songs

play before the unavoidable slow one comes on and we freeze.

Annabelle takes a fraction of a step toward me. "I won't bite," she says.

My hand rests on her shoulder. "I make no such promises."

That earns me another dimple and together we sway a slow circle. Annabelle has a glint in her eye, the kind that comes from sneaking cookies out of the kitchen. "If I didn't know any better, I would think you actually enjoyed those songs," she says.

I raise an eyebrow, amused. "Good thing you do know better. Which reminds me: What did you think of that Fiona Apple song I sent you?"

Her hair swishes against her back, brushing the top of my hand and I want to grab it and never let go. "It was moody. But it also somehow felt like I was walking inside of a dream. There's that line, something about love costing too much when you're starving. I can't get it out of my head."

Light from the disco ball streaks across her face and I stop holding my shoulders so rigidly. "I knew you'd like it."

A drumbeat crashes into the end of the song, splitting our bodies apart and we're back to dancing like idiots. The air in the room is hot, almost too thick to breathe, but I understand something I never have before.

Normally I'd be alone, hating the idea of people getting dressed up to go dance in a building that sits empty every other day of the year. Now I see the appeal. Right now, we all belong to something bigger than ourselves, even if just for one night.

The cracks surrounding my heart have gotten so big that an entire person has found her way past them. I don't feel afraid of that, just breathless and sweaty and happy.

A trip to the refreshment table results in crackers in paper cups and small glasses of water. Reaching for another, I ask Annabelle if she wants more, but her attention is outside, watching the flickering outline of the bonfire in the distance.

"Want to go out?" I ask, and she nods.

This is not the kind of bonfire meant for someone to stand over, warming cold hands. It is a mountain of flames, large enough to burn for days. We claim an unoccupied log and sit. Annabelle looks at my sleeves rolled up to my elbow, no jacket, no typical sweatshirt. "You'll get cold," she tells me.

My knee presses against hers. "You do realize we're sitting inside a furnace."

An orange glow dances across her face, bending shadows into light. It highlights her jaw and the sweep of hair across her shoulder and I'm content to let the minutes pass. I don't need to fill it with anything because I feel strangely full inside. But the longer I watch the flames the more they remind me of the click-slap, click-slap, click-slap of Nat messing with her lighter. She would do that when she was nervous. Or making promises she would never keep. I don't want to spend energy thinking about Nat, not tonight. Not when I'm enjoying trying on a new me for size.

Annabelle is lost somewhere in the shimmer of the fire, and I wonder what hidden messages spell themselves out in the curl of each flame. What is she thinking? I'm about to ask when Sasha slithers in front of me.

"Vance, Vance, Vance." Sasha's breath pushes against my face, a sour-sweet, bottom-of-a-shoe stench that turns my stomach. It's what Nat always smelled of. "I've been meaning to ask you something, but haven't found the right time," she says.

She trails the back of a chipped fingernail along my face, and I lean so far back that I tip off the log. Standing up, I wipe away clumps of grass clinging to my jeans. "You should go home," I tell her.

Sasha shrugs, swaying as she does and Derek appears at her side, swaying a little himself. Whatever she drank dulled the edges of her voice, turning it flat and loud. "Should is a funny word, MiniVan. For someone with such a love for writing, I would have thought you would understand that. So many things you *should* have done."

Annabelle's face is twisted in confusion and not for the first time I want her to know the truth. But for Annabelle to know the truth it means I'll have the last leg kicked out from under my life. I'm tired of holding up the pillars that support Trent, keeping him spotless in Annabelle's memories.

Sasha's body jerks toward Annabelle. "I know a secret," she says, pressing a finger against her lips. "I know what Trent didn't want to tell you."

# twenty-three

. . .

## ANNABELLE

Sasha is ringed by flames. Her mouth keeps moving but all I hear is the shouted celebration coming from inside the building. She puts her hand on my shoulders and dips her head opening her mouth to tell me Trent's secret when Vance pushes himself in front of her.

"Trent was going to break up with you." The words rush out like something slimy spilling over the edge of a counter. But it's Vance who says the nasty words. Not Sasha.

Derek lunges, spinning Vance away from me. "I told you not to tell her!"

All these words are fireworks exploding inside my heart, my brain, and the sky while the celebration explodes all around us. Derek and Vance have been keeping secrets from me? And Sasha knew this whole time. The ground tilts away while logs shift from the pressure of the flames shooting embers out in every direction.

Vance shoves Derek's hand off his arm. "Then what was Sasha about to say? Huh? If she knows anything it's only because you told her."

Derek's voice is a wrench tightening around every word. "I had to. That night you helped me, she heard us talking and remembered snatches of it the next morning. She wouldn't let it go. I had to tell her. She promised she wouldn't say anything."

I start to shake. Not from the cold or from standing too close to the flames. But because everyone knew the truth except me. *Trent was going to break up with you.* Of all the things that could have been the cause of Trent not acting like himself, I cannot believe it is this.

My voice is the ocean, cresting, and breaking. "Is that true?"

"The truth is Trent loved you," Derek says as Roman candles rocket through the sky.

Sasha's eyes are daggers aimed at everyone but mostly Derek. "You told me he was cheating."

Nausea flips my stomach inside out and I collapse onto the log, legs splayed in front of me, my head dangling between them, hair in the dirt. I'm trying to breathe. I'm trying not to vomit. My chest tightens. *Cheating.* None of this makes sense. Trent was a lot of things, and loyal was one of them. I stand up, dead leaves tangled in the ends of my hair, and find Derek in the shadows. "Trent was cheating?" I choke out the words, imagining him with someone else is a cut too deep.

"No," Derek says, and I almost collapse from the relief of the single word but Derek keeps talking. "At least not like you think. He wasn't cheating on you."

Sasha pounces, spewing what she knows at my feet. "Trent was paying Vance to write his papers."

Every game Trent played was by the rules. Why would he cheat at school? The edge of every memory I can call to mind of Trent starts to burn. This doesn't make sense. It's like I don't even know who he was anymore.

My head is splitting and I hold my breath until everything slows, turning the flames into drowsy curls. Cheating. Breaking up. Vance. Papers. Lies. Lies. Lies. When I finally exhale, all that remains is anger. It is a simmering ball, slamming through my chest, sudden and overwhelming, ricocheting off my ribs until it rolls to a stop in a newly constructed house inside my heart— a house that is dark and heavy and holds every ounce of my anger.

I thought Derek was my friend, but maybe he only belonged to Trent. I don't know what has happened between Sasha and me, but I never imagined our friendship would turn into this. And what about Vance?

I shove my hands into his back. The lyrics we were talking about earlier, about how hunger hurts, flicker to life, like one of those trick birthday candles that can never be extinguished.

"You knew I was searching for an answer, but you let me—" I choke on anything else I could say.

Vance doesn't say anything, and I glance down at my shoes in the dirt. It's almost been a year, but I feel the same earth-shifting slant as I did in Mr. Logan's office and on the bridge. This is another moment when my life shifts, becoming something I can't recognize and do not want. I skim the toe of my shoe across the grass like maybe I could find myself in the tangle of blades, but it's just dirt and grass. And by the time I look up, everyone is gone. I'm all alone next to the flames.

# twenty-four

. . .

## VANCE

Murphy scares the life out of me when I climb onto the roof.

"You're home early," he says from the bench press. "You okay?"

It's only half past midnight, but I assumed I'd be alone. Murphy is always asleep by now. But I also assumed when Derek told me not to say a word to Annabelle that he'd keep his own lips zipped.

"Peachy," I answer.

Murphy reaches under the bench, opens a cooler. Glasses clink together and he hands me a bottle.

"What? No." Everything about tonight is wrong. Murphy is drinking? I want to yank the bottle from his hand and chuck it off the roof.

Murphy's laugh is a rumble through his chest, and he slaps my back. "Root beer." He places the bottle's lid on the metal peg that holds the bar and hits the cap with his free hand, popping it off. A small curl of vapor drifts out of the neck when he hands it to me.

Murphy answers my question of what he's doing up here before I ask. "It was this time of year when I moved up here from Seattle, and Founder's Day always gets me a little sentimental. Plus there's something about holding a long neck." He tips his back. "I'm not saying I miss that life—I don't, but sometimes this"—he raises his bottle—"feels like home."

Home. His old life, who he used to be when he was young, impulsive, and drunk. When he was with Nat.

Home. The only thing I've ever wanted and, with what just happened at the bonfire, I'm guessing I have minutes left here, not days.

Murphy takes a sip and then asks, "Did you and Nat ever have any special traditions?"

He must really be feeling nostalgic tonight because he never brings her up. "Does me wondering if she'd come home or not count as a tradition?" I'm still thinking about what Murphy just said, about a glass bottle feeling like home. When I close my eyes and remember Nat as my home, I see blonde hair, ratty couches, and tipped-over bottles. I think maybe Murphy does too. But it wouldn't be the only memory of her that he has.

My time is almost up, so I better make the most of this moment. "What was she like *before*?" I ask.

Murphy sets his drink between his feet, rubbing both hands over his face. "Did she ever sing to you?" I shake my head. Sometimes she sang along with the radio, but I don't think that counts as singing to me. "She had this rasp you wouldn't believe. We used to sneak into clubs, and she'd convince the bartender to let her sing. Of course, that was sort of the beginning of the end. People started buying her drinks."

The beginning of the end. Exactly what tonight is.

Murphy picks his drink up, taking a long sip. "Nat came back, you know?"

"What? When?" My heart races at the thought of Nat waiting for me in Murphy's living room, her hands gripping the arms of the couch, eyes darting for the nearest exit.

"Years ago. I still lived in Seattle. I saw her hit bottom before, but that time . . ." He cups his hand over his lips, shaking his head. "She had just found out she was pregnant with you."

I hardly hear Murphy over the blood roaring in my ears.

He grabs another root beer, knocks the cap off, and takes a swallow. "She was scared. She didn't want to drink while she was pregnant, but she couldn't do that, not by herself. Not if she stayed with your dad. I never saw her fight so hard for it. But she did. She stayed with me for months." He drains the bottle. "I thought she'd stay for good. But one morning"—his head dips like he's about to pray—"there was a note on the counter telling me to never change my phone number and that was that."

And that was that—the beginning of the end of Nat and me.

What would my life have been like if she stayed with Murphy? The word *family* flares inside my chest.

Sometimes when I went to the library to watch YouTube videos, and all the computers were occupied, I'd pull encyclopedias off the shelf while I waited. There was one that showed the progression of time. You could peel back a clear plastic sheet, and all the cars vanished, peel back another layer, and every other man-made structure was gone, leaving the land as it once was, untouched.

Nat could have stayed. It's dizzying to think about everything that would have been different and every-thing that would have stayed the same. Because the truth is in every clear plastic layered version of my life that I can imagine, Nat never stays.

Murphy presses the cooler lid closed, standing from the bench.

Nat knew she'd never be able to stay sober. She did for a time, and I'm thankful. But she also knew that if she asked Murphy to keep his phone number the same, he would do that for her because he would do anything she asked. It gave Nat an insurance policy to pass down to me written on the tag of a sweatshirt when she had nothing else to offer.

Insurance policies. Like Derek holding onto the speech I wrote for Trent. Now Annabelle knows the truth, and maybe she'll be the one who will want to take her newfound knowledge to Mr. Logan. I wouldn't blame her if she did.

Murphy walks toward the ladder. He's going to go to sleep and I should at least tell him thank you—for the root beer, but more specifically, for the past three years of my life.

"Hey, Murphy?" One of his hands clutches the cracked handle of the cooler, the other rests on the curve of the ladder. But I can't do it. I can't make myself say what I really need to. "Want to go watch Fight Club?"

Murphy turns, a wide-open smile spread across his face, answering with one of his favorite quotes from the movie. "This is your life and it's ending one minute at a time."

He has no idea how right he is.

# twenty-five

. . .

## ANNABELLE

There's not a stitch of a breeze as I walk along a road that disappears into the darkness. I've never been here before, but I know this road will go on forever. My bare feet leave soggy imprints on the ground but something's not right. The ground is too soft, too squishy to be a road. Where am I? Diamonds spun from moonlight glint atop the water gathering at my ankles. Then without warning, a surge rushes toward me, and cold, silky fingers from the river slide up my legs, sweeping to my knees, then my hips, before skating up my spine, pulsing under my chin.

There is no time to take the breath I need before the water covers me.

I wake up gasping, shaking in my bed, pulling my knees to my chest. I grab my phone to check the time. Eight minutes past two.

I pull the duvet over my head, trying to make a bubble of protection, but it just reminds me of how alone I am. Memories from the bonfire race through my mind.

*Trent was going to break up with you.*

*I told you not to tell her.*

*Trent was paying Vance to write his papers.*

My life is an echo chamber of everything I've lost, and I shove the blanket off my head. I reach for the spiral notebook on my desk and click on my lamp, regretting the influx of light as soon as I turn it on.

My dad is the reason I write lists. I had just learned to write, and he let me help him plan our summer road trip. He ruffled my hair, gave me a pencil and a piece of paper, and told me, "Can't go wrong if you have a list."

Turns out that's not true at all.

I flip the notebook over to the front and shuffle through pages from when my life made sense. I knew who I was. I knew who Trent was—at least I thought I did.

Wake up. Work. School. Trent.

Page after page after page of the life I miss. Until one page stops me cold.

*SUMMER: Farmer's market - doughnuts. Camping/Rainier? Floating. S'mores. Firepit. Gum wall.*

I forgot Trent and I were making a list of things to do before he left for college. I forgot that he grabbed the notebook from my hands, shielding it from my view, writing something before he kissed me. I could taste cinnamon on his tongue from the latte I made for him.

And now, staring me in the face, is his idea for the summer we never got to enjoy.

He wrote: *I don't care, as long as I'm with you. Also. Skinny dipping.*

I swat the notebook off my leg as if it's a tarantula crawling across my skin, and leap to my feet. Why would he write that if he wanted to break up? Why was he cheating? Why did everyone keep the truth from me?

I rush to the bathroom at the end of the hall, strip my pajamas to the ground, and twist the shower on. Hot needles prick against my back and for a moment every muscle I've held tight uncurls. But the feeling doesn't last. A knife-edge of unease twists in my stomach. I thought I knew who Trent was. I thought I knew who Vance was. But I don't think I know anything at all. I stand in the shower until the water is no longer hot. It turns tepid then cold, and I shiver uncontrollably under the ice that numbs my skin.

I'm shivering in my room, wrapped in a towel, pulling on a pair of jeans, and hunting for a shirt. Opening drawers then closing them, dumping my laundry basket on my bed, sifting through the over-turned contents. I don't care what I wear except that nothing is right. I finally pull on the striped shirt I wore a few days ago.

The question I wrote on the mirror mocks me as I stare at my reflection. Dark circles mark the skin under my eyes and my mouth turns down. I feel like I've been trying so hard, but all this time I've been failing, and my so-called friends have had a front-row seat to watching me spin in circles like an idiot. Swiping my hand through the words, I reduce my written question to fragments.

What does hope look like? It looks like unrecognizable letters.

It's too early to be anywhere but there's no way I'm falling back to sleep, so I push my feet into my shoes and leave. As I walk the path that bisects the town from top to bottom, I realize I'm heading to Mrs. Hernandez's house. I can't exactly knock on her door at three in the morning and am about to turn around when I notice her living room light is on.

I knock once, twisting the knob, and poking my head inside. "Mrs. Hernandez, it's me."

"Capítuloito? So early." She calls out, her voice a scratch. "In here."

Her living room has a bay window in the center surrounded by built-in bookshelves. Every inch is filled, some sections spilling onto the rug. Mrs. Hernandez is standing on top of a step ladder, reaching for a book on the top shelf.

"Here, let me help," I say.

She puts her hand in mine, and it feels like a bird, weightless against my skin. "Thank you." Her exhale wheezes, and she folds herself into the couch.

I step onto the ladder. "Which book do you want?"

"All of them."

Of course, she wants to read them all. "Okay, sure, but which one did you want me to get for you?"

She doesn't answer and I look down. One hand is pressed to her chest, her eyes closed, and a cellophane crinkle rattles in between each breath she takes. Maybe I'm not the only one wondering why being alive is such a painful experience. Sasha's words from months ago blink to life, a neon sign at the back of my mind. *You're not the only one.*

But I am. I have been, haven't I? I twist my still-wet hair into a knot. "Mrs. Hernandez?" I don't want to wake her if she fell asleep. What was she doing awake at this hour anyway?

She opens her eyes, a smile covering her face. "Sorry, got a little winded."

I smile back, reaching my hand to the row of books behind me. She presses her hand to her knees, pushing herself up, heading to a stack of boxes I didn't see piled at the opposite end of the room, pushing one across the floor with her foot to where I'm standing atop the ladder. "All of them."

The clock ticks above the fireplace and my heart

clicks along with it except in double time. "Are you . . ." I don't want to say it. "Moving?"

She reaches for my hand, patting it, tugging me back to the carpet and the couch. "Soon, my Capítuloito, soon."

I yank my hand out of her grasp as if it burned. "No. Why? I need you."

"Do you remember my Ernesto?"

A smile whispers across my lips. Mr. Hernandez always had the creepiest Halloween decorations making me both dread and long to trick-or-treat at their house.

Mrs. Hernandez is also smiling, maybe remembering the same thing I am. "People have this strange way of thinking that the rules, or warnings, or whatever you want to call them don't apply to them." She sighs deeply, rubbing a circle above her heart. "Lung cancer for him, emphysema for me."

My lungs feel like they are trapped in a vice. Life is filled with too much death and dying. "Are you . . ." I can't even finish. I don't want to make it true but she understands.

"Eventually, but not today." She nods her head to the stack of boxes. "My sister lives in New Mexico and my doctor says the warm, dry air would be good for my lungs. Plus, I won't be alone." She stands up. "Come, I'll make us some tea."

The click-click-click-woosh of the burner ignites,

flames licking the underside of the kettle, and it reminds me of the bonfire. Revelations I can't understand about the boy I loved and the boy who saved my life twist my stomach into knots. And now I've learned that Mrs. Hernandez is leaving. It's too much for me to hold and my words are practically a shout: "He needs to pay for what he did."

Mrs. Hernandez almost drops the mug she's about to set in front of me. "What are you talking about?"

So, I tell her everything I learned last night.

"If Vance wasn't writing Trent's papers, none of this would have happened," I say.

"Maybe. But that's a hard rope to walk." Mrs. Hernandez blows over the rim of her mug before drinking. "Do you think you can remember something I am going to tell you?" She turns away as a cough with jagged edges cuts through her lungs and I nod.

"Your pain can be a mystery." She stretches one of her hands across the distance between us, thumping my sternum like a drum. "This pain, it can try to become many things. A mouth that would eat you. A knife you swallow that cuts in secret places. A mountain too big you give up trying to climb it." She continues drumming a cipher over my heart. "But if you let it, this pain becomes the wind." Her eyes drift out the window and mine follow her gaze to the dark shadows of branches swaying in her yard. "You already have the wings, Capítuloito." She stops tapping, grabbing my hand in hers. "Then you fly."

I am barely breathing. Afraid to move in case I break the spell of her words. I've never heard anyone talk about pain so clearly. It is a mouth. A knife. A mountain. It is the water I sank in and a bonfire of lies that turned out to be the truth. It is a boyfriend who was lying and friends who betrayed me. It is my life.

Mrs. Hernandez leans in front of me, placing her hand on my cheek. "Capítuloito, too often we want nothing and everything all at the same time. Nothing to change, everything to stay the same. Nothing to hurt, everything to last."

I can't stop shaking. My body is too full of truth and information and all the hurt I keep avoiding. I'll need to release something or I'm going to implode. But I don't know how to do that or what to say, so I just push back from the table, my chair toppling to the ground, and leave.

My feet are slow but my mind is racing. All I can think about is the bonfire and the fact that Trent was not who I thought he was. And Vance wasn't either. I hear Mrs. Hernandez's words as if she were walking next to me. *We want nothing to hurt and everything to last.*

I'm so tired of my entire life hurting. For too long my heart has been a locked cage, and everyone has been making decisions for me.

Derek knew the truth about Trent and every time I tried to talk to him, he walked away from me. Vance knew the truth and he distracted me with something I thought was friendship but that can't be the name for what we had.

Everyone I know is a liar. The night is dark and so are my thoughts. I know the truth now and the truth is as suffocating as wondering what Trent was hiding. I know Vance was cheating, and all these months he's been keeping an eye on me so he could keep the secrets all to himself.

My heart is hammering in my chest. Everything hurts. My head, my heart, my memories. Mrs. Hernandez's words whisper through my mind again. *Too often we want nothing and everything all at the same time. Nothing to change, everything to stay the same. Nothing to hurt, everything to last.*

My life cannot keep playing in a loop like this. It's time to make a change. It's time for Vance to understand what the truth feels like.

# twenty-six

. . .

## VANCE

Founder's Day weekend is over, but you'd never know that the celebration from this weekend had ended. Seniors buzz through the halls in a fresh wave of excitement. This is our week. We only have to endure finals before freedom will be handed to us in the shape of a diploma on Friday.

The constant pulse of chatter surrounding me is a swarm of mosquitoes I can't stand and for once, I'm early to class. As soon as I walk in, Miss Cripps sends me to the office to collect the papers she left on the copier. From halfway down the hall, I see Annabelle standing at the secretary's desk. There are a lot of possibilities as to why Annabelle could be standing there but only one that matters.

Annabelle learned the truth over the weekend.

Mr. Logan's door opens, Annabelle walks in, and I turn around exiting the school just as the first bell rings. Miss Cripps will have to get her own papers.

There's a dampness in the air that my hoodie doesn't shield, but I'm not going to slink back to Murphy's and risk him seeing me. If this is it, if Logan is having it all spelled out for him, I'm not going to sit around waiting to be expelled. He will have to come find me.

I tried being a new version of myself and look what happened. Images of dancing with Annabelle flood my mind and I force them away. I tried to let someone in, tried to make room for another person in my life, and it went up in flames.

It's my own fault. What did I think was going to happen? Secrets layered with more secrets, sprinkled with the lies of a dead boyfriend then baked in a grief-shaped tin is not a cake anyone wants to eat. And yet I took a bite. And now Annabelle is in Logan's office telling him I spent all of last year writing Trent's papers. Probably blaming me for everything that happened. Fine, if that's what she thinks, that's who I'll be.

I'm done trying.

I'm done being disappointed.

I'm done with people.

The river is large enough to hold my mood and I walk along it until the sky opens. I'm soaked by the time

I make it back to Murphy's. His truck is gone, and the café is closed, neither of which is normal for this time of day. Is he out looking for me? I need something hot, so I unlock the back and slip inside. The electric kettle is quick to boil and while I wait, I open the register. Murphy won't play the music I uploaded to a thumb drive, so I shoved it under the cash drawer and now I might as well take what's mine. When I lift the tray out, I uncover a slip of paper.

The IOU Trent wrote.

I press my thumbs against my eyes. I know what it means to hold onto relics from the past.

When I was eight, I stole something from the neighbor I'd been thrust upon when Nat supposedly went to buy groceries. Vivian's apartment looked like one of the stalls at Portland's Saturday Market that Nat sometimes took me to. A variety of fabrics as flowy as the house dresses she wore were scattered around the room, draping over stacks of canvases she had leaning against the walls. Throw pillows scattered the floor, and a small circular table sat in the center, every inch covered with painting supplies. As we waited for Nat, Vivian let me thumb through a stack of paintings that were smaller than a postcard, but not by much. I couldn't take my eyes off of one in particular. A man, who looked like a knight, rode a white horse and was shoving a spear into the heart of a dragon, blood dripping from the wound. The knight's face was calm in contrast. It wasn't the victory of the knight that initially drew me to the painting; it was panic I could see in the dragon's eyes. It was a look I knew all too well. I was familiar with dragons.

When Vivian had given up on Nat returning and went to find her shoes, I slipped the card into my pocket. Every night after that I slept with the painting tucked inside my pillowcase. That and the Nirvana hoodie are the only artifacts of my life that I've been able to keep.

It isn't much, but I understand the desire to hold onto the past. I also know that keeping these artifacts is worthless. If anything, they weigh my memories, chaining me to places and times that I should cut out of my heart and forget.

It's easier to walk away when there isn't much to carry. At least Nat got that part right. Life is easier with no strings attached.

It would be easy enough to slip Trent's IOU back under the cash drawer, but anger simmers ahead of me, a mirage that looks like an answer.

I'm done trying to find a place for myself in this town. Life hurts less when I am on my own and I flick the sticky note back and forth between my fingers.

Thinking. Deciding.

Every time Annabelle opens the drawer and sees it, she takes a step back in shock. I crumple the paper in my hand, throw it in the trash, tie the bag closed and walk to the dumpster. The lid clangs shut, and I regret nothing. If anything, she will thank me. This will release her from threads of her past that will wind so tightly they will cut off her circulation.

I've just done her a favor.

# twenty-seven

. . .

## ANNABELLE

I rip a banana from the bunch on the kitchen counter as mom's slippers scuff across the floor. She's never up this early. "How come you're awake?" I ask, as she enters the kitchen.

"Couldn't sleep." She pulls the belt of her robe tight before putting her arms around me. I'm stiff as stone but melt in her arms as she holds me. Did I do the right thing yesterday when I walked into Mr. Logan's office? I feel sick because I'm not sure. Mom sweeps the hair I didn't brush away from my face, examining me only as a mother can. I'm afraid she'll see that the seams holding me together are coming undone.

There used to be an entire troop of stuffed animals living on my bed. I had so many I could have opened a zoo. But Blinks was my favorite. I took that elephant everywhere and slept with it next to me for more years than I will admit. I loved that thing even when the seam down its back separated and mom sewed it back together because sometimes "well-loved" and "shabby" mean the same thing.

Right now, I am Blinks.

Mom's hand is still on the side of my face. "Are you doing okay?" she asks.

"There's so much," I stop, not knowing what to say, afraid I'll say too much. *Ignore. Survive. Keep doing what I'm doing.* I repeat the phrases in my mind until they are the only words I understand. "There's so much going on at school with finals and everything, but I'm good. Everything is fine." Covering the truth with lies has become remarkably easy. Even though I hate this version of myself, reality is much worse than lies that let people think I'm okay. Is this how Trent felt about cheating? Did it eat him up inside? Lying to my mom twists my already knotted stomach, so I wave the banana in the air as a quick goodbye and walk to work.

The scent of freshly brewed coffee swirls the air, welcoming me along with the notes Vance plays on the piano.

"Hey," I say.

Talking to Vance isn't something I meant to do. The word just slipped out, a hardwired response to seeing another human being. But it doesn't matter. His only reply is the straight line of his back.

Vance stays at the piano while I unlock the register. My feet are glued to the floor as I rummage in the bottom of the drawer, shoving loose papers and receipts from side to side. "Where is it?"

All these months Trent's IOU has been hidden in this drawer. A surprise, a reminder, a treasure, an omen. It has been all of those things depending on the day I happen to see it. And now it's gone.

I ask again, this time much louder. "Where is it?"

Vance keeps playing and I rush to him, striking my hand against the keys, making all the wrong sounds but it gets him to stop playing.

Vance stands, thrusting his hands into his pockets. "I threw it away."

My face falls under the weight of what he said, and my body drops to the ground, and I pound my fist against the floor. The sound that tears loose is a scream. It's a growl. It is everything I've been holding inside.

My last seam has ripped open and I cannot keep myself together. The veins on my neck strain as I jump to my feet. "You're a jerk, you know that? I thought maybe you weren't, but you are."

His eyes are stone. "Yeah, well, get in line."

I shove my hands into his chest. "I don't have to get in line. I'm standing right here telling you."

He starts to walk behind the counter. "One day you'll thank me."

There's a knock on the door. We haven't unlocked it yet, and I don't care that Officer Daily-Drip-To-Go is waiting outside. "I will never thank you. You had no right to do that but I'm pretty sure you know that because you seem to know everything. About everyone. All the time." My throat hurts from screaming. "Well, here's what I know. You're a coward. And if you so much as speak one word to me ever again, I'll do what I couldn't do yesterday and tell Logan the truth."

Vance takes a step back as if I slapped him and something slides across his face. Not anger. Shock maybe and I stomp to the door to let in Officer Dobb. He eyes Vance and me, his hand resting on his belt. "Everything okay with you two?"

"Fine," Vance and I shout in unison.

I snap a lid on the to-go cup and slide it across the counter while Vance rings it up. Officer Dobb leaves with a backward glance, probably uncertain if he should leave us alone.

Yesterday I was so sure I was doing the right thing by going to Mr. Logan. Except when I stepped inside his office, my body remembered what it felt like to collapse onto the carpet, crushed under the news of Trent's death. Telling Mr. Logan what I knew about Vance would get him in trouble, but it would also reveal details Trent kept hidden. What would happen to Trent's memory? Would his family be informed? And how did Vance get wrapped up in all of this anyway? Was it his idea or Trent's? So, I walked out of his office, the truth hammering at the base of my skull.

Maybe I was better off not knowing the truth, but that would mean Sasha was right and I like that idea about as much as I like Vance right now. I'm furious. Vance took something from me. Something that was never his to take. Something I'll never get back.

But Trent took something from me too: the ability to truly know him, mistakes and all.

Untying my apron, I toss it toward the rack, not caring if it lands on a hook or not. I grab my backpack and run. I need to get away. My pace is wild down the street, my backpack thumping against me as I whip onto Ridgeline Road.

I need to go faster.

I need to get further away.

I need my body to ache.

Pulling in huge gulps of air, my lungs burn. It's a comforting sensation to feel them scorched. And for a moment it calms everything rattling loose. My lungs are the only part of my body I feel. I do not feel my feet hitting the pavement or my arms pumping. I only run.

The road blurs in a wash of tears as I push myself harder. Further. Faster. Flying up the last rise, rounding the curve before the bridge. Skidding to a stop, I swipe sweat and tears from my face. The bridge looms in front of me and my chest heaves as I inhale pain and regret.

I'm really on my own now. Trent is dead, and I can't hold any memory of him without wondering if it was all a lie. Mrs. Hernandez is moving away. And Vance, the one person I trusted, took the last thing that was mine.

I hold my breath until the lack of oxygen sets my ribs on fire. I don't think, I just run. I slam my body against the stones, grip my hands over the rough-cut rocks, my finger digging into the cracks between the stones as I pull my torso over the ledge. I lean so far I almost fall. Again.

I take a breath. All I have to do is hold on.

I take a breath. All I have to do is let go.

I take a breath.

# twenty-eight

. . .

## VANCE

Alone in the café, I drag the marker over the page.

~~In the dark~~ **I** ~~made out the edge of a well, the kind
you drop in a~~ **wish** ~~or two inside.~~ **I** ~~was tempted to walk
past, I do not have have time for superstitions. Yet I~~
**could** ~~not deny the draw to pause and speak a hope into
the depths. To~~ **tell** ~~the secret~~ **you** ~~want me to keep
hidden. I closed my eyes over the image of your face
asking me~~ **why** ~~and let the truth slip from my lips.~~

But Annabelle said not one word, and these are
words so I slam the book shut.

Nat and I lived in California when I was in third
grade, and I learned a new set of words. June Gloom.
The Five. Fault Line.

I learned that faults are fractures inside the earth and
that there's nothing anyone can do to stop one from

cracking open, nothing anyone can do to keep an earthquake from destroying everything in its path.

Every day my life feels like I'm waiting for an unavoidable earthquake.

Murphy appears through the back door with the daily haul of pastries. "No Annabelle yet?" he asks. I'm not about to tell him what happened this morning, so I shrug. "That's not like her," he says. "I'll cover until she gets here."

I shrug again and shove the paperback into my back pocket. Saving myself from expulsion almost doesn't seem worth all of this. Maybe I should throw myself on the grenade of not graduating in order to save the memory of Trent, and release Annabelle from whatever agony she's locked inside of.

*Should.* The same word Sasha threw at me. Life is filled with a lot of *shoulds.* Nat should be my mom. I should be able to graduate. I should be able to tell Annabelle the truth. I should confess and take whatever consequence comes my way. I should ask Murphy if I could live with him even if I got expelled days before graduation.

My thoughts are a jumble when Murphy says, "Time's up."

I know he's talking about my shift ending, but inside this web of thoughts, his words land like a brick. Those two words throb behind my eyes.

Then Murphy says, "When you talk to Annabelle at school today be sure to ask her if she's okay."

He hasn't been paying attention the last few days if he thinks Annabelle and I are still friends. I scuff my shoe on the bottom of the counter. "Sure thing, boss. Anything else?"

Murphy flips a towel onto his shoulder. "What is up with you lately?"

"Nothing." Except for the fact that I'm waiting for the rest of my life to implode. I lift the apron over my head and exchange it for my backpack. The deal was I could live with him until Nat came back or I graduated. There were never any stipulations made for what he would do if neither of those happened. So any way I look at it, the end is in sight. Besides, Murphy told me the truth whether he knows it or not.

"Time's up, right?"

Murphy stares at me for a long time, opening his mouth like he's about to say something but his eyes slide to the clock. "Right. Time's up."

And that's all I need to hear.

# twenty-nine

. . .

## ANNABELLE

The sunrise is a bruise across the sky.

My legs dangle over the ledge of the bridge. As I clawed my way to the top of the bridge, my shirt snagged on a rock, skin scrapping against stone, and now my abdomen throbs and I can't hold one single thought in my mind.

Trent. Lies. Vance. IOU.

They race in a loop until it blurs into a knot of confusion. I should call Murphy to tell him I won't make my shift and pull my phone from my pocket. But instead of calling him, I spin the phone in my hand to the rhythm of my circulating thoughts. I close my eyes and see the slant of Trent's crooked smile. I want to open my eyes and watch him materialize in front of me. But who would he be if he did? Would he tell me why he chose to cheat? Would he still want to break up?

It's hard to think about those questions. Answers would be nice, but I'll never have them. A cluster of birds make an arch above me, and I tip my chin to watch them. I still can't believe Mrs. Hernandez is moving. She understands my heart, but she still hasn't told me what hope looks like. Maybe no one knows and asking me to look is just something that sounds nice.

I pocket my phone, the thought of checking in with Murphy already forgotten, and I continue to watch the clouds turn into purple, pink, and orange wounds against the sky.

By the time I exit school, the sky is pockmarked with gray clouds. A voice behind me calls my name. I spin, squinting, raising a hand. My dad's jeep idles against the curb. "What are you doing here?" I ask.

He pats the passenger seat. "I have to go pick up some parts in Rye and I thought I'd drive you to your appointment."

Right. Wednesday. I forgot what day it is. Too many thoughts roam the landscape of my mind for me to remember my weekly counseling appointment. Grabbing the roll bar, I step up, lowering myself onto the seat. I wedge my backpack next to my feet and strap the seatbelt across my scraped-off skin as we drive away.

Dad bumps his elbow into me. "How was school today?"

My cheeks puff. "Oh, you know. Finals."

"I can't believe you graduate in two days."

Me either. Graduation is a strange topic at home. It's not like we avoid it, but it's not circled on the calendar as it should be. What comes after the end of high school is a large blank space that I don't know how to fill in. I never sent in any applications.

Closing my eyes, I let the wind rush over my face, tangling my hair. Riding in my dad's jeep always feels more like flying than driving. There is no roof or doors to close around me. I love the scurry of air, and for the rest of the drive, my heart doesn't tap messages about Mrs. Hernandez leaving or Trent and his lies or everything Vance knew and never told me. I simply let the wind whip my hair.

We slow and Dad drums his fingers against the dash. "I'll be back in an hour to pick you up." I don't say anything. There's just the click of my seatbelt releasing. I should have at least thanked him for the drive.

This old Victorian house has been converted into offices. The top floor is studio space that artists can rent, and the main floor contains the offices of Craig and his colleagues. Slumping on the ottoman by the picture window, I wait.

Seeing Craig is a familiar routine. We talk a lot about

running, and I pretend the progress I've made physically translates into my emotional healing, but it doesn't. I've just gotten good at saying what people want to hear.

So, when I take my regular spot on the blue velour sofa in his office and he asks his regular opening question of how my week was, I respond with my regular answer. "Fine."

But my heart rebels at the lie.

This week has not been fine. Not even remotely, but I can't backtrack and change my answer now. He's asked another question, one I didn't hear but he crosses his legs, looking at me with an expectant face. Outside, clouds roll across the sky, darkening the room several shades until they pass, and the room is bright again.

Storm clouds gather in my mind. I used to have a simple life. It made perfect sense to me and it was all I needed. Why couldn't that have been enough?

Trent said he loved me, but he was hiding things from me.

Vance has been my safe space, the one person who made me feel like myself, but he let me grope around in my grief looking for the light switch when he knew the truth all along.

Mrs. Hernandez has X-ray eyes and sees me, but she's about to be a thousand miles away.

"Why do people have to die? Or leave you behind?"

My question jumps out and now I'm looking at Craig

with an expectant face. I'm so tired of holding my breath, holding my pain in, and more words rush out. "I mean I get it. One day you're born, and you get however many days and then one day you die. And don't come at me with the whole circle of life song, because I understand. What I don't get is *why*. Why do you have to love someone? Why does it have to hurt so much?"

I come and sit. I nod. I say I'm trying. I go home. It's the same song every week.

Not today.

Craig tilts his head. If he doesn't know I've been pretending all these months, he does now. He answers my questions with questions, and I answer his as generically as possible. This is our routine, but I've just broken it. He opens his mouth to say something, but I'm afraid he'll ask a question and I'm so tired of questions. I want answers and jump from the couch, itching to run out the door.

Craig pats the air in front of him with his palms facing me like you would do to calm a frightened animal. "Have you ever seen footage after a tornado rips through a town?"

He points to the couch I leapt from and I sit, gripping my knees like it's the only thing keeping me from floating away as he continues.

"The camera zooms way out showing a row of houses, or what used to be a row of houses, except now they are piles. And there's always one person sifting through the wreckage. Mangled walls, shredded furniture—you can't imagine that all this debris used to fit together and be their house. But there's that guy, picking things up, searching, trying to find something that survived. And wouldn't you know, he pulls a toaster out from under a splintered wall and holds it like it's an artifact fit for a museum. He'll start to laugh, sort of hysterical. Happy, but not happy. Confused. Grateful. Because here he is, standing on the leftover pile of his house and there's not a single scratch on his toaster."

Mrs. Hernandez told me I have wings and now Craig is telling me there are toasters waiting to be uncovered. What does any of it mean and what does it have to do with my life? "What is the toaster supposed to be? Love? Death? Me?"

He leans forward. "What do you think?"

I think I'm going to scream. "I think there are no guarantees. There is no such thing as safe. And if your house gets destroyed, what good is a toaster? That's what I think." It's all true because, from my vantage point of standing on the leftover pile of my life, there is nothing intact to pull out from under the walls.

I don't want to be in this room anymore because none of this matters.

Once I'm outside I hear footsteps behind me, and I

look to see Craig following behind me. "I'm fine, you know. You don't have to follow me," I tell him.

"Can't let you disappear from our appointment though, can I?"

I whirl to face him. "But I'm fine!" Even I know I'm acting unhinged. People who are fine do not shout at their counselor on the side of the road. But when I start walking again, I'm glad Craig lets me go, even though he still follows me. The road ends in a T intersection. Unsure of what direction Dad will come, I lean my back against the pole of the stop sign, sliding to the ground. Craig sits in the grass with me, but I don't look at him.

My head aches. Why did Vance have to throw away the IOU? It was the last thread connecting me to Trent. I feel like I'm losing my grasp on life. Everything feels upside down and inside out. I pull a blade of grass from the earth and wrap it over my finger, making a tiny cast. Roughly this time last year, a cast covered my wrist. Being physically broken made sense in a lot of ways. It's the healing that's been harder to understand.

The wind picks up, pushing itself through the branches above, sounding like a wheeze reminding me of Mrs. Hernandez.

Do I want everything and nothing all at the same time? Could I hold onto the memories of Trent without dissecting them trying to find lies hidden in their fabric? Could I forgive Vance and still feel the jagged edge of pain when I remember how he lied, and what he took from me?

Am I strong enough to do any of this instead of beating my head against the ground, wishing for a life I can never get back?

Clouds are being pushed together by the wind, and that's when I see it. A single cloud, bunched in the middle, with wisps flaring out from the sides. It looks exactly like a pair of wings. Mrs. Hernandez keeps telling me I have them, that I can fly, and I have no idea how. I close my eyes and see Vance standing on a bridge next to me. His shock of black hair flopped across his face, his hand outstretched, the breeze lifting my hair off my shoulders.

Maybe I did fly. From the way I tipped off the edge, I should have had more severe injuries. Or worse, been pulled out of the river in a body bag. Maybe Mrs. Hernandez has been right this whole time.

I hear the rumble of my dad's jeep before I see it. "Craig?" I ask, watching the wind pull apart the wings. "Do you think that person whose house got destroyed by the tornado would be okay if everything in their house got ruined but everyone made it out alive?"

His hand is soft on my shoulder. "Absolutely."

Have I been holding onto the wrong things? The IOU wasn't Vance's to throw away, but a slip of paper won't bring Trent back. "Even though it's those same people, the people they love, that will somehow hurt them one day?"

His hand squeezes. "Yes, even then."

I finally look at Craig, and a raindrop splats on my shoe, then my cheek. "Is finding a toaster what hope looks like?"

The jeep's engine is loud now that my dad is on the grassy shoulder next to the stop sign. Craig doesn't answer—he just smiles at me like I told him he won the lottery. Getting to my feet, I climb into the jeep.

"See you next week," he says and, for the first time, I'm looking forward to it.

I knock my elbow against my dad's the same way he did when he picked me up. My heart is twisting in a new direction, or it's finally starting to untwist from all the pain I've been stuffing inside of it, refusing to let it out. "Should we try to outrun the rain?" I ask.

Dad revs the engine, and we become a bird gliding across the pavement. My arms lift above my head, but we will never be fast enough to outrun the downpour that erupts from the clouds above. In a matter of minutes, we are both drenched and laughing and he slows to a less reckless speed.

Tears and rain are streaming down my face but for the first time, in a very long time, I feel free.

The next day Mr. Logan's voice cuts through the school's intercom. I knew this was coming. Everyone knew this was coming. All of West Aldrin High pretends to pay attention in class and not notice the lack of band students in the second to last period of the day. As soon as Mr. Logan shouts, "Lumberjacks! Are! You! Ready?" The marching band is in the hallway and begins to play. At which point, my high school career is officially over and the hall floods with cheering students.

No one knows how this tradition started, passed along from one administrator to another, and kept alive because everyone loves the rush of adrenaline it brings. If my life were a musical, this would be the scene with glitter cannons, where everyone bursts out of classrooms wearing matching outfits, doing a choreographed dance routine.

It's so familiar, yet it's the first time the celebration is for me. I did it. I survived senior year. My fingers lift my necklace, the coin cool between my fingers, a stark contrast to the fire I feel building in my chest. I feel like a foreigner watching the entire school dance in the hallway.

One summer, a young man from Kenya stayed with us. I have no idea why he was there or where he went after our house. I only remember following him around like a five-year-old puppy, repeating everything he said. The words he taught me slid over my skin, my mouth rounding in vowel and consonant combinations that seemed more appropriate for words than the sharp-angled sounds English provides.

Door—mlango. Cat—paka. House—nyumba. Sleep—lala. Goodbye—kwaheri.

This is what it's like to look for hope.

It is learning a new language within my own life. The music sweeps through the confines of the hall. A cymbal crashes and I hold my breath. This is the last time I will ever experience this event. Should I celebrate? Should I mourn all that is coming to an end? I don't know what direction to point my heart.

Too much of life feels balanced on the blade of *hold on* or *let go*.

Every note of every instrument fills every inch of space in my heart, and it overtakes me. I've felt lighter since talking with Craig, but there's a tightness in my heart I can't seem to shake. As I listen, the thudding music transforms into a key, unlocking the last remaining deadbolt on my heart. And once that door swings open, every emotion and every memory is freed from their cages. They rush through me the same way the music rushes through the hall.

I start sobbing and need to get somewhere I can be alone so my emotions won't turn into another social media clip. Trying to maneuver through the band would be like swimming upstream, so I squish myself behind a line of dancing classmates next to me, scraping along the wall until there is a door behind me.

I back into the bathroom and the door closes over the music, muting it to a manageable level.

"Well, well, well, look who the cat dragged in."

I spin around. Sasha sits on the counter, both knees pulled up to her chest, unscrewing the cap of a flask.

My mouth drops open.

Her snort almost sounds like a laugh. "Oh, please." She slowly raises it to her lips, daring me to stop her, but I don't. I'm too shocked to do anything. After a very long guzzle, she wipes her hand across her lips, screwing the cap back on. "That's what I thought."

Sasha hops down and for the first time I notice how carefully she is holding herself together. It's something she wouldn't want people to see. It's a belt cinched tight around the center of her. She's afraid and hurting. I only recognize it because I've finally allowed myself to acknowledge my own pain and I'm beginning to understand all the ways pain shapeshifts. Black hoodies. Bridges. Lies. Toasters. Wings. Truths kept hidden.

"If someone catches you," I wave my hand to the flask she is stuffing into her backpack, my hand flitting back to my necklace.

Her eyes roll. "Please. I've been doing this all year. What are they going to do now? Not let me walk tomorrow?"

I flick back through every encounter I've had with her and now I wonder if there was something else lingering under her anger toward me. "All year? But why?"

"Nope. You don't get to do this. You don't get to suddenly pretend like you care. You're your own kind of messed up, and in case you didn't realize it"— she walks closer and whispers in my ear—"we're not friends anymore."

The full force of her words pushes me back. All year, the gap between Sasha and me grew into a rift, and right now it is the exact width of three bathroom tiles, but might as well be the Grand Canyon.

"Here's a piece of free advice. Mind your own business." Sasha's arm grazes mine as she walks past. She pulls open the bathroom door and lets in a rush of pep band music. "Stay out of my life, just like you have been." Then she's gone.

The band takes a collective breath between songs, throwing silence into the bathroom. The soft plink of water dripping from the faucet turns into tiny explosions. The next song starts, and muffled music fills the bathroom again, like the grout between the tiles running up the wall, filling every empty space. I lean on the counter and turn the water on, wetting my hands, and press them to my flushed face.

I am messed up.

It's easy to believe Sasha because it's true. It's even somehow comforting to sink into those words. They feel like being wrapped in a blanket straight from the dryer —hot and soothing, but also stifling. I hold my breath until the edges of my vision turn a shade darker like a preset filter. Bracing myself against the edge of the counter, I exhale.

I can't hide from everything that hurts. Not anymore. I tried and nothing good has come from ignoring my pain. Sure, I've made mistakes, and yes, I am messed up. But that is not all I am. I'm here, right now in this bathroom, standing on the leftover pile of my life with nothing much to show for myself. But I'm not giving up.

Shoving my hand into my backpack, I search for the marker I took from my mom.

Across the bathroom mirror, I write.

*I am loved.*

*I am brave.*

*I am here.*

Taking a deep breath, I look at the tears clinging to my cheeks and leave them where they are. I think I'm beginning to understand, and write one more thing: *Hope feels like finding toasters after tornados.*

The ruckus in the hall has stopped, and students exit the building, strutting into the parking lot as if they swallowed the drumline. In the middle of the parking lot, I see Derek about to get in his car. Mrs. Hernandez never judged me for my selfish choices but gently encouraged me toward healing. And none of that would even matter if Vance never saw me, took a chance, and stepped onto the ledge.

I need to find Vance and talk to him. Really talk to him and give him a chance to tell me his side of the story. But first things first.

Derek turns at the sound of my approaching footsteps, obviously surprised to see it's me. "Remember when you, me, and Trent went camping?" I ask.

An instant smile lights his face. "You mean, remember when you forgot to ask your parents if you could come, and we all got busted?"

My smile matches his. "Fun while it lasted though, right?"

"Right." The memory inflates Derek like a balloon. I haven't seen him this happy in months. "Remember when Trent let me cut his hair but the guard on the clippers slipped and I had to shave his head?"

I shake my head at the memory of a practically bald Trent. Now that the door of my heart has been unlocked, more memories beg to be remembered. "And when the two of you thought knee-high socks and baggy athletic shorts were the height of fashion."

I forgot Derek's eyes always squish closed when he laughs. "Do not disrespect the socks." Emotions are coins and there are always two sides. His eyes are still wrinkled closed, but tears leak out. His voice is so quiet. "I miss him so much."

Derek's head is tipped to the asphalt, his shoulders trembling, and I see another casualty of my tunnel vision. I am not the only one who lost Trent, and I wrap my arms around Derek. "Me too."

I love that Derek and I can say Trent's name and have a hundred stories to swap. It's a comfort knowing Trent will be kept safe inside our memories. Even though pulling these memories to the surface hurts, it hurts less than trying to keep them locked away. Sharing Trent with Derek makes my pain more tolerable.

It's something I can write on my lists when I get home: *Hope is having someone to remember life with.*

I step back and Derek wipes his face with the end of his T-shirt. "I should have told you the truth. Vance thought you deserved to know but I made sure he wouldn't tell you." His voice dips. "I couldn't watch the truth do to you what the truth about her dad did to Sasha."

Sasha. She's the whole reason I came looking for Derek. "What do you mean? What truth about her dad?"

Derek looks at me like I'm not serious. But when my face stays blank, he whistles. "Well, that explains a lot."

When he's done telling me the story about her dad's affair, I let go of his arm, leaving half-moon fingernail marks on his skin.

"I didn't know." I feel stupid and small for not knowing something so important about my best friend's life. For her not being able to tell me, and me not being there for her. My mind tries to find clues she left for me so I could follow her into her own pain, but if she did, I was blinded by my own pain, unable to see anything else. "She was drinking in the bathroom."

Derek's words slide over the end of mine. "Annabelle, don't."

Don't what? Pretend as if I care? I'm mad at Sasha, but I still care. "She could talk to someone." Derek's shoulders droop again, and he shakes his head. I wonder how many times he's had this conversation with Sasha while I was MIA in her life.

I'm not the only one missing. I need to find Vance. I clutch Derek's arm. "Keep trying. She'll listen to you. I know she will."

Mrs. Hernandez and Craig have seen me at my worst, and they never shoved me away for not healing fast enough. And Vance. Was it torture for him to keep the truth to himself? Mrs. Hernandez is right as usual. I've wanted nothing in my life to hurt and everything to stay the same. How blind could I have been?

Derek nods. It's not much, but it's something and I turn to go. I'm three parking spots away when Derek shouts, "Hey Annabelle?" He jogs over to me. "For whatever it's worth, I don't think Trent would have broken up with you. He was—"

"Acting like he wanted everything and nothing at the same time?"

Derek locks his hands behind the back of his head. "Wouldn't have said it like that, but yeah, that's exactly what he was acting like."

# thirty

. . .

## VANCE

I'm leaning against a tree at the end of the parking lot, waiting for Annabelle. I wanted to see what her reaction would be if I started walking home with her. It would involve speaking to her, which I'm not supposed to, but there's something I want to ask her.

I watch Annabelle run across the parking lot making a straight line to Derek. They talk, she smiles, then clutches his arm like a life raft, hugs him, and I slam my fist against the tree. She has her people. Any question I need to ask her is pointless—I already know the answer.

Where do I belong? Not here. I was a fool to believe it could be anything different.

I walk all the way down Cut Canyon, past Murphy's, to the gray cinder block building at the edge of town. I saw an old Volvo with a *For Sale* sign parked in front of Davis Auto Repair yesterday.

Fifteen minutes and one handshake with Annabelle's dad later and I'm the owner of that vehicle. But my stomach turns to rock as I walk to the only home I've had these past three years. Graduation is tomorrow and after that, I'll be gone.

# thirty-one

. . .

## ANNABELLE

I've looked everywhere for Vance. There is only one place left to check.

I poke my head over the brick wall, a spy ready to take the castle. Vance is flat on his back, hissing air out of his mouth as he lifts the bar of the bench press. We haven't been on level ground, and I'm the one who told him to never speak to me again, but there are things we need to discuss.

"Hey," I say.

His reply is a breath through clenched teeth. The bar touches his chest ten more times before he sets it on the rack. He sits but doesn't turn. "What do you want?" he asks, his voice as flat and hard as this roof.

While I hunted for him, my mind buzzed with everything I wanted to say, but now that I'm standing here all my thoughts have slipped away. He's not wearing a shirt, and I can see how tightly he's holding the muscles along his shoulder blades. The heat of his anger shimmers across his skin in a slick sheen of sweat.

He stands up and stares at me with granite eyes. Pulling my hair off my shoulders, I twist it in my hand, letting it fall back into the same place. "So, graduation, huh?" He blinks slowly. Taking a breath, I puff my cheeks and exhale as Vance takes the weights off the bar, stacking them in the corner of the roof. "Look, I didn't come up here to stare at you like an idiot. I was wrong to threaten you without even hearing your side of the story." I think about talking to Derek in the parking lot and how both he and Sasha don't belong to me anymore. My voice wavers. "Somehow you ended up being my only friend. I miss the songs you make me listen to. I miss you and your sweatshirt. Not that I don't appreciate this look because it's a good one." What is wrong with me? My face turns to fire and his hand hovers over the weight, a momentary pause when he almost stops stacking them and picks up the conversation.

But he doesn't.

I press on. "You won't talk to me. I get it—I told you not to." I twist my hair again. "But you get me in a way no one else does, not anymore at least. I want to understand what Trent made you do. Or maybe he didn't make you. I don't know." I coil my hair in my hands. "The point is: I'd like to understand."

Vance holds still for a very long time, and I think silence is the only thing he and I will ever share. "You don't need to come up here looking for pity points or forgiveness while you're on your healing journey or whatever it is you're looking for."

Whatever it is I'm looking for? I'm looking for Vance. I'm staring at him wondering where he is. Where is the guy who used to be my friend and mocked me for not knowing R.E.M. was a band? Where is the guy who translated my emotions into notes? Where is the guy who helped me throw rocks and danced like a fool? I can't find a trace of him in the hard lines of his face.

Vance is done stacking the weights, but he still won't look at me. "Just go back to your people, the ones Trent always approved of."

"What are you talking about?"

All I need is an opening. If he can tell me what he's thinking, if he gives even the slightest opening, I can slip through the crack, and we can figure this out. I want him to hit his fist into my shoulder, complain about all this drama, and tell me what obscure band is currently on repeat. We could work this out if he'll talk to me.

"You should leave." He walks to the opposite edge of the roof, keeping his back to me.

"I want to understand what was happening."

He crosses his arms. "Go."

I climbed up here to talk to him, to find a way back to

the place where we forged a friendship but apparently Vance is done. I tried to build a bridge in his direction, but half-built bridges don't go anywhere.

I scramble down the ladder, and I run through the alley, not knowing where my feet are taking me until I enter the parking lot. A truck backs into the ramp, depositing a boat onto the water. A few classmates congregate on the dock. My body knew where it wanted to go long before my mind did. I sprint the width of the parking lot to the unmarked trail between bushes and head deep into the trees.

I choose a random place to veer into the untouched woods, picking my way over uneven terrain. Branches reach out, snagging my hair or catching the strap of my backpack. I wipe a spiderweb's gossamer thread off my face, shuddering as it multiplies across my skin.

Then I see the river.

It's not the same stretch Vance took me to, but it's the river. My reflection wavers on its surface and I hear it speaking as it rolls over rocks.

*Slip into my grasp. Everything would be solved if you slid away.*

Vance's reaction surprised me, and stings in a way I was not prepared for. Why does he think there is nothing worth salvaging between us? Surely there is more tucked into the remains of our friendship other than kept secrets and misunderstandings. Even a small shred of kindness could, over time, expand, and once again be big enough to cover both of us.

My heart starts pounding at a familiar tempo. Crumbling relationships is a song I don't want to keep singing. Sasha and Vance. People from my past and present are both telling me they don't want anything to do with me. What am I supposed to do with a wound that cuts so deep?

The river pushes past my feet, tempting me, calling my name, roaring in my ears. This time there is no bathroom to escape into to mute the world around me, and I press my hands over my ears, but the loudest sounds are the words inside my head. Words that tell me this is all my fault. If only I could have understood sooner. If only I hadn't let go of Sasha. If only I had accepted Trent's death for what it was: final. With the trees as my only witness, I scream and crumble to the ground, pulling my legs to my chest.

When will my life stop breaking apart?

People say we should trust our hearts, but I'm not sure I should. Not with pain so thick and raw surging through my arteries, threatening to pull me into a comfortable land of locked doors and overwhelming darkness. I want to lie down, covered by the shade of a multitude of trees, and not be found. The sun shifts in the sky as I sit alone. I could so easily fall back into the pit I've been wandering around in this entire year.

There's a magnetic tug from deep within my chest to slip into the empty, quiet darkness.

But there is something new forming inside my split-open heart, something gaining strength.

Getting up, I look for rocks and hold one in my hand. It's smooth and round, perfect for skipping, but I don't want to bury it under the water, so I tuck it in my pocket. One day I want the sight of the rushing water to once again feel like carefree enjoyment instead of a reminder of everything I lost.

Hope is a slippery word. As slippery as some of the rocks I've been picking up. Then I have an idea. Digging into my backpack I pull out the marker I used earlier. I wonder if anyone saw the message I left on the bathroom mirror. I cannot keep hiding from my pain, and in sharp quick strokes, I write the word *hope* on the rock. When the idea of hope grows foggy again, I'll hold this rock and remember.

So much can happen by accident—finding your way or losing it. I don't think it's an accident that I am finally starting to find my way, even in the midst of this new round of pain. I've had support all this time, even when I didn't recognize it or think I needed it. And now I can make the decision to hope, even when I have no idea where it will lead.

I put the rock back in my pocket and gather a pile of stones. When I have enough, I begin writing.

Some I label with broad ideas. *Love. Anger. Fear. Pain. Regret. Sadness. Disappointment. Lies. Blame. Secret. Friendship. Cheating. Family.*

On others, I write specifics. *I failed. I'm sorry. I love you. I lost you. Wings. Breathe. I wish you were here.*

I pick up *anger* and throw it into the river. One by one, I hold a rock, feeling how solid each word is before throwing it. I offer the river everything that has weighed me down, and the river accepts them all, no questions asked.

I make a circle with the remaining rocks. *Love, friendship, family, I love you, I wish you were here, breath, wings.* Then I find one more rock and write *hope* on it, placing it in the center. I cast a shadow over the ring of words that I am choosing to define me. These do not sit heavy in my heart.

I need a few more and I write names on them, setting them like sun rays around the circle. *Mom. Dad. Murphy. Meredith. Trent. Mrs. Hernandez.*

On the last rock, I write his name. *Vance.* What should I do with it? Throw it in the river or set it on the ground? He doesn't want me in his life anymore and the river is there, always ready to receive. Vance is a mystery I don't know how to solve. He has always been there when I needed him and I'm not exactly sure what he means to my heart, but it's not nothing.

I don't throw the rock with his name, but I don't put it on the ground with the others.

Climbing over fallen trees, I make my way back to the trail, still holding the rock with Vance's name. Not so long ago I would have chucked it into the water without so much as a backward glance, but I don't want to be the sort of person who tosses people aside like gum wrappers anymore. It would hurt less to drop the rock to the forest floor and forget about him. We shared a friendship and now it's gone—I should move on. But I still don't see the appeal of moving on. Not like this.

I want to be better. I want to keep flexing the wings Mrs. Hernandez insists that I have and finally fly on my own.

The rock with Vance's name feels heavy and uncertain. There is more to his anger than he is letting on, but I don't understand what. Whether he wants me to or not, I'm not going to let him push me away this easily like I did with Sasha. I've carried the rock all the way to my room, and I dig the other one out of my pocket, putting both on my desk.

Vance and hope.

Neither makes sense. Both hurt in surprising ways. And I'm not giving up on either one.

# thirty-two

. . .

## VANCE

Blue and silver streamers cascade off the podium while bunches of matching balloons bounce at either end of the stage. Today is graduation.

I didn't sleep last night. Not that I have a record of sleeping well, but last night I couldn't find a stitch of sleep to hold onto. It makes me edgy. At work this morning, I cleaned the counters when they weren't dirty. Tied closed mostly empty trash bags, flinging them into the dumpster. Jumped every time the door opened. I relaxed a little after Murphy told me Annabelle asked for the morning off, but not much.

I almost caved yesterday, acknowledging her attempt to regain a footing in each other's lives, and let her back in. All I had to do was lift my head and take a small step in her direction, and she'll take one toward me and if we did, we'd find a way to be friends again.

I hate the jerk I'm being.

But there's no point in offering her something I can't stick around and fulfill. Today is graduation. Day zero. Early this morning I shoved everything I owned into my duffle bag. It sits waiting in the back seat of my car. I should have left then when Murphy was out at the bakery. When there was no one to watch me go or to try to stop me. If he knew what I was about to do, would he try to stop me? I can hardly swallow.

I push off the door frame and walk to the band room where everyone is getting ready and slip in unnoticed. People bend together taking selfies, signing yearbooks, and acting as if there is something to celebrate, which of course there is. I watch it like a movie I've never been a part of. The credits are rolling and suddenly I want a speaking part. I want to be someone in the film other than who I've been cast as: a boy in the back taking up space. I want someone to ask me to sign their yearbook but what would I write? *I never knew you, but have a good life. -Vance.*

It doesn't matter. No one asks.

My arms swim in the oversized sleeves as I zip the blue gown. At least now I look the part, even though I'm still standing on the outside. I should have skipped this, already been miles away. But all I've ever wanted is to have a normal high school graduation because all I've ever wanted was a normal life. A mom who stayed, a place to call home. Normal. But that's always been too much to ask for. It's the same desire as showing up to a bonfire thinking that by showing up, I could turn over a new leaf. It didn't work then, and it won't work today.

I try not to scan the room for Annabelle, but I find her standing on the fringe of a group. Not excluded, but not included. What is she thinking? Does she feel as if she is masquerading in her life the same way I do? She must feel the pressure of my attention because she turns, and her face softens with a smile. Before I can shake my head or turn my back, she is standing in front of me whooshing her sleeves back and forth.

"These gowns are something else," she says.

I freeze, making my body a statue under the obscene amount of fabric. Inside, I'm a precariously stacked game of Jenga. One wrong move, and I will crash to the ground. I've been keeping my earbuds in round the clock this week, reducing my conversations with Murphy to the bare minimum. The music kept me from hearing my heart breaking. I don't have them in now, and all I hear is the cracking, howling pain. I bite the inside of my cheek and remind myself that this is not my home.

Annabelle doesn't accept my silence and tries again. "Do you ever wonder? I don't know, maybe it sounds stupid, but do you ever wonder if we'll make it?"

Today is our high school graduation. We are standing

on the square in the game that can literally be labeled We Made It. But I've been asking myself that same question my entire life. I never knew if Nat or I would make it to the next square in the game or not. Annabelle has been to the bottom, her rose-colored glasses broken at her feet, and now she knows something I've always known. No square is safe, and the game can change rules without warning.

I need to put space between myself and Annabelle. She understands more than anyone I know or she wouldn't be standing there asking me this question. I need to shut the door and throw away the key because I cannot stay. It's not even possible. And I only know one way to barricade a door.

I blink once. Twice. "Nope. Never wondered about that. The only people who would ask something like that are lost causes." Then I shove myself to the far end of the room.

Minutes later, cheers explode around the gym like popcorn kernels of happiness from family members as we file in. We thread ourselves into rows of folding chairs, standing until the music ends. Annabelle is several rows ahead of me, and I stare at the back of her head, but she never turns.

I don't pay attention to Mr. Logan's speech about how bright my future is. I'm busy counting minutes, not days. Then the names are announced, followed by whistles and claps. Classmate after classmate crosses the stage and I don't clap for a single one. More names. More cheering. Then finally, I'm climbing the steps. For a split second, I think I'll cross the stage to crickets. It would have been fitting, but applause follows me.

I don't scan the bleachers to try to find Murphy. I don't want to see the expression on his face. I'm scared to find relief settled in the corners of his eyes. Life forced us together but now Murphy can hold his head high. He did everything he promised he would. The only person in my life who holds that title.

This is it.

There's nothing left to wait for.

Staying in West Aldrin with Murphy and Annabelle is not in the cards. The only card I have left to play isn't a card at all. It's a postcard-sized painting folded in my back pocket. One night, I was bored and searched online for paintings of knights, dragons, and white horses. Turns out that what Vivian painted is of St. George. Legend has it that the dragon was ravaging the town, demanding a human tribute to satisfy its longing for blood. The town paid until the princess was offered up to the dragon. That drew the ire of St. George. He had to save her, so he killed the dragon. But not before the dragon had already ripped apart countless other families in the town.

It might as well be my story. Except there is no knight. No saint. Just dragons.

There is nothing left.

I have to go.

Instead of snaking my way back into the line of chairs, I step to the side and slip out the door. In the hall, I throw my cap to the floor and leave the gown where it falls. I stop short of the double doors, grab the painting out of my pocket, and flick it to the tiles. Crashing through the door into my newfound freedom, I am instantly soaked.

Shaking the water from my hair, I rev the car to life, and as I whip out of the parking lot, my duffle bag tumbles to the floor. How many times have I shoved my life into that bag? It's remarkable how easy it is to reduce my life to what I can carry, but so much always gets left behind.

This time it's Murphy, Annabelle, and a place that could have been mine in another life.

There could have been another way, a door number two. I could have asked to stay, but it felt like begging and that's something I'll never do. Murphy never brought up our agreement, which translated into a pretty solid "No" in my book. Leaving allows me to be free from everything that could have been—especially the pity I might have found on Murphy's face if I had asked to stay.

I am no longer an agreement or a problem to be solved.

I am not a son or a friend.

I am on my own and there are no more days to count.

# thirty-three

. . .

## ANNABELLE

I'm sitting in a folding chair, clutching my diploma, trying to pay attention, but my thoughts keep floating away. *Lost cause.* Is that what Vance thinks I am? A few weeks ago, I would have agreed and his assessment might not even have stung. But his words are Velcro in my heart, clinging to tender wounds, hard to rip off and throw away.

I blink back tears as Mr. Logan introduces our valedictorian.

Derek shakes Mr. Logan's hand before stepping to the podium. "It's been a crazy ride, Lumberjacks!" The senior class erupts. Derek pumps his hands in the air, trying to quiet everyone, but what he says next drains the room to silence. "Last year, my best friend, Trent, never had a chance to read this speech." Derek smooths a wrinkled sheet of notebook paper on the podium. His voice cracks. "I think you should hear it."

I hold my breath as Derek starts.

"Life is a race toward an unknown end. We make plans and memories, and hopefully, we'll make some money along the way, or our parents will be forced to let us move back in." Laughter rumbles out from the bleachers. "But as we race toward our future, we keep checking our rearview mirrors looking back to everything we left behind. We'll spend our entire lives checking our phones, our bank accounts, and our inboxes. There will be eviction notices and blank postcards, announcements, and regrets. So, what makes life worth all of it? What makes our life stick together and mean something? People. The people sitting next to you, the people you love and chose to let into your messy, beating heart."

Last year I would have jumped to my feet, like everyone has now, and clapped. I would have wished I could put my fingers into my mouth and whistled extra loud. And after the ceremony, I would have kissed Trent and told him his speech was perfect.

Trent could never have written that.

I jump to my feet along with the rest of my class but instead of cheering, I look behind me for Vance. Maybe he's sitting, covered by the sea of students wearing ocean robes. Climbing on top of the chairs, I clamber to the aisle, racing to his row. And right there, between Rachel Poague and Sean Purvey, is an empty seat where Vance Powell should be.

I rush out of the gym, but the ghostly remnants of a cap and gown on the floor stop me. Vance has vanished into thin air. Was he planning this all along? The afternoon we spent at the river comes rushing back. He knew the exact number of days until graduation, and I thought it was a hurry-up-and-get-here kind of anticipation, but I think I was wrong. This entire year I've been so focused on myself that I haven't seen any of the clues laid out in front of me.

Vance wrote that speech with his own messy beating heart when he didn't have anyone to let into it, and now he's gone.

But he just walked across the stage. I watched him get his diploma. Maybe there's time to catch him. I drop my cap, unzip my gown, letting it fall next to his, and almost step on a patch of color out of place on the gray and white floor. I bend to pick up the small piece of paper, not really looking at it, when my parents call my name, worry etched in their voices because I'm running away from another celebration.

"It's okay. I just need to go find Vance. I'll be right back."

Pressing the painting to my chest, I shove myself through the double doors and I'm waterlogged by the time I get to the café. My hair hangs in wet cords taped to my cheeks, my navy T-shirt dress shrunken against my skin. I can see the café is empty, but I press my face to the glass anyway.

And there, leaning to the side of the cash register is what looks like a paperback book.

I yank on the door, even though I know it's locked, then fly around back, standing on the bucket of used grounds next to the door so I'm tall enough to grab the spare key above the door.

Inside I don't even take the time to dry my hands before picking up the book. A thumb drive is shoved between two blacked-out pages.

~~"There will be a reckoning!" The Viceroy screamed into the crowd, spittle flying from his lips. "Upon this day~~ **I am** ~~reclaiming the blood right and the land that once forgot how such payments were to be extracted. You had the chance to flee, and now you will be~~ **sorry** ~~you did not take heed."~~

I flip back and forth through the entire book, looking for more dark lines crossing out words, leaving me a message, but that's it. Three words.

*I am sorry.*

A hand comes down on my shoulder and I flinch. I didn't hear the door open, but Murphy stands next to me. "Where would he go?" he asks. Beads of water track down Murphy's scalp and across his face. His eyes flick from my face to the book and back to my face. "Where would Vance go?"

My heart sinks like silt to the bottom of the river. "I was going to ask you the same thing."

"Me? Why me? He spends all his time with you."

It's a punch to my gut. Used to. Vance used to spend time with me until everything broke and we burned down our friendship with a Founder's Day bonfire. "Not lately. Besides, you're like his dad or something. I know you're not. But you are the closest thing he's got."

I don't know where Vance would go, and I start shaking. Not from being soaked through and cold but from the realization that I maybe don't know Vance at all. I can make a list of bands he would rather poke his eye out than listen to. I know he makes a killer latte that he'd pour down the drain instead of drinking. I know he never goes anywhere without his sweatshirt.

I know he took a risk and saved my life.

Vance was there when I needed someone the most and when I couldn't find my way—more than once. I don't know what would have happened if he hadn't appeared at my side that day on the bridge. I turn the flash drive over and over in my hand. It's not the same one that our morning playlist is on. "Do you have your laptop?" Murphy nods and we walk to the back room. He pulls it off the shelf, setting it on the table. I lift the lid, plug it in, and click play.

Drifting piano music plays as feet crunch across gravel. I gasp—those are my running shoes. My own measured breathing can be faintly heard, a metronome behind the notes. I know this moment. I felt free as I ran, and I needed to remember that feeling, so I recorded it and sent it to Vance.

The melody is familiar. It's the same notes Vance has been playing and replaying, trying to perfect for months. He figured out whatever he needed to because the music is seamless. Some of the pictures are mine. Clouds. Branches dripping with sunset leaves, my shadow stretched across a road. Some of the pictures I've never seen before and Vance starts speaking over the images, through the notes.

*You should know you weren't completely right*
*About what you thought you knew*
*Or what you thought was me*
*There was one thing you did get right,*
*One thing I think you understood.*
*Something that if I would admit it*
*To myself, I've always been afraid of.*

More pictures flick across the screen. Chairs overturned on the tabletops inside the empty café. A streetlamp casting a pool of yellow light. A solitary bench. Me, draped in a gray sweater, reaching my hand into the river.

Then Vance's voice again.

*"I watched a hundred birds scatter*
*Across the sky and I watched you run*
*I watched you fall*
*And then I watched you come alive*
*I could never say it and I should have.*
*You're braver than I'll ever be."*

When it stops, the silence is all-consuming, so I play it again, listening as Vance weaves a story. Why couldn't he have said everything in this recording to my face in the band room instead of calling me a lost cause? My next thought buckles my knees. *Lost cause.* Were those words meant for me or himself? People don't want to disappear unless they think they are out of options. Or if they think they're a lost cause.

I disconnect the flash drive and slip it and the card I picked up from the hall between the pages of the novel. It's all I have left of Vance.

By the time I return to school, people are spilling from the gym, lingering in the hall to avoid the downpour. My parents wait by a row of lockers, and I lean into my mom's embrace even though I'm soaked. She doesn't seem to mind as she wraps her arms around me, and I breathe the words against her collarbone. "He's gone." She rubs my back, not trying to ease my hurt, just holding me tight while fresh needles of loss prick my skin.

I press back from her hug. "I have to go do something, then we can go."

Tracking wet footprints across the gym, I make my way to where Derek stands surrounded by his family, Sasha's arm looped through his. He turns when I tap his shoulder. "Can I talk to you?" I ask.

Derek and I take a few steps away. "You're going to ask me why I read Trent's speech, aren't you?"

We both know he should have put air quotes around Trent's name and I nod. That is exactly what I wanted to ask.

Derek takes the folded paper from his pocket and hands it to me. I rip a few of the spiral notebook tassels hanging from the edge, letting them fall like confetti to the floor. "I've been doing a lot of thinking." He lets out a long breath. "Trent was my best friend, a good guy, and he loved you. Those are facts. But I think we got a few things wrong. I think the author of this speech deserves more than we gave him. Plus, having that in my back pocket all year literally saved me from writing my own speech." He winks and I make a strange gurgling sound halfway between laughing and crying.

I walk back to my parents. It's time to go. We stop at home so I can change and I'm warm and dry in my sweatpants and Post Malone T-shirt, bringing Trent along for the graduation celebration he never had. In the back seat, I watch drops of rain create their own rivers chasing each other to the bottom of the window.

Cliffsburg is a nothing town further east with a single gas station, a bar, and a post office the size of a stamp. But at the gas station, they sell cinnamon rolls by the dozen in simple brown boxes with oval stickers that say Handmade by Ethel. Trent swore they were the best he ever tasted, always covering his heart and adding, "Sorry, Mom." When my parents asked me what I wanted to do after the ceremony to celebrate, eating one of those was the first thing I thought of.

So many what-if questions pester my mind like a swarm of gnats around my face. What if Trent never drove away that night? What if he told me the truth? What if he was about to snip the string binding us together and we both flew higher than either of us imagined we could?

The questions crawl under my skin, laying eggs of doubt. And doubt is a storm cloud trying to extinguish my tiny flame of hope. It's fitting that the sky is so dark today.

I'm still holding the novel, bulging from the painting and the flash drive tucked inside its pages. What if I understood why Vance knew the exact number of days until graduation? What if he never agreed to what Trent asked of him? What if Vance never saw me running through the woods? What if Vance told me everything he had to say instead of leaving it for me to find?

What if.

Maybe he'd be in the back seat with me, instead of being another person removed from my life.

The rain sputters to a stop as we pull into the gas station. A sliver of light burns a line across the horizon creating a ribbon of gold under the black canopy. I get out and snap a picture of the smoldering sky. Vance's speech rattles around in my heart. It's people that make life bearable. It's also people that make life breakable. I guess that's what makes life so beautifully gut-wrenching.

I tap open my messages. If Vance is gone, fine, that's his decision, one I don't understand. But this is my decision. He's out there somewhere and if he means what he wrote in that speech and his poem, then I have to try.

I type: *Why did you leave like that?* I erase it, replacing it with: *Where are you?* I erase it and leave the screen blank. Nothing is right and I pocket my phone.

It's been an entire year of missing Trent.

Counting when I lost Vance is complicated. The bonfire? The fight? The roof? Today? Dad holds the door to the gas station open. "You coming?"

I jog over. "Why would someone run away?" I ask.

Dad puts his arm around my shoulder. "Probably for a lot of reasons. Fear. Or maybe the allure of chasing a dream. Or they've been hurt. Or maybe they don't believe they belong."

Murphy isn't Vance's family, and sometimes he wonders if his mom is even alive. Vance made the choice to leave months ago, and I never saw it coming. And even though he was always guarded, the parts of himself he allowed me to see proved he's someone worth holding onto. Underneath all the rocks he stacked around his life—and sometimes threw—beats a battered heart, and I know what that feels like.

I am not a lost cause and neither is Vance. Even if that's what he wants me to believe.

I take out my phone out again, and I send Vance the only message that makes sense: *Come home.*

# thirty-four

. . .

## VANCE

I hold my phone as if it might bite.

I thought I might find a place in Seattle, but it was suffocating to walk the labyrinth of tent cities sprouting along the sidewalks, people pressed too close for my comfort. It would be easy enough to find places to disappear but somehow the city made my skin crawl.

Now I'm parked at a rest stop south of the city, farthest away from a line of idling semis, and I finally turn my phone on. I'm afraid there will be a message. I'm afraid there will be nothing.

Five voicemails and seventeen missed calls from Murphy.

One text from Annabelle.

Tears wash down my face. Two simple words from Annabelle crush my heart.

*Come home.*

I don't know where home is. Annabelle claims it's West Aldrin, but how can that be? How can home be a place I never fit inside of? A place I was never asked to be a permanent part of? I wipe the back of my hand across my face. I have no roots anchoring me to a piece of land and answering the question of where I'm from was never cut and dry. Nat and I drifted in and out of too many places to count. I never belonged to any of them except for one.

If I were to sit you down and tell you the entire story of my life, I could start it how all good stories start. Once upon a time.

After shutting off my phone, I shove it into the glove box before twisting the key. People say you can never go home again, but I'm about to try.

Night swallows Portland as I cross the I-5 bridge. It's late and I'm too tired to find my way in the dark. Taking the Broadway exit I drive until I spot a Fred Meyer and park under a streetlamp in the far corner of the grocery store lot. Leaving had not been what I expected, but what did I think would happen? A going-away party? Someone clinging to my leg, begging me to stay? Slipping away unnoticed sort of exes those options out. I should feel satisfied, but that isn't the word coloring my thoughts. It has to be the exhaustion of not sleeping that is finally catching up with me. I'll feel better in the morning. After locking the doors, I stretch out on the faux leather back seat as much as the confines of a backseat allow me to stretch out and sink into a dreamless sleep.

Portland doesn't look familiar, even in the light of a new day. I drive past shopping centers that are no longer shopping centers. What I remember being a dry cleaner is now a vitamin shop and dispensary. I do remember the railroad tracks and the way they jarred my body as I rode my bike across them. Three more blocks and I pull to a stop in front of my old house.

The one place where I had a family.

The place where my life broke—for the first time.

When I lived here, it was painted brown, had a mostly dead lawn, and a bent, metal gate that never latched. I remember that when I played in the backyard, the house was large enough to block the sun. Today the house looks small. A little white house with yellow trim and rose bushes making a fence never needing to be latched.

My fingers hum with the desire to push open the garage door and see my bike still inside. The day before my dad walked out, he gave me the bike of my dreams. Black with blue accents to match his Charger. For one whole day, I loved that bike. More-than-words loved it. But after that, I hated it as much as I hated my dad who never wanted to see me or Nat again.

The chipped orange counters in the kitchen are probably long gone. Sometimes I sat on them. Sometimes I dragged a chair to the edge to make myself tall enough so I could pour something for Nat. Shot. Pint. Fifth. Those were the first units of measurement Nat taught me, and none of them ever came in handy in second-grade math. I never knew who she needed me to be, even when she told me exactly what she needed me to do. *"Baby, pour me a glass. Make it a big one."*

In this house, I had a mom and a dad and a bedroom and a bike. I never knew most families had things on their walls. Paintings, posters, photos, signs of life, love, and family. Not until a birthday party at a classmate's house and I saw pictures on every wall. I came home with a stomachache from too much cake and noticed the emptiness inside our house for the first time.

Inside the walls of this house, there had been quiet days, and loud days, and angry days. Quiet days were the days I was on my own because my parents were too hungover to wake up. Loud days were the days I lived for but were hard to come by. They were the days Nat swung me from her arms and every ounce of her love belonged to me. Angry days were the days I tried to stay hidden, dodging the hit of a hand or the sting of words because both left marks.

Tied in a knot of memories, I jump when someone knocks on the window of my car. A woman wags her phone at me.

"You've been staring at my house all morning. Leave or I'll call the police."

People see what they want to see and she sees Suspicious Youth. I offer an apology. "I used to live here." But she doesn't care; she wants me gone. Her shout chases me as I drive away. "I don't want to see you again, you hear me? You don't belong here."

I already know that.

History is repeating itself, and I take a last look at the house in the rearview mirror. Once again, I'm leaving it behind with a swarm of complicated emotions flapping in my chest.

All I ever did with Nat was leave. There were times when she woke me in the middle of the night, telling me I had five minutes to grab whatever I could. Everything else got left behind.

I have no idea where I'm supposed to go.

*Come home.* Annabelle's text haunts me.

I could find a job and an apartment anywhere, but I want more than a room surrounded by noisy neighbors. My heart longs for a family, for a place where I can leave my socks on the floor and stop being a stranger or a guest or an agreement. It's hard to remember if I ever had that sense of belonging when I lived with my parents. I mostly remember swinging from one extreme to another, my arms aching from holding on.

One single day burns in my heart. A day we spent

together as a family at the beach. It was an unexpected slice of normal instead of our usual turbulent sea. This is exactly what I've always wanted.

Normal.

So, I change direction and drive in search of the waves.

# thirty-five

. . .

## ANNABELLE

The morning after graduation, I stare at the piano in the café. The longer I stare, the more I envision the slope of Vance's back as he curled his body toward the keys, and the more I can hear the music he perfected and left behind on the flash drive. I lost track of how many times I listened to it last night.

A bony-knuckled hand rests atop mine and I look to see Mrs. Hernandez smiling. "That was a good ceremony yesterday. I especially enjoyed the speech." The way she says it makes me think she knows the truth and I wonder what she and Vance used to talk about. I grab a plastic cup, about to fill it with water, but she shakes a finger, slapping a crisp ten-dollar bill on the counter.

Squinting my eyes I ask, "What's this for?"

"Today I want one of his expensive coffees." She jabs a finger in Murphy's direction. "You choose which one.

But only if you make one for yourself and come with me."

Murphy swipes the money off the counter, giving it a snap, holding it to the light. "I don't know Maria, are you sure this is real?"

I don't know why but I start crying. It's such a small and insignificant moment of life, and you would think it doesn't mean anything. But if I've started to learn anything, it's that these are exactly the moments that matter.

I swipe the back of my hand across my eyes. "Deal. But on one condition." I shove my hand in the back pocket of my cut-offs, pull out my own five-dollar bill, and slap it on the counter. "Wherever Mrs. Hernandez and I are headed, you're coming with us."

Mrs. Hernandez claps her hands, and Murphy shakes his head in disbelief.

There are two customers in the café. Mr. London Fog is scrolling through his phone at the counter by the window and Ms. Chai-and-a-Muffin sits in the wingback chair.

Murphy walks around to the main section of the café. "Sorry, folks, there's a family emergency and I have to close." He holds the door open for them to exit.

Family. Somehow that is exactly what we are, and I wish Vance were here. IOUs and toasters are nice, but what Vance wrote in his speech is true. I have to hold onto my people.

I tug out my phone and check for a reply from him, but just like every other time I've looked, there's nothing. I shove it back in my pocket and start working on three cardamom honey lattes for us to take wherever we are going.

Mrs. Hernandez sips her drink as we walk. "There might be something to these overpriced fancy drinks." She coughs and takes another sip. "This is delicious."

Murphy offers her his arm. "Any chance if I start supplying you with one of these, you'll reconsider and stay?"

She tips her head to his shoulder for a brief moment. "Wouldn't that be wonderful?"

Our pace is slow, but we make it to her house and I ignore the moving van that sits in her driveway. When we walk around to her backyard, I half expect to see Vance standing there with a shovel, but I don't. He's gone. A table is covered in orange fabric. A cake and a punch bowl rest on it, and streamers twirl down from branches. Leaning against the base of a tree is a piece of plywood covered with balloons.

My parents stand from the deck chairs they were waiting in. Dad and Murphy slap each other on the back while they hug, and my mom wraps her arms around me then Mrs. Hernandez.

Mrs. Hernandez asks us to take a seat, and I sit cross-legged on the grass in front of her just like I used to at story time.

"Capítuloito. It's about time we have something to celebrate, and this party is for you." I glance at my parents, and they give me a look that says they know as much as I do, which is nothing.

Mrs. Hernandez continues. "My Ernesto and I never had children of our own and for years it was a pain that tried to eat me. I tried many things to fill the pain or take it away or make me feel like my life meant something. Then one day, quite by accident, I found a notice that they needed help at the library." She brushes her hands together as if to say, "The rest is history."

She reaches into the pocket of her cardigan, pulls out a dart, and crouches in the grass with me. "Sometimes you have to try something unexpected in order to find what it is you've been searching for. Sometimes you have to destroy a dream and sometimes life does the destroying for you." She turns my palm over and carefully presses the dart into my hand. She leans her head in the direction of the balloons attached to the plywood. "Throw this and see what you can find."

For a moment, I don't get up. I'm thinking of Vance and how he told me to throw rocks into the river until my arm was sore. But I brush that thought away, and get up and throw the dart. I miss the first time. But the second throw hits the mark, a balloon explodes, and confetti and a slip of paper flutter to the ground.

Mrs. Hernandez laughs, a familiar wheezing cackle that feels like summer wrapping its warmth around my shoulders. "Read it," she says.

Unfolding the slip of paper I read, "La Tomatina." I scrunch my eyebrows together. "What does it mean?"

Her face is glowing. "It means there are so many possibilities." She nods her head toward the waiting balloons. "Again."

I pop another balloon and find on this slip of paper: *physical therapist.* Another one says: *buy out Murphy and run the business.* Murphy gives a good-natured growl and asks what sort of game this is, all while grinning ear to ear. Another balloon popped: *run a marathon.*

When it's all finished the grass under the tree is littered and I'm holding a stack of possibilities in my hands.

Mrs. Hernandez comes up to me. "Maybe there's meaning in one of these." She lifts her eyes to the sky. "Or maybe there's none, but be brave enough to try. You have the most beautiful wings."

I try to keep the tears from falling but give up and let them escape. "I don't want you to go." My voice sounds like someone is strangling me. "This is your home."

"This is my home." She bookends my face with her hands. "Right here." Then tips her forehead so hers is touching mine. "You'll tell him all this for me, won't you?" I shake my head, not understanding at first, but then my eyes widen in understanding. She's talking about Vance.

"But he's gone."

"Wings, Capítuloito. Don't forget about wings," she whispers before stepping back, clasping my hand in hers, and making another announcement. "It's time for cake."

After we eat, I help Mrs. Hernandez wash the dishes and tell my parents I'll be home soon. When the last dish is dry, packed inside a box instead of the cabinet, I ask her what's been burning in my chest. "Have you heard from Vance?"

Her sigh crackles. "No."

"But you think he'll come back."

"Thinking and hoping are not the same. Are you still searching?"

I collapse into the only chair left in the kitchen. "Yes, but it feels confusing."

"Most good things in life are." Mrs. Hernandez pulls her phone out of her pocket. "I didn't know Vance was planning on leaving. I could tell he was wrestling with something heavy, but I didn't know what. One of the last times he came over he helped sign me up for Instaland."

I laugh at her renaming of the app. "Vance signed you up for Instagram?"

She rests her hand on my face again. "The world is shrinking, and we don't have to be apart."

I don't really want to think about what it will be like to miss her. I don't want to see the *For Sale* sign go up in her yard. Or not to be able to run here and talk about life. I hug her, thanking her for the surprise party, promising I'll stop by before she leaves.

Later that afternoon, I clear everything off the bulletin board above my desk and pin each slip of paper to it. So many possibilities written in Mrs. Hernandez's neat cursive. I've never had a specific vision for my future. I've only wanted a simple life. Even as a child, when someone asked, I never had a ready-made answer of an astronaut, teacher, veterinarian, or mermaid scuba diver. My only answer was that I wanted to be happy. My parents applauded while everyone else laughed. I guess they knew happiness was a bonus, not a guarantee.

I google La Tomatina, shaking my head at the idea of traveling to Spain to throw tomatoes at strangers. I search a few of the other possibilities, but I keep circling back to two tabs I've left open. One details a career in physical therapy. The other is for a trade school in Rye that offers certificates in auto body technology. The idea of fixing broken things—people or their vehicles—is one I can't shake loose. Is this what I'm supposed to do? I don't know that I would have ever considered either of these possibilities before.

The word worms through my chest.

The life I had before was an exceptional chapter in my life. It was filled with Trent and extraordinary days of first love, but it's time to put that book away and fly on my own wings.

# thirty-six

. . .

## VANCE

If only life could be like navigating a highway. Directions. Scenic viewpoints. Warnings. Signs letting you know how many miles until an exit. It's hard to get lost when you follow the signs.

I can't even turn on a playlist as I drive. I'm unsure what songs should make up the soundtrack of driving this two-lane road twisting through a mountain pass surrounded by trees I cannot look at. When I catch a glimpse of the tangled branches, all I think about is another two-lane road winding up a ridge. I never imagined living in a place like West Aldrin with more trees than people and someone as reliable as Murphy. I never attempted to settle in or let my body relax because I knew it would never last. The drumbeat of leaving was the backbone of my life. Endings always came, ready or not, and I needed to be ready.

My arm hangs out the window, fingers curving against a breeze tinged with the ocean. I have no idea if this is the same beach we came to as a family. But it's sand and waves and briny air.

I find a place to park, blocks from the surf, and reach under the passenger seat for my sweatshirt, but it's not there. I'm sure I stuffed it under the seat before leaving. I never looked for it last night, too tired to search before I slept. I smack my palm against the seat. Never in all my years of leaving have I forgotten my sweatshirt. Maybe it's better this way—a clean break.

My hands are clenched in my pockets as I pass clumps of people crowding the beach. They are bright splashes of color against the muted sky, merging with the gray-blue wash of the ocean. Kids and kites and laughter bombard me, turning into messages. A family huddled together becomes: *You don't deserve what we have.* Siblings that scream and chase and bury each other in the sand turn into: *No one wanted you, no one wanted you, no one wanted you.*

I push further down the beach away from the messages flashing on the sand until I am finally alone.

The day my parents brought me to the beach was a rare moment. It wasn't a quiet or loud or angry day. There had only been a bucket and a shovel and sand stuck between my fingers. I dug holes and piled sand in heaps and chased seagulls that ran before they flew, all while Mom and Dad watched from the blanket they shared.

The day had been perfect, the kind we could have hung on our wall. After the sun went down, Nat pulled me into a shop telling me to pick a bag of taffy, but I didn't want candy. I wanted something beautiful from the rotating rack that mirrored what I felt. I lived an entire day inside a picture-perfect postcard, and I wanted one to take home.

Nat didn't buy one. She laughed as she paid for bags of the chips and taffy we would call dinner on the drive home. She didn't understand that I craved something real, not a temporary rush that would never last.

Sitting alone in the sand now, I scoop it with my hands and let it sift through my fingers until my hand is empty. The strange thing about picture-perfect is that it's always a lie. There is always an unseen moment before the shutter clicks. Quiet, loud, angry. And an unseen moment after. Abandoned.

Somehow, I need to hold all the still frames that make my life, even if they are uncomfortable. As much as I want them to be sand in my hand, disappearing through my fingers, it's not possible.

There is one other picture-perfect moment in my life. Dancing with Annabelle under the thrown stars of the disco ball. But even that had a before and a very broken after.

I cuff my jeans and tuck my socks into my shoes and walk to the water. *No one wanted me.* The white crest of a wave rolls onto the beach, pushing a line of water and foam toward me. The waves are consistent. The rhythm of the tide coming in, rolling out, every single day. I understand rhythms. I use them when I play the piano and appreciate them when they fill my earbuds. My life was defined and uprooted by the rhythms of Nat's addictions.

*I deserve what I got.*

It's easy to think that. I even see those words flash across the sand in family-shaped messages. But that doesn't make it true. I deserved a family, stability, and love. Everyone deserves those things. Life lied to me, over and over and over, just like the waves lapping across my toes.

If life lies, where does the truth hide? My heart pounds with an answer. The first night I lived with Murphy, we sat on the roof drinking peppermint tea and Murphy told me it would only work between us if we were honest with each other. He said he would never lie to me, and he never did. But I constantly looked for ways he would disappoint or leave me behind because it was all I knew adults would do.

My face is wet, and I can't blame it on the breeze lifting off the waves, spraying me. The first voicemail from Murphy was a repetition of him saying my name followed by a stretch of silence so long all I heard was him breathing. I imagined him taking the steps to the house, turning circles in the living room, looking for signs of me. Then he spoke again. "I don't understand why you left, except maybe I do. I wanted to give you your space, hold doors open, and not pressure you. I have no claim to you but don't you understand, Vance? I can't imagine any other life than with you in it."

I've listened to that voicemail so many times it's imprinted on the walls of my heart. I hear Murphy's voice in the whisper of wind over the waves.

What if pictures were never supposed to be perfect? What if all of us are looking for picture-perfect lives in all the wrong ways? Could I retrain my eyes to focus on what I have instead of everything that has been taken away? What would happen if I tried?

I shift my eyes to the line where the water meets the sky. What do I have? A car. Maybe Murphy and West Aldrin. My heart skims across the surface of regret— Annabelle. Being friends with her was its own kind of home for my heart, and that is exactly what her message said.

*Come home.*

Is there still a chance?

It's not that I didn't have anything, it's that I threw everything away because I was scared to keep it. No one taught me how to stay.

Take what you can carry. Slip away into the night. Leave and never look back. Those are the foundations that built my world. I never wanted to be like Nat, but standing on the beach, I realize it's her skin stretching across my bones. I abandoned the life I had in exchange for nothing, which is a trade Nat constantly made.

Another wave washes over my feet and I break a steadfast survival rule. I look back at everything and everyone I threw to the ground in an attempt to protect myself, and my heart seizes. How could Annabelle tell me to come home after I called her a lost cause? How could Murphy say he can't imagine life any other way? I can't go back with my tail between my legs.

Can I?

I pluck a broken shell off the wet sand. Murphy taught me how to make chicken parmigiana, lent me the keys to his truck, and never once told me it was time for me to pack my things and hit the road. I followed the pattern I'm most familiar with because it's how I expected life to play out. But I can't say it's the only way I know—not anymore, not after living with Murphy. He showed me there is another way. A way that champions staying and giving people chances and seeing someone's potential for change.

The monotony of the sky shifts, igniting as it nears its end. I close my fist over the shell, and its sharp edge digs into my skin. I need to hold all the pieces of my life together without minimizing the awful while also accepting the good.

It would be more pleasant to forget, to wipe my mind clean and pretend my past is not my past. It's what I told Annabelle to do with Trent when I tossed the IOU. I didn't feel regret then, but now it weighs me down. The breeze pushes the hair off my face. Could I really go back and face Murphy and Annabelle after walking away from them like they meant nothing? Murphy keeps calling, leaving me messages, trying to reach me.

My entire life I've thought I wasn't enough. Not special enough for my dad to stick around for. Not loud enough to make Nat stay and love me.

Never enough.

The burning ball of the sun sinks below the waves and I half expect a hiss of smoke to curl from the water. Allowing someone else to hold the line and measure me means they can shift their expectations without warning. The truth is, I've made mistakes. We all have. But it's also true that I didn't deserve the life Nat gave me.

I was thinking about blank postcards and Murphy when I wrote Trent's speech. How we need to hold onto the people we invite into our messy beating hearts. I didn't even know Annabelle when I sat at the river that afternoon and scribbled the lines across the page. I invited her in, and it was worth it. I wrote that speech for myself, not Trent.

I wait until the sky is black before walking back to my car, passing a twenty-four-hour convenience store. I walk a block past it, stop, turn, and retrace my steps. Taking a breath, I pull the door open and march straight to the counter, my heart in my throat. I can't call Murphy from my phone. The instant I do my name will flash across his screen.

"Do you have a phone I can borrow?"

The girl behind the counter pops her gum and sets a cordless receiver on the counter, twirling her purple-tipped hair.

Calling Murphy right now is the same song, different verse. The same coiled ball of nerves weighs my stomach. What if Murphy answers? What if he doesn't?

One ring.

Two rings.

Three.

Murphy's voice cuts through my panic of waiting for an answer. "Vance? Is that you?" Silence hovers between us. "I'm not going anywhere. I'm right here Vance, and I'm not going anywhere."

My throat closes over anything I could say, and I hang up without a word. Leaving the phone on the counter, I hurry out the door, retreating to the beach and the waves. I need the repetition of them crashing on the sand to help me think.

I tuck myself into the shelter of a dune surrounded

by seagrass and pull my arms tight around my legs. Murphy answered the phone wanting whoever was on the other end of an unknown number to be me.

Not Nat—not this time.

Murphy wanted it to be me.

I breathe in the ocean-infused air as if I'm drinking it. I can live the rest of my life in Nat's shadow, never being able to stay in one place, closing doors on the people brave enough to knock on my walls, and running away to escape the heat of staying to face what life brings, even its consequences.

The wind shifts, tousling my hair and raising goose-bumps on my arms. Thinking about going back to face Murphy and Annabelle is about as comforting as sitting in a sand dune on a windy night without my sweatshirt for protection.

I've never returned to any place I lived before. If I go back to West Aldrin, I'll have to stop hiding. I'll have to apologize. It will mean completely obliterating my walls and not making side-eyes at the door, counting days, or waiting for an unexpected end to chase me away.

The choices Nat made shaped me and they broke me. But living by the rules she passed down does not have to define me or be the skin over my bones.

Not anymore.

# thirty-seven

. . .

## ANNABELLE

If it were up to me, summer would be year-round. I love when life gets stripped down to the bare essentials of swimsuits, barbecues, and the river. Long lazy days. Even longer nights. Nights I used to spend curled against Trent gazing into his backyard fire pit, sparks skyrocketing across my skin or shooting to the sky.

This summer will be nothing like that.

I have possibilities pinned to my board and the list in my notebook consists of: *Work. Run.* But today is Wednesday so I also write: *Craig.*

He asked to meet at the river because according to him, summer is for getting sunburned, not spending hours inside his office and I couldn't agree more.

Children splash at the river's edge, and gangly teenage limbs protrude from inner tubes bobbing on the surface. It's the portrait of every summer I remember. I kick off my sandals and carry them at my side. I find a spot to sit and watch while I wait.

It's easy to feel Trent's presence along this shore. We spent a staggering number of hours here and ghosts of our past selves haunt the landscape. The summer of my teal two-piece. The time Trent cut his foot on a rock and hobbled home. Holding my breath to go under and coming up riding atop his shoulders. The summer sun kissed my skin almost as often as Trent did, but not quite. These are ghosts I'm making peace with. Learning to live with them when they appear in the corner of my vision, instead of trying to pretend they don't exist.

"So, this is your river." Craig plops himself next to me and I jump, startled by his sudden presence. He's wearing mint green swim trunks covered with lobsters, a line of white zinc sunscreen smeared down his nose.

A sound comes out of my mouth that I try to turn into a cough. "You look ridiculous." After I gave Craig a chance, I learned that he actually knows what he's talking about, that he's on my side, and is also very funny. Who would have guessed?

His hand flies to his chest. "Those are not the words I would use." He shifts so he can see me better. It's a different location, but it's the same start to our time together. "How was your week?"

Fine. Okay. Nothing much.

My standard answers bubble to the surface, beachballs that don't want to be kept underwater. But I don't let them out anymore. "It was really, really hard."

"Tell me about graduation."

I feel myself pulling my shoulders up toward my ears and have to force my body to relax as I take a deep breath. "Should I start with the part where I cried? Or the part where Vance called me a lost cause? Or the part where he disappeared? Or the part where he left behind something really amazing? Or the part where I cried?"

Craig nods and that's my cue to tell him all of it.

After I release the week's events, Craig instructs me to put a hand over my heart and close my eyes. "Go back to the moment with Vance, the one before the ceremony in the band room. Don't edit it or rewrite it. Stay inside of it. You'll know when to open your eyes."

This is something new Craig is helping me learn. The ability to sit in the discomfort of a moment, a memory, without instantly wanting to bolt.

I follow his instructions, taking myself back to the music room. Back to the slippery blue fabric that swooshed with every move and Vance's hard face. I breathe shallow and fast, wanting to get up or open my eyes and not be trapped inside a moment I don't enjoy. My heart hammers under my palm as I breathe in. Then out.

In.

Out.

*Lost cause. Lost cause. Lost cause.*

In.

Out.

Over and over, until there is an echo of Vance's words. But my pulse slows to a steady thump-thump-thump and I open my eyes. "When you told me doing this exercise would feel sort of like running up the ridge, I didn't believe you."

"Healing comes in a variety of ways." His smile is kind and full of understanding. Then, without saying anything else, he gets up, and runs until his legs splash through the water, arching his arms over his head, pushing under the river.

This must have been his plan all along. I told him I'm afraid to get in the water. Afraid the river will hold on, wanting to take what it couldn't claim the first time. A line of sweat trickles down my spine. It would be so refreshing to slip under the surface. Everyone in the water splashes and shrieks, and I would be okay. The river is, after all, just a river.

First my left foot then my right steps into the cool rush. I close my eyes at the familiar pulse of water over my skin. I keep going. Up to my knees. My chest. I pause, hold my breath, and disappear. Resurfacing, I push water and hair from my face, letting out a shout of exhilaration.

Tipping back, I float like a starfish, spinning circles,

suspended between the sky and the bottom of the river. Craig's voice comes from somewhere to my left.

"Do you think you can live here?"

"On the river?"

His laugh is always a rush of air out of his mouth. "Well, I guess, if you wanted to. But I mean here, floating in the middle of two opposite things. Pain lives on the bottom of the river—you've been there. Forgetting every hard memory, or every love-soaked one lives up in the clouds—you've been there. Two extremes. But here. You're between them, acknowledging both."

The clouds circle above me, the water swirls below me, and I am held by the river. Could I live like this? Could I keep both pain and forgetting in perspective and keep my head above the water? The longer I float and the longer I watch the clouds roll across the sky, I know this is something I can do.

My hands and feet are wrinkled by the time I return to the shore, water sloughing off my tank top and cut-offs, laughing as I lower myself next to an already-dry Craig. "The river is a much better situation than your office."

"Agreed. So, in that case, I'll meet you here next week." He stands, tipping a finger from his heart to me. "I'm proud of you."

Tears sting my eyes as I wave goodbye. I'm content to

spend the rest of the afternoon being baked dry by the sun. I spread myself on the ground to do just that as a group of girls walks behind me. One girl asks what everyone is going to wear. Another girl is glad this will be the last party Sasha is hosting; her going away party is tonight.

I sit up. My mind spins with the gossip dropped at my feet and what Craig and I just worked on. Friends with Sasha and Definitely Not Friends with Sasha are two opposites inside my life. I can't say I'll miss her. It will be a relief to not brush shoulders with her anymore. But living between Friends and Definitely Not Friends means acknowledging the reality that both exist and finding a place to float.

If I pause to think about the decision I've just made, I'll end up letting anxious thoughts steal my intentions, but I don't want to be left holding more regret.

I can't change the past. I can only choose today.

Dripping my way through the aisles of West Aldrin's Cash-And-Carry I pay for my purchase. "Hey, Max, can I borrow your pen?"

The freckle-faced cashier unclips a pen from his apron and hands it over. I rip the plastic off the box and shove its clinging bits into my pocket, clicking and unclicking the pen against my thigh. This is the right thing to do. Sasha is a big girl and can make her own decisions when she opens the box and finds Craig's phone number written on the inside flap. Sasha might keep it or toss it.

All I can do is offer it.

The trunk of Sasha's Prius sits open, revealing an abundance of black trash bags which I assume are the entire contents of her closet. As I step onto the porch snatches of an argument leak out the open window, but I press the doorbell, trying not to listen.

Sasha yanks the door open. "I told you to wait—oh, I thought you were Derek." Her eyes slide to the porch swing that sits empty and maybe where Derek was instructed to wait. "What are you doing here?" She raises a finger. "Better question: Why are you all wet?"

I wipe away droplets of water still clinging to my arm. "Therapy swim in the river."

"I'm in the middle of something so if you stopped by to tell me you had a holy moment in the water, good for you. Not my thing, but you do you." She starts to shut the door.

"I heard you're leaving. Finally, huh?" I instantly regret my choice of words. "Not finally like, hurrah you're finally leaving. I just mean you've always wanted to live someplace else." This is not my best attempt at a conversation. "Where are you going?"

"Malibu." She puffs a mouthful of air up, forcing a dangling twist of hair on her forehead to flutter. Right now, I can't help but see Sasha age seven with her hair tied up in a bandana like that, curly wisps escaping. I always envied her tangled mass of red curls that refused to be tamed. But Sasha never wears her hair curly anymore. At school, it always has to be down and straight and perfect. "My dad lives there now with that witch of his. But whatever. I got into Laguna College of Art and Design, and it makes sense to stay with Dad for the summer. Mom's trying to convince me I shouldn't. She thinks, and I quote: It will end in disaster."

"I can picture you in California." The quiet that settles between us could be filled with a hundred disappointments. A hundred lies. A hundred memories. I'm searching for toeholds in this new terrain of talking to someone I've known my entire life but is now a stranger. I extend the brown paper bag folded in my hand. "I wanted to give this to you before you left."

She pulls the box out. "What is this?"

"Peppermint tea."

Sasha blinks at me like I am an idiot. "Obviously. But why are you giving it to me?"

"Someone told me it tastes like regret. It's my attempt at an apology. You needed me to be your friend and I was . . . I don't know what I was. Lost? Blind? I'm sorry. I never meant to hurt you."

Sasha shuffles the box between her hands before putting it back inside the bag, blinking her eyes rapidly.

"You should stay out of the river. Seriously. It does something to you."

I back down the steps. I want to say something else. Not goodbye. Even to Sasha, even when I'm glad she's moving away to embrace the future she always dreamt of having. There have been too many goodbyes for me to stomach. "Do you remember when we got invited to Lucy Jackson's sleepover?"

The memory flashes across Sasha's face. "That was ages ago. We were kids."

"We played light as a feather stiff as a board, and you freaked out, running for the stairs, but her basement was pitch black and you smacked your head on the wall so hard it started bleeding."

Sasha's hand lifts to a tiny scar at her hairline from that night, nodding.

It's a small memory, one of the hundreds from when we were inseparable. "I remember too."

I'm at the end of the driveway when Sasha yells. "I don't understand you, Annabelle Davis!"

I turn back to Sasha one last time. "Try not to devour all of Southern California on your very first day." And that convinces a smile to appear on her face.

There are a lot of types of broken.

Some broken things get thrown away.

Some get forgotten.

Some get repaired.

In my room, I pull off my wet clothes and replace them with dry ones. Broken always means different even when it's fixed. My wrist sometimes clicks when I rotate it, a reminder that it used to be broken.

I don't know what kind of brokenness I share with Sasha. Friendships are built on what gets remembered together. Apologizing might have been too little too late. But I remember what Sasha and I once shared, and she remembers too. Maybe that's all I can ask for.

In my notebook, I write: *Hope is floating on the river and keeping a place for broken pieces—even if they stay broken.*

I drop my pen on the paper.

Peppermint tea flavored apologies mean that Vance is walking in circles through my thoughts. Where is he? I bet he would have joined me in the river, swimming in our clothes, finding ways to survive between the bottom of the river or the impossibly high clouds. Picking up my pen I write: *Maybe peppermint tea should taste like hope instead of regret.*

Last year I deleted social media because it was another source of pain, another reminder of who I no longer was. But even Mrs. Hernandez has *Instaland* now and I bet there are all kinds of people out there, people like me, who need to find a safe space between painful, opposite realities. People who need to find a slice of comfort and compassion in a squared-off landscape that thrives on comparisons. What if instead of saying nothing, I open that door and hold space for myself, inviting others to find their way?

Once I have downloaded the app, I choose the name @hopelookslike and fill out my bio. *Annabelle Davis. Bravely broken. River floater. Rock thrower. Bad dancer. Friend. Snipe hunting for hope.*

I select an image of the river glinting in the sun and type: Rivers are roads and roads lead you home.

Somehow, I am doing this. I am floating between two opposites, finding my way along a twisty, bumpy path, but I know it's the right path.

I tag Mrs. Hernandez in a comment on the picture, hoping that when her flight lands in Las Cruces she will see the notification. I know Vance has Instagram but whether or not he is checking it is another story. He still hasn't replied to my text. Murphy hasn't heard from him. But I go back to the post and tag him. Maybe it will help him find his way home.

# thirty-eight

. . .

## VANCE

Eat's Diner off Pier Fifty in Seattle has mirrors opposite the counter. Which means I have a front-row seat to watch myself eat a burger. I push a fry through a mound of ketchup, leaving it on the side of the plate so I don't have to see myself bite, chew, swallow.

Four nights ago, I called Murphy and fell asleep in the sand. Then I spent the rest of the week at the ocean, walking the hard-packed sand every day until my legs were worn. Until I forced myself to say the word *family* without it catching fire in my throat. Families still clustered on the beach, and the pain I felt in my chest at the sight of their happy enjoyment was still present. It's a gaping hole that nothing seems to fill. Not true. I found people to fill it. People I was an idiot to leave behind. What magic spell holds some families together while others explode is something I'll never understand.

I don't want to be the sort of guy who hides from the truth. Even the truth of where I come from, and what I'm afraid lurks in my DNA. I also don't want to be the guy who can never stay in one place, a vagabond wishing for more.

I pick up the fry and shove it in my mouth. I've made it as far as Seattle. Only a few hours stand between me and Murphy's house, but I'll sleep in my car again tonight. Convincing myself I'm not pressing on because it's too late. Which is true. But the closer I get back to West Aldrin the blurrier the idea of *home* becomes and the harder it is to know if I'm grasping at the right thing. The word *family* still burns my throat.

The door swings open and two people walk in as I'm about to take a bite of my double cheeseburger. A woman slumps onto the stool next to me, and the guy she's with leans into her shoulder, saying something against her hair before heading out the door. There is one other customer in the restaurant, sitting at the far corner booth. An abundance of other seats are available. But the woman slouches next to me. The smell of cheap perfume failing to cover the stench of stale cigarettes hits me like a brick wall. It's a familiar and nauseating scent. I set my burger on the plate.

A question drags across the woman's tongue. "What time is it?"

"Six minutes after one." I steal a glance at her in the mirror and crash through my life. The last time I saw Nat I was fourteen, and we lived in Denver. She leaned over me while I slept, waking me by brushing a section of hair off my face and kissing my cheek. She told me she was going out with friends. She told me to not forget about school in the morning. Another kiss on my cheek and three simple words: "Be back soon."

I never saw her again.

Until a few minutes after one in the morning in this nowhere diner somewhere in Seattle.

She looks the same. But different. Aged not only with the passage of time but also by her choices. Wrinkles crack the edge of her mouth. A cloudy sheen masks her eyes. But it's the same face, the same scar on her chin, the same blonde that comes from a box.

I pull myself taller, pushing my shoulder blades back, and turn to face her. I want her to see me, to see what I've become. Let her examine the boy she didn't think twice about leaving. Nat's eyes squint, then relax. She slips a little off her stool and readjusts. Her words stick together. "I used to live with a guy who had eyes like yours."

My shoulders slump. How can she look at my eyes and only see their source? How can she draw into her depths and find an ex-boyfriend but not me? I'm not a replica of either my mom or dad. My features blended into something of their own creation. Except for my eyes. They are a direct copy-paste from my dad. Frustration pushes the question out. "Was his name Eddie?"

Nat sits up straight. Not sober straight, but shocked straight. She slaps my arm. "How did you guess that?"

I used to imagine what Nat would say when she came home. So many days have accumulated since she kissed my cheek. I had already eaten all the food she left behind, which wasn't much. Would she ramble on about losing track of time, not having a ride, or some other senseless explanation for being gone for weeks? Even during the first couple of months living with Murphy, I stayed awake knowing Nat would never return but wishing she would. Hating the fact that I longed for and despised her in the same breath.

None of my made-up reunions went anything like this. I grip the counter for support, stuffing the truth that Eddie is my father into the dark folds of my heart. "Lucky guess."

Nat digs in her bag and pulls something out. "Lucky guess or not, you gave me the chills when you said his name." She sets a slightly crumpled photograph on the counter next to my plate, tenderly smoothing it out. "That's my son."

I watched Nat slip and right herself into a sitting position on the stool several times and now I'm the one almost falling to the floor. A young Vance stares at me from the photograph. I have no idea when the picture was taken, or where. There are few clues to go on. I'm standing under a blank blue sky with shaggy hair, wearing black shorts and a red shirt, smiling at the camera.

Nat picks it up. "He's such a good kid."

I swallow my heart, unable to speak. Then finally squeak out, "How old is he?"

Her face falls like she's been caught stealing and will have to lie. "He's five. No. Seven?" The picture shakes in her hand.

I could do a lot of things. I could be angry and part of me is. I could howl in agony, and part of me wants to. I could pick up the picture, press it between my hands and tell Nat I could guess her son's name. And if I do that, I will convince her I'm far better than a lucky guess. Or a mistake. But I don't do any of those. I cover Nat's hand with my own. Cover over the picture of myself. Cover over the fact that Nat can't remember how old I am.

Nat remembers the smiling boy in the picture is her son and that's the part I choose to hold onto. My voice wavers. "It's okay if you can't remember."

The door swings open again bringing in a gust of air. The man walks to where he left Nat and sees the picture in her hand, his voice is gruff but not unfriendly. "Sorry, kid. She'll show that picture to anyone with a pulse. Isn't that right, babe?"

Nat presses the photograph to her chest, then turns it one last time for me to admire. "Course I do. Look how handsome my baby is." She puts it back in her purse.

I hang my head to stop the dizziness creeping up my spine trying to encircle me. Nat slip-hops off the stool, taking faltering steps away without another glance. Walking out of my life. Again. I blink at my fuzzy reflection wavering on the glass as the man pulls the door open.

"Thank you." The words got stuck and I had to shove them out, so they land with a smack on the floor causing Nat and the man to turn around.

I stare at my mom. *Thank you for letting me be your one brave act. Thank you for giving me a chance. Thank you for giving me the gift of Murphy.* But all I say is, "Thanks for showing me that picture."

Nat stumbles the few steps back and rests her hand on my cheek. "You're a good kid." Then walks back to the man, clutching his arm to steady herself.

I could have told Nat who I am. And when she put her hand on my face I wondered if she knew. But her eyes were empty and telling her would be meaningless. She won't remember this tomorrow. Telling her I'm her son won't make her stay. Or be my mom. I don't need her shame for not recognizing me. I could run after her, follow her, but for what? I've never been what she wants the most.

Nat is my past. She's my mom.

But she is not where I belong.

I am simply a stranger at a nowhere diner somewhere in Seattle.

A person with a pulse.

Nat could never hold onto anything. Everything she owned got lost or left behind. Sold or ruined. But somehow, she has managed to keep a picture of me all these years.

*She'll show that picture to anyone with a pulse.*

For more years than I want to count, my heart has been a tire slowly leaking air. But Nat kept my picture. In her own complicated way, she keeps her baby close. She doesn't know how to keep me in any way that matters, so she does it in the only way she knows how. Frozen in time. Forever young and smiling whenever she looks.

My heart is a flat tire, shrunken and misshapen, but somehow rolling along. And for the first time, it stops hissing air. I push away the plate of food, no longer hungry.

Nat's choices are not mine.

I know that now.

I had to learn it my own hard way. It's not like I'm going to rush out and buy an *Everything Happens For A*

*Reason* bumper sticker, but I had to leave everything behind in order to somehow find her. The universe is strange like that. And tomorrow I'll drive through familiar trees to see if there is a future waiting for me in West Aldrin.

# thirty-nine

. . .

## ANNABELLE

The sky is a milky blue as I walk to work. I'm thinking about how the river is just a river, but it is actually much more than that when my phone chimes. I read the notification twice and sprint the rest of the way.

Murphy almost drops the bag of beans he's pulling out of the cabinet when I crash through the door. "Someone chasing you?" he asks.

I rush over, holding my phone in his face, bouncing on the balls of my feet. "What do you think this means?"

I nudge the phone into his hand. "You're going to have to tell me what I'm looking at, kiddo," he says, squinting at the screen.

I explain about my new Instagram account and how I tagged Vance in the picture then jab my finger at the phone. "There's a comment and it's from him."

Murphy's eyes widen and flick back to the phone.

**vance.shaped.box** *You drown not by falling into a river, but by staying submerged in it - Paulo Coelho.*

It's been a week without any sort of communication, and I ask again. "What do you think it means? Do you think he's coming home?"

Murphy whistles, handing my phone back. "I don't know what I think. But I sure hope so."

Tapping the heart next to the comment I pocket my phone. I've successfully avoided looking at the hooks next to the back door since graduation, grabbing my apron as quickly as possible, keeping my eyes from lingering on the black sweatshirt dangling by its hood. But my hand slows, reaching for the empty sleeve, and I echo Murphy's words. "I hope so too."

Apparently, no one needs a drink today and my shift crawls by at the speed of a sloth. I check the time like clockwork but that doesn't make it move any faster. I check Instagram. My messages. Then Instagram again. But there's nothing. Desire is the downfall of hope. Or the anchor of it. I'm not sure which. But desire is definitely glued to hope. One small taste of Vance making an effort to communicate, and I lick my lips, wanting more.

I want his comment to mean something, and I need to be ready in case it means nothing at all.

What would it be like to see Vance again? Would he tell me why he left? Would he explain all the times he kept the truth to himself? The bell above the door clinks and my head shoots up.

After Mrs. Herbal-Tea and her infant daughter find a seat, I turn to Murphy. "Do you think I could head out early today?"

"Need to go for a run?"

I cover my face with my hand. "That obvious?"

His smile is contagious. "Not exactly covert."

I hug him and hurry outside, blinking against the sun as I fly down the steps and through the ally. Never noticing anyone else.

Until he speaks.

"Running away?"

I whirl at the sound of Vance's voice. Relief floods my veins but my heart pounds with caution. The last time I looked for him, he was gone. He told me I was a lost cause then vanished. As much as I want to be happy, I'm also cautious. So, I measure my words. "Running away is what you do."

He winces. "Accurate assessment. But I came back because I forgot something."

There's the truth.

He only returned to claim what he forgot. He doesn't care about what he said, or the fact that he left. I turn away, hope seeping out of my heart like tea in a broken mug. I shouldn't have assumed he came back for any other reason. "It's on the hook."

"What is?"

I pick up my pace, not wanting to stay and listen to whatever lame excuse he'll offer this time. "Your sweatshirt. It's in the back, on the hook." The reflex that jangled my bones a moment ago propelling me out the door so I could pound my feet against the pavement intensifies. I need to get out of here so Vance can get what he came for and go.

"Annabelle, stop." Vance jogs half the length of the alley until he's in front of me, putting his arms on my shoulders. "I didn't come back for my sweatshirt. I came back because I want to stay."

His words make the alley spin. I reach out and steady myself against his arm. "What?"

He gently tips my chin until I'm looking at him. "This place is home." I watch his Adam's apple dip. "At least I want it to be. Driving back, I had everything I needed to say all figured out. It was an eloquent yet understated speech." His winks. "But my mind went blank the minute I parked. You surprised me when you ran out, and I got mouthy. Bad first instinct."

His words are a whiplash, but I am grinning stupidly. It feels as if a balloon is expanding in my chest and there is only so much space before it will burst. I need to make sure I heard him correctly. "You didn't come back for your sweatshirt?"

He stands his ground, hands still on my shoulders.

"Don't get me wrong, it's a nice hoodie and I've missed it. But that's not the reason I came back."

The expanding balloon presses against everything inside me. It squeezes my pain, my dreams, my fears. Things I have wished for, things I long to do over. The pressure has nowhere to go, and it bursts and leaves me panting. Vance's eyebrows raise at my breathlessness, but I don't care. This is the most alive I've felt in months. My question comes out in huffs. "You came back because you want to stay?"

He looks past me. "I need to talk to Murphy, but that's the idea."

I back up from him, laughing even as tears wet my cheek. I want to draw a circle around this moment so I will never forget it. I've spent weeks, months, trying to figure out what hope looks like, but is this what hope *feels* like? A strength born of suffering fluttering wildly inside the walls of my chest, feather-light and unshakable.

Vance came home and he wants to stay. But what about the way he left? There are a lot of questions he needs to answer. "You acted like an idiot."

He nods. "I did."

"You called me a lost cause and then vanished."

His chin touches his chest, then he raises his head, his eyes a soft, searchable gray. "I said that because that's what I've always believed about myself. Not you. I pushed you away so I could leave, no strings attached. There is a lot I need to explain. And I will, I promise. I know it doesn't make up for what I said or how I treated you. But I mean what I said." He steps closer. "And I'll say it again because you deserve to hear me say it to your face. You're braver than I'll ever be and I'm sorry I hurt you."

I close my eyes and everything from the past year flashes across the screen of my heart. Trent. The bridge. Secrets. All the hidden and unavoidable pain. Peppermint tea. Friendship. Acceptance. Recovery. Wings.

Hope.

There's something I have to say to him, and I open my eyes. "I'm sorry, too. I never should have threatened you. You were always there when I needed someone, and I threw that away rather than trying to understand. Will you forgive me?"

His face dissolves into an emotion I can't place. Not sad or happy or upset or exhausted. But he nods and every line of his face relaxes into the Vance I've always known and have missed.

Throwing my arms around him, hope beats a new tempo in my chest. I hold onto him a moment longer before launching out of the embrace and run the opposite direction down the alley. Flinging the door open I shout, "Murphy, get out here. Vance came home!"

# forty

. . .

## VANCE

Murphy collides with me on the back step, almost knocking me over with the force of his hug. I have never been so happy to be crushed.

"Hey Murphy, since it's so slow, you want me to go ahead and close?" Annabelle asks. Murphy agrees and I follow him up the stairs so we can talk. But before I enter the apartment, I smile down at her. "I'll see you in the morning."

An envelope sits on the pillow in my old room. Murphy grabs it, handing it to me. I pull out a *Congratulations to the Graduate* card. Inside Murphy wrote: *To the future,* and something falls to the floor that I bend to retrieve.

"I didn't have a chance to give it to you after the ceremony. Thought we'd have time to talk," he says.

I lift a key from the carpet. "What's this?"

Murphy sits on the end of my bed. "I bought Pockets, and I thought you could help me figure out what to do with it."

Next door to Murphy's is a flower shop that has been abandoned the entire time I've lived here. *Pocket Full of Posies* is painted across the window in what I assume was once blue but has turned a putrid shade of green from the sun. "You bought the building next door without knowing what you are going to do with it?"

"Seemed like a good idea at the time. But then—"

"I took off."

He nods. "I thought maybe we'd expand. Or I don't know. I wanted to hear your ideas of what we could do."

I press my thumb into the cut mountain ridges of the key. "You want to start running your business decisions past me?"

Murphy gets off the side of the bed, closing the distance until he's in front of me. "I want to run every-thing past you. You're my . . ." He doesn't say the word like he's afraid of what I'll do if he says it.

"Family?" The word singes my throat and maybe it always will. But today it's the kind of flame that could illuminate a room instead of burning it to the ground.

"I should have talked to you about this more." He fans his hands between us making *this* mean us, or life, or both. "I never wanted to close the door on Nat coming back for you, but maybe I was wrong to hold it wide open. You deserve so much more than what you got, and I don't know what you want out of life, but if you want this . . ." He flaps his hands between us again. "It's yours." His voice lowers and his hands rest on his heart. "I'm not just talking about buildings."

"You mean you?"

He nods and tears sting my eyes. No one ever wanted me enough to stay. Nothing in my life has lasted except Murphy, and he's telling me there are no time limits to this agreement. The words won't come out, so all I do is nod and I'm crushed in his arms. Again.

I'm not alone.

We spend the rest of the day talking. I tell him how I walked the shore while I wrestled demons. He wants to know what it felt like to see Nat after all these years and I'm surprised to hear myself say, "Strangely okay." My heart is reinflating little by little, and I know there is more healing ahead of me. Seeing Nat helped in its own strange way. She is who she is—my mom, a stranger, an addict—and making peace with all of that will take time. Healing is not a pill I can swallow once and be done. Old wounds will be quick to bleed but I'm not going to keep tying a tourniquet around my heart trying to keep it from hurting.

It's good to talk to Murphy even when I feel the muscle memory of trying to deflect his questions flair up. He's in this with me, and I'm not going to doubt that again. It's hard to believe I'm switching teams from *Never* to *Always* but it's a trade I'm happy to make. But there's one more thing I need to ask. "I don't want to assume that I still work for you but, can I have tomorrow off?"

I've never heard Murphy laugh so deeply, and when I tell him why, he agrees without hesitation.

Even with a documentary about the 1964 Alaska earthquake playing on my laptop, I cannot fall asleep. So, I sneak downstairs to the piano. The painting I flicked to the floor is now framed, resting on top of the piano. This time when I look at it, I focus on the town in the background. Not the calm, victorious knight, or the bloodied dragon, but the town, filled with people who could finally take a breath without the worry of the dragon. I crack my knuckles and close my eyes, then bend my fingers into my favorite chord progressions. My pulse slows at the sound, matching the rhythm of a new melody.

I'm still emptying my heart into the notes when Murphy enters the café. I had no idea I passed the remainder of the night playing.

"You ready for today?" he asks.

The music stills, and I'm unable to keep a smile off my face. I feel mildly nauseous but I'm ready.

Murphy twists his keys in his hand before heading to his truck for the bakery run. "Good luck," he says.

The song I am writing is unfinished, but it will have to wait. I walk to the counter. I need to do this quickly in case Annabelle shows up early. I switch the electric kettle on, willing the water to boil faster than it already does. Bending over, I write something across a piece of paper and slip it into the cash register. When the water finishes, I make a to-go cup of tea. I fill another cup with iced water and push a straw through the lid before I head out the back door. In the alley, I take a tentative sip of the piping hot tea and have no idea what it tastes like today.

# forty-one

. . .

## ANNABELLE

I run to work. Last night it took all of my self-control to not call Vance repeatedly or go knock on the door. He needed time with Murphy, and I respect that, but now it's my turn for answers.

"Morning," I call out, as I enter through the back door.

Murphy stands at the front counter. "Hey, kiddo."

Tying the apron around my waist, I scan for Vance but he's not here. Pulling out the bag of roasted beans from the cupboard, I open it and lean my face into the abyss. The aroma centers me like it does every day. I shouldn't feel so wound up. Vance will be down any minute. I pour Officer Daily-Drip-To-Go his drink.

I bite my lip so intently, that I wonder if I left marks. What did Vance say yesterday? See you in the morning? See you later? I swallow.

"Is Vance coming down?"

Murphy strides past with an empty pastry plate, heading to the back room. "Could you check to see if I put the receipt in the cash drawer? I can't remember if I did."

Did he not hear my question? I would have asked again, but the bell above the door sounds, and in walks Mrs. Soy-Vanilla-Latte. I punch the button, the drawer wooshes out. I lift the cash tray and almost drop it. A crisp blue sticky note rests on top of the punch cards. I grab it, replace the tray, and shove the drawer closed, ignoring the woman waiting for me to ask what she wants even though I already know.

My hand trembles as I read.

*IOU an apology (several). Find me where I found you -V*

Shoving the note in my pocket I rush to the back, pulling the tie on my apron to release the fabric wound around me. "I have to go."

But Murphy already knew that because he is holding the door wide open, a goofy smile on his face.

I'm glad I wore my tennis shoes today and not my sandals because I'm running up Ridgeline wondering what Vance will say when I get there.

When I round the corner, he slides off the bridge onto the road and I skid to a stop, bending in half, catching my breath.

"Nice job, turbo," he says.

I pretend to glare. "You're jealous because all you ever do is lift heavy objects above your head."

Vance thumps a fist against his chest. "Certified neanderthal trainer. I bet I could make that the next health sensation. It'll be bigger than pilates, you'll see." He bends to the ground, lifting a clear plastic cup of water. "You earned this." I yank it from his hand, draining half in a matter of seconds.

The rush of the river slipping over rocks is a hush below us but somehow seems loud in the quiet morning air.

I finish the rest of the water. "I've been pretty mad at you."

"I've been pretty mad at me too."

I narrow my eyes. "That only makes me feel a little better."

"There are a lot of sad details, so many they could fill a new Dashboard Confessional album, but those will have to wait because I need to say two things. One. I'm sorry I never told you the truth. After everything that happened, you deserved to know all of it."

My head dips. "Thank you."

"Two." He takes a deep breath. "This one is a little longer." He fiddles with the to-go cup in his hand before he sets it on the ledge of the bridge with a sigh and starts to speak:

*They say home is where the heart is*

*But mine was never where you'd think to look.*
*I confused the idea of house with home.*
*And when that vanished I thought,*
*Mom will be my home.*
*But she left and she left and she left.*
*Once. Often. Forever.*
*I was scared*
*Or hurt*
*Or stupid*
*Or all of them together*
*And I didn't understand that home replaced an agreement*
*But the only place*
*I want to build my house,*
*Is in the valley of a dimple*
*next to your eye when you smile.*

Nothing exists except the silent shadow of Vance's words pulsing between us. He pushes the hair off his face and takes a step back as if he's about to vanish again.

I rub a hand over the rocks of the bridge. I've stood here twice this past year while my heart has split open. I wedged my fingers between the rocks and scraped myself across them. I've climbed this ledge looking for a way out of the pain I didn't want to be real. And now I'm standing here listening to Vance talk about his life, his pain, and what he wants.

Me.

I twist the straw in the cup until it makes a horrible screeching sound and set it at my feet. "I don't know how you do it, but that's twice now."

Vance's face crinkles. "Do what?"

"Take everything you feel inside and make it sound so beautiful."

His shoulders lift and there's a light in his eyes I've never seen before. "We cannot question the gifts God gives." I smack my hand against his shoulder. "But seriously, I don't understand it myself, it's like music, it just happens."

I lift my hand, shielding my eyes from the sun. "Will you do it again?"

The corner of his mouth curls. "Write you a poem? Absolutely."

My lips mirror his but then I shake my head. "No. I mean walk away without any sort of warning or explanation."

"Never. More like the exact opposite. I was wondering what you would think if I stayed here, and we figured this out. Together." His hand grazes my arm before tentative fingers weave through mine.

So many possibilities for pain or betrayal or love exist in life. I don't know what my future holds. It is a shape I cannot fully see, and right now, I'm okay with not knowing. All I can do is hold onto the people I invite into my messy beating heart. I've lost too many already, and I'm not going to let that happen again.

I step closer, and so does Vance, until there is little oxygen between our bodies, only a rising heat. I can feel his heartbeat, or maybe it's my own. I don't have any answers for what comes next, but I know one thing.

Vance and I are kindling stacked in a fire ready to ignite.

# a note from the author

When my kids were young enough to need a mid-day nap, I would jog on the treadmill as they slept, and that is how this story came to me. While I was running a certain song came on, and as it played I imagined a river, a bridge, and a woman submerged in the water. The image was soaked in grief and I wondered: Who is she? What is her story?

Then the song would end, my kids would wake up, and my day would rush along in a blur. But that little scene never left my heart. Years went by, and one day I was sideswiped by a pain I never saw coming. As I learned to heal, I returned to the bridge where this story began.

Every story is significant to an author, but *Erase The Empty Sky* will always hold a special place in my heart. This is the first manuscript I ever wrote, and writing it taught me how to tell a story, but only because Rachel showed me the way. I found my author's voice by giving voice to Vance and Annabelle. This is a work of fiction, but so much of it is a mirror to my own heart, my own journey with grief, my own struggle to understand hope.

It is a hard reality, that grief will find all of us. We can not outrun or avoid it. Maybe you know this all too well, maybe grief has already found you. And for that, I'm sorry. But another wonderful reality is that hope is real, and stronger than you might imagine.

One day I stumbled across this quote, and it is a bit unclear who to attribute it to but it seems it should go to someone named Matthew from a tweet.

"People speak of hope as if it is this delicate, ephemeral thing made of whispers and spider webs. It's not. Hope has dirt on her face, blood on her knuckles, the grit of cobblestone in her hair, and just spat out a tooth as she rises for another go."

Hope knows how to fight.

Whether you are already well acquainted with grief or if it is not yet a shadow at your side, my prayer is that the story Annabelle and Vance have to tell within the pages of *Erase The Empty Sky* has been a comfort to your heart.

Never give up on hope.

# acknowledgments

Jennie Wexler, working with you during Author Mentor Match, was a dream. Your insight made this story stronger. I'm so glad you picked Vance and Annabelle.

Lindsey, I'll never forget opening Instagram and listening to you talk about how much you loved an early draft of this story. Social media can be a wild landscape, but I'm so glad it gave me the gift of your friendship.

Dario, your support and encouragement have been such a gift to me.

Kate, thank you for always reading and praying.

Jo, I hope you found all the secret messages I left for you inside the story.

Liz, thanks for walking across Paris with me.

Mom and Dad, thank you for always pointing my heart to the Author of Life.

Zachary, Declan, and Imani, I love you more than I'll ever be able to say, but I'll tell you every day.

David, I mean what I said, I'd do it all again.

To my living hope Jesus, thank you for never leaving me to wander on my own.

# about the author

Hannah Stone is a poet and award-winning author who writes stories that wrap around your heart. She lives in the Pacific Northwest, where she shuttles kids to activities while dreaming up her next novel.

Connect with her at hannahstonewrites.com or on Instagram at @hannahstonewrites.

instagram.com/hannahstonewrites

www.ingramcontent.com/pod-product-compliance
Lightning Source LLC
Chambersburg PA
CBHW051302130726
47987CB00004B/1623